HARD SHOULDER

HARD SHOULDER

John Douglas

Hodder & Stoughton

First published in 1996 by Hodder & Stoughton
A division of Hodder Headline PLC

10 9 8 7 6 5 4 3 2 1

A CIP catalogue record for this title is available
from the British Library.

ISBN 0-340-66050-3

Typeset by
Letterpart Limited, Reigate, Surrey

Printed and bound in Great Britain by
Mackays of Chatham PLC, Chatham, Kent

Hodder and Stoughton
A division of Hodder Headline PLC
338 Euston Road
London NW1 3BH

For my brother Gordon, and
my son David

He that travelleth into a country before
he hath some entrance into the language,
goeth to school, and not to travel.
Francis Bacon
Essays, Of Travel.

The Joys of parents are secret,
and so are their griefs and fears.
Francis Bacon
Essays, Of Marriage and Single Life.

ONE

Why did it have to rain at funerals? Weren't things awful enough without having to huddle under an umbrella while someone consigned your daughter to the mud and worms?

It was June. A wet June. A lot of people had come to the funeral, most of them friends of Julie. Oh, there were Ronald's friends from school and some relatives, but anyone passing the sorry gathering would have guessed immediately that a young girl had died. The number of sniffling teenagers sheltering from the rain in their regulation school mackintoshes lent the scene a formality its pointlessness didn't deserve. It was a funeral; someone had died; who the hell cared that people were smart?

Ronald looked at the droning priest, burying maybe his third person of the day. Shaking his head, Ronald cast his gaze instead up to the slate-grey sky and the relentless drizzle. God's tears? No chance. If there was a God He wouldn't kill eighteen-year-old girls on the verge of life. Beautiful, loving, innocent souls on the threshold of adulthood and about to discover their worth and purpose. God couldn't exist. At least, Ronald hoped He didn't – because if he ever found out that He had been sat up there twiddling His thumbs while his daughter had been bleeding to death in her crashed car, then he would gladly set fire to the first church he could find.

The priest finished and Ronald threw flowers on the box containing his only child's shattered body, then walked away down the path to the waiting cars. The second funeral in twelve months. Last July it had been Ruth, his wife, but at least she'd had fifty years of life and her death was a blessed release from the cancer that had eaten her alive.

Ronald stooped into the Daimler and waited for his wife's sister and her sloth of a husband to join him. Lately he had taken to categorizing people as animals. His sister-in-law was a smug she-cat, married to a sloth. Their two children, the squabbling piglets, hadn't come, thank heavens. Of course, his own daughter had been a beautiful lithe swan about to spread her wings for the first time. Now she was a dead duck. He grimaced at his analogy: a rictus grin that was a match for that of any corpse buried in the hill above the car. And Ronald? He was a dodo, of course. Fat, ugly, useless and too stupid to realize how easy it was to die. He checked his watch, but it measured time by the minute, the hour. He had years yet. Years . . .

He looked out at the miserable crowd streaming away from the graveside. Fifty all told. He couldn't name half of them, wouldn't know more than a dozen to talk to, and didn't want to meet any. They were here on sufferance. It was his daughter who had died. *His*. They could cry a river but when they woke up tomorrow they could look at their children and their wives and think how lucky they were, not like that poor sod Ronald. They were lucky. Ronald was the one on his own with no wife, no child, no reason to continue.

And then he looked back at the hillock of covered soil that would soon lie on top of his sweet Julie. He stared at the duvet of dirt, then leaned forward and buried his head in his hands and wept. He might be alone but his darling daughter was dead. Over and gone forever. He had no right to feel sorry for himself: he was still here. And his sudden guilt made him cry all the more. The living may miss the dead but half of it is regret that they've been left to carry on. The two people who had underpinned his entire life had been taken from him in the space of eleven months and now he was left to shuffle along without hope or purpose. At fifty-one he was as dead as his daughter. He burrowed his head further into his hands and wept some more.

Days passed. Ronald changed from a dodo into a fish. Or at least he tried to drink like one. Scotch was consumed. He took the phone off the hook. He missed school and didn't answer the door. He started cleaning out Julie's room no fewer than three times but each time began sobbing so uncontrollably that he had to shut the door and retire to the emotional vacuum of the kitchen.

He spent four days in the kitchen, one day not even bothering to travel upstairs for a piss but using the sink instead. What did he think of as he stared at the blue walls and the days-old dirty dishes and the bottom of his glass?

Death. His own. And the ways.

TWO

So it was true! Even as Cally urinated in her knickers and laughed hysterically, she took bitter satisfaction in the realization that she wasn't mad and that what she had claimed to have been doing was fact, not fantasy. She really had killed all those people.

She controlled her laughter and stared up at the intruder, horrified yet fascinated. All these years, all those deaths, and all because of that. Suddenly the deafening noise subsided, as did the tinkling of broken glass inside the room and on the patio below. In the silence, all she could hear was Dr Rogers jabbering about his 'darling fishes' and his feet sploshing on the soggy carpet. One shiny blue fish caught her eye, stranded between her feet, thrashing its tail and gasping its last, its wet black eye staring up at her. Maybe it was begging for help, or maybe its little brain couldn't understand what was happening. Either way she envied it: another minute and its misery would be all over.

Cally looked over at Dr Rogers. He was on his knees now, trying to scoop up the numerous brightly coloured fish that flapped and fretted on the sodden green carpet. Only minutes before he had been so cool and professional, so sure he could solve her problems; all he had needed was proof. Now that he had it, he wasn't able to cope and had focused his attention on his fish instead. Pathetic.

Cally stood up, careful to avoid stepping on the still struggling fish, yet aware that she was not going to make any attempt to save it. Let Dr Rogers look out for it; they were his fish. About time he was of use to someone.

She looked back at the intruder, but it had gone, leaving no trace other than the smashed windows, shattered glass cabinet doors and, of course, the remains of the aquarium.

What should she do now? Run away? Wait until Dr Rogers had

calmed down? Cally walked over to the window, the faint mist around her feet swirling up into nothingness, the carpet squidging under her feet. She looked out on the hills behind the house and breathed in clean air.

It was a sunny, summer afternoon. Sheep on the hill in front of her *baaa*'d contentedly, somewhere in the distance traffic zinged on tarmac, and birds, initially silenced by the exploding windows, had resumed their calling. Back to normal. If only everything were that simple . . .

Then they came in, two of them. A man and a woman, both dressed in white, both stopping dead in their tracks as they surveyed the wreckage of the room. The woman let out a gasp, then slowly backed out. For his part, the man shook his head at his employer chasing tropical fish. Then he saw Cally standing by the window, and his eyes widened. Cally barely had time to open her mouth to speak before he had dashed across the room, glass crunching under his feet, and slapped her so hard across the face that her head banged into the bookcase and she dropped to the floor, her world quickly filling with blackness. The last thing she felt was wet carpet on her cheek, the last thing she heard was her psychiatrist, his voice high and insistent.

'*Stuff the girl! Save my fishes! Save my precious little fishes!*'

THREE

Ronald was woken by letters thudding onto the doormat. Dragging himself into the hall he found a grand total of twenty-one letters which had accumulated since the funeral. So, sitting at the kitchen table, cup of coffee to hand, he worked his way through the pile.

Most of them were condolences from people he recognized only as names on the Christmas card list. There were half a dozen bills, a lot of junk mail and a letter from his headmaster suggesting he take a couple of weeks off to get over his loss but to please get in touch as soon as possible otherwise his job might be in jeopardy. And there was a package from a photographic processing company, Betapix, addressed to Julie. Her holiday snaps.

Ronald dropped the package on the table as if it were alive – as it was, with memories – and took a long sup at his still too hot coffee. He didn't care. Pain was all in the mind and part of his mind had died over the last week. He slowly finished his Nescafé, then steeled himself to look at the last remembrances of his daughter. It didn't hurt as much as he thought it would, despite the munificence of smiles.

Julie had not only been a hard worker at school – she had been set to gain excellent A-level grades and had been accepted provisionally by Nottingham University to study History. Her reward was a new Yugo 64 – buying second-hand was out of the question as neither she nor her father knew one end of a spanner from the other – and she had looked after her 'fart-box', as Ronald called it, with the kind of care and attention she presumably would have lavished on her children, had she lived to raise a family. She had taken the car with her on her first holiday without her parents: a driving tour of Scotland with her best friend, Caroline.

Ronald had, of course, endured all the usual parental nightmares over the possible outcomes of this venture. But it had all gone smoothly enough, the two girls having a wonderful time, motoring around seeing the sights and spending their nights in out-of-the-way bed-and-breakfast establishments. And then, with that dreadful irony that can only happen in real life, Julie had been killed on the M6 on her way back from dropping Caroline at her new home in Nantwich.

Life. Stuff it.

Ronald went through the forty-eight shots slowly, savouring each glimpse of his daughter's last few days of life. Mother, daughter and father had enjoyed many a family holiday in Scotland so he recognized most places. Julie and Caroline had started in Edinburgh, gone north through St Andrews, Dundee and Aberdeen, then cut across country to the Isles. Some shots were shaky, a couple over-exposed but on the whole they were bright and cheery. He separated out all the shots with only his daughter in them and lined them up across the table. Nine pages from the last chapter of a girl's life. *His* girl's life.

Ronald remembered the police investigation. How they had found no traces of paint on the car, no skid marks and no debris on the road to point to a collision. Nor had Julie been drinking or taking drugs and the car was in perfect condition before the crash. All the evidence had pointed to a simple loss of control. Up to that moment he had refused to accept such an obvious solution. He needed someone other than the meaningless whims of fate to blame. Let it be a car mechanic rather than karma; not so much *c'est la vie* as *c'est la V12* going too fast. But now, sober and all cried out, he knew it wasn't so. He stared at his daughter's last days.

She *was* pretty, it wasn't just a father's pride. Pretty, and bright, just like her mother, his dear Ruth. He stared at all the shots containing Julie on her own. Two at Queensferry; one outside St Andrew's University; two of the Tay at Dundee; two on a ferry; and two in Sauchiehall Street. They had obviously had a good time. But something was odd. What was it? They were all of Julie, different places, different clothes, so what was bugging him?

A truck. Yes: there was a white truck in every shot. The same truck, though he couldn't tell what make. Coincidence? No, not in five places, spread over a couple of weeks. Okay, so maybe the girls weren't as pure as he thought. One of them had a boyfriend who was a trucker and . . . and he took a forty-ton truck around Scotland to be with them? Not likely.

Half an hour later he had examined every shot minutely, using a magnifying glass. Out of forty-eight shots, every single photograph that contained Julie on her own showed the truck somewhere in shot. Nine in all. In one photo it was just the merest hint of its bumper, in another a reflection in a shop window and, in a third, the top of its cab spoiler just above a wall. This was no coincidence. Either the truck had been following them around or they had joined up with its driver. But if that was the case, why no shots of him or his truck proper? Surely the girls would have wanted a memento of such a dedicated courtier. Ronald decided to ring Caroline.

She knew nothing about a lorry or its driver. Had she got any photos of the trip? Yes, she had, but no – after she had checked – there was no white lorry. Her father had then come on and asked Ronald to leave her alone. He knew Ronald was going through a bad time, and God knew he sympathized, but upsetting his daughter with stupid—

Ronald slammed the phone down. Sanctimonious prat. So what was he going to do? He separated the photographs into two piles. Okay, Ronald, think.

Firstly, the truck only appears in pictures with Julie in them. Never with Caroline, or when the two girls are both together or when the photos are just shots of places. Right? Right. And second, those shots in Dundee . . . He put them in the right order. The first showed Julie assuming a muscle-man pose in front of a statue of a naked man. The truck was in the background about fifty yards away. The next shot was of Caroline pointing up at the statue's private parts. The truck was not there. The third shot was of Julie again. The truck had reappeared. So what was wrong? In the background a bus was stopped at a bus queue. It was a long queue, only reducing by three people between shots, a woman in a pink coat and a punk bringing up the rear of the queue in each photograph. That was it!

The shots were taken maybe fifteen seconds apart, and yet the truck disappeared in the second shot when there was only Caroline, then reappeared in the last when there was just Julie again. How could a truck move so fast, and why? More to the point, Ronald thought, scanning the shots with his magnifying glass, how could it move at all when there was no driver in the cab?

FOUR

Life had taken a turn for the better for Cally, there was no doubt about it. Any food she wanted, videos, sweets, magazines. True, she couldn't leave the hospital but where the hell would she go anyway?

Handland Hospital was comfortable and, whilst it betrayed its blunt Victorian origins, Cally's room and the ward were bright and well-equipped. And, as Dr Gantry kept telling her, she was a guest, not a patient. Except, of course, when she took part in his experiments. No, not experiments, *studies*. She had problems, his job was to find solutions to them. Yeah, whatever, doc. He hadn't had much success so far, but at least he hadn't wimped out like that bastard Dr Rogers.

Cally switched off her television. Bloody soaps. She hated programmes that reminded her that most people had ordinary problems like late homework or which boyfriend to choose. God, what she would give to have normal worries, instead of the nightmare that was forever hovering in the background. People had died because of her and she prayed Dr Gantry could do something before even more were killed.

He was a weird old bird, was Dr Gantry. Tall, skinny, sixty, he had thin grey hair, a thinner, greyer moustache and always wore pinstripe suits and bow ties. Cally didn't know whether she liked him, but he'd been amicable and given her as free a rein as she could expect. All in all, he was about the best friend she'd had for some time. One day, she might even trust him. And when was the last time she could've said that of a man?

She flicked through a copy of *Smash Hits*. Fashion, lads and lyrics floated before her uninterested eyes and annoyed her further. The drugs seemed to have robbed her of concentration lately. It pissed her off. She dropped the magazine, got off her bed, wandered over to the window and looked down three floors into the courtyard of the hospital.

Eleven cars were parked there, ranging from a burgundy Land Rover Discovery to a silver BMW to a Ford Sapphire, none of them with a registration older than J. There was definitely money in this place. Cally glanced up at the other walls surrounding the courtyard. Grim was the word. Outside, from the gardens, it looked a nice enough building, even if obviously institutional. But here, inside its heart, it looked exactly what it was: a prison. Look hard enough and the bars and mesh at virtually every window became apparent, despite the bright curtains and flower boxes. The rings of nails around the drain pipes were another giveaway. Handland was a mental hospital, the majority of its patients in for the long stretch. Cally wondered how long she would be looking out of this window, waiting and wishing. Weeks? Months? She let out a sigh and turned to the wardrobe-door mirror to check her naked body.

A video camera was blinking its presence in the corner but she had got used to being monitored. Cally was skinny, no question. Not slim or slender, but thin. Scrawny, even. Her breasts seemed an afterthought, the nipples masculine. She turned and surveyed her bottom. She got curvy down there but who was to know? Even her periods were just dribbles. Okay, she didn't want to wake up in a scene from *The Godfather*, but if you have the headaches and the cramps, they justify a result. Anyway, who was she going to show her body to, other than the medical voyeurs watching her every move? Maybe one of them had a thing about teenage girls. If only he knew . . .

Cally opened the wardrobe and pulled on light blue jeans and a Motorhead sweatshirt. She ran a comb through her short blonde hair, smiling as she remembered the dark triangle between her legs that gave the lie to her head-hair colouring, then slipped on some laceless trainers – a fashion statement rather than a precaution – and walked onto the ward.

The usual bunch of half-dazed, unkempt excuses for human beings shuffled about or watched TV or stared out of the windows through the wire mesh. It was a mixed ward, though sexuality had little place in the doped and damaged minds of the patients on Ward M. She looked around for Mark.

He was the only patient she could get on with, if just sitting with Mark could be called getting on with someone. All he ever did was draw. Hand him a pencil and a sheet of paper and point him at the window and he was as happy as pie. He was supposed to be autistic. Cally didn't know what that meant but his drawings were wonderful, accurate down to the finest detail, and he would only stop when you removed his pencil. He never objected: he just drew or he didn't. And he never spoke, unless 'fug' counted as speech. What it meant no one knew – or wanted to know, it seemed – but it sufficed on all occasions when he was forced to say something shyly.

Mark was there. Good. He was drawing a collection of books on a table. The staff usually plonked him down with his pad and pens and let him get on with it: one less patient to worry about. Over the fortnight Cally had spent with Mark, she had come to realize that there was more at work than an ability to copy. To prove her point again, she walked in front of him, placing herself between him and the table.

'Hallo, Mark,' she said.

No response.

'Hallo, Mark,' she repeated.

Still no response. She gently lifted his head until he made reluctant eye contact through his dark, shaggy fringe.

'Hallo, Mark,' she said.

'Fug,' he said quietly.

She smiled and he smiled loosely at her smile. He was probably thirty or more but had the innocent expression of an infant. He might not have been all there but what was there was sweet and unsullied and Cally gravitated towards him for it. Too many people in her life had been tainted or out for what they could get but Mark was a true innocent. She felt an almost sisterly affection for him. She let go of his chin and he resumed drawing.

'And how are you today, Mark?' she asked.

No response. She tickled his side. He gave a shiver of pleasure, another half-smile creasing his chubby face.

'Fug,' he finally said.

'Yeah, fug,' she said sadly.

Mark was one hell of an artist. There were seven books on the table and he was drawing each one of them in felt tip, not just getting their relative positions and scale right, but also copying the covers. One was a Biggles hardback and he had done a picture of an aerial dogfight every bit as good as the original. Cally sat for five minutes, watching. She assumed he retained a picture in his head of what he was drawing even when his view was interrupted. She had first spotted this odd ability when he had drawn a view of the building from outside on window-cleaning day.

He had taken three hours to do his huge picture, almost two feet long and accurate down to the tiles on the roof and the different curtains. By the time the picture was finished their side of the building had been cleaned and half the windows that had been open were now closed, but Mark's drawing showed them open. He had obviously taken a shot in his mind of the building with the windows as they were at 9:00 a.m. and that was what he had used for reference as he drew. It was amazing to watch and it was also very therapeutic.

Although Dr Gantry was sympathetic and had Cally in therapy with two sessions every day – to say nothing of the sleep monitoring each night – she refused to tell him everything. But with Mark she could gabble away, safe in the knowledge that, even if he understood what she was saying, he wouldn't tell anyone, not unless they understood the language of 'fug'.

Cally lazed back in the chair next to Mark. Poor bastard. If the connections in his head had been set up right he could have been an artist or an architect. Mind you, she thought sourly, if the connections in *her* head had been set right, where might *she* be now instead of in a loony bin? She closed her eyes and tried to relax. She had dreamed of Chloë again last night. She had woken up crying. A nurse was beside her instantly, ready to take notes, but Cally had burbled something about a puppy. Chloë was private: she was the only innocence Cally had left in her life and no one was going to sully it, unless Dr Gantry could *prove* he had the right to interfere in that precious memory. True, she knew her problems had started with Chloë's death, but it had nothing to do with the girl herself. She had been as innocent as Mark still was; a victim of circumstance.

Someone shook her arm and Cally sat up with a start. It was Dr Gantry, his false smile as transparent as ever. It seemed to her that it wasn't so much insincerity as simple overuse, like a beauty-queen smile: done for effect but, because it is done so often, ending up having no effect.

'Sorry to startle you, Cally. I want you to meet someone. This is Nurse Bigg. Elizabeth Bigg. She's to be your personal nurse from now on.'

'Personal nurse?' asked Cally.

'Yes. I'm not happy with the progress we're making and I want Elizabeth here to be with you to see what happens.'

Cally nodded, although she didn't understand what he meant. Then she looked up at Nurse Bigg. The name was right!

Nurse Bigg was built like a man, meaty forearms and legs forcing their way out of a barrel-shaped uniform. Her mousy hair was unflatteringly short, a nurse's cap, stranded on top, too small for her round head and she had little eyes that peered through slits as if her ruddy face was a mask.

'Hallo, Cally,' she said, her voice a sing-song that would have been more at home in a girl of Cally's build and age.

'Hallo, Nurse Bigg.'

'Call me Elizabeth.'

Carry smiled, though not for reasons of friendship. She was remembering the number of times adults in roles of authority had asked her to call them by their Christian names – and how many times they had screwed her up.

FIVE

Ronald had been to G-Mex – The Greater Manchester Exhibition and Events Centre – before, but each time he had entered from the front. This time he got to enter through the back, thanks to Raymond, one of his less successful GCSE students. The Northern Truck Trade Show was due to open in a couple of days and if there was one place where there would be someone able to identify his mystery truck it would be there. Five minutes of mindless chit-chat and a warning not to touch any of the stands for fear of upsetting the unionised workmen later, and Ronald entered, pass pinned to his anorak.

There was no denying that G-Mex was impressive. A single-span arched roof of translucent plastic two hundred feet across and some hundred yards long, supported by immaculate Victorian wrought ironwork, it offered a huge uninterrupted space within which to hold shows and concerts. At that moment, however, the scene was one of chaos, like the building site it was. Exhibits in various stages of construction, vehicles standing around seemingly abandoned, only half of them trucks, and the sound of hammers, electric drills, saws and the shouts and whistles of workmen struggling to fill the echoing cavernous space.

So, what to do? A lot of the people looked like builders, but there were also men in suits. He decided to try them; if a company was putting thousands of pounds into a stand for a show starting in two days, truck company representatives were bound to be present – and who better to identify the truck in his photographs?

Thirty-five minutes later and Ronald was in trouble. He had shown his photograph to at least twenty people and not one – not a single one – could identify the truck. Most admitted they couldn't even *see* a truck and some gave him weird looks. One even challenged him over who he was and why he was there and then stalked off.

Ronald just stood and stared at the truck in the photograph. It *was* there, large and white and as plainly visible as any Ford, ERF or Foden currently parked in the hall, except it didn't *look* like any of them. Nor did it resemble any other truck in the building and in the literature he had picked up from a couple of completed stands.

Raymond came up to him. 'No luck?'

'No,' said Ronald. 'What do you see there, Raymond?' He showed him the shot.

'I'm sorry, Mr Blakestone, but, like I told you, I don't see a truck. Sorry. Look, I've had a complaint, a guy on the Volvo stand. Wants to know why you're here. I'm afraid I—'

'It's okay, Raymond. I was going anyway. Looks like I've wasted my time.'

The sunshine that greeted them as they left the building did nothing to lift Ronald's mood.

'Sorry you couldn't find what you wanted, Mr Blakestone.'

'No, thank you, Raymond. At least you helped.'

Leaving a bemused Raymond, Ronald walked across the car park which was full of trucks and trailers. A gaggle of drivers were gathered in a group by a parapet, laughing and joking. Ronald decided to give it one last try. He walked up to the men, and coughed to make his presence known.

Immediately their laughter stopped and five large men turned to look him over. There was also a woman with them, the only smoker. She was blonde, mid-thirties, and looked every bit her age, a welter of make-up failing to conceal a well-worn face and an undernourished body. Her short black skirt and tight red satin blouse did her no favours.

'Hallo,' Ronald said to the men. 'Sorry to bother you. I'm trying to trace a truck. No one inside was able to help.'

'Bunch of tossers,' said one.

'Yes, I suppose so,' said Ronald, siding with his audience.

'Here, let's have a look,' said another holding his hand out for the photograph.

Ronald let him take it and the men passed the shot round, all of them shaking their heads or looking puzzled.

'Sorry, mate, can't help,' said the last man, handing it back. 'To be honest I can't see a truck, just some light.'

'Oh, it's there,' said Ronald deflated.

'Maybe *you* could spot it, Annie,' said the first trucker. He took the shot back and passed it to the woman. 'You've seen the inside of more trucks than most.'

The woman punched him. 'Cheeky fuck!' she said hoarsely.

She looked at the photograph and instantly her whole demeanour changed. She handed back the shot as if it were aflame and shook her head vigorously.

'What?' said Ronald.

'Never seen it. Never,' she said and walked a couple of steps away and turned to take a long drag on her cigarette.

Ronald looked at the truckers for help but they were equally baffled. He took the shot from the trucker's hand carefully and edged around the men to Annie's side. She turned to him and blew smoke in his face, patently ignoring the photograph he was holding up for her to see again.

'You recognize the truck?' coughed Ronald.

She stared at him, dragging on her cigarette. Then she spoke, her voice hostile. 'What's the truck to you?'

'Do you recognize the make?'

'Who died?' she said.

Ronald was stunned. 'How did you—'

'Who died?'

'My daughter.'

'Car crash?'

Ronald nodded, confusion playing on his face.

'No cause? No witnesses?'

'No. Yes. I mean . . .'

'If I tell you what it is, will you leave it alone?'

Ronald didn't answer. He didn't know what to say.

Annie ground her cigarette out urgently with a high heel and let out a last long stream of smoke. She seemed to age visibly.

'Nefast,' she finally said.

'What?'

'Nefast. The make of truck.'

'How come you can see . . .'

'Because I've seen too much. And I've seen it before. Leave it alone.'

She started to walk away. Ronald grabbed her arm, her blouse riding up to reveal scabs on her arm. She pulled her sleeve down hurriedly and broke free of him. Ronald could sense the men bristling behind him and, turning, found all five truckers glaring at him.

'He bothering you, Annie?' one said over his shoulder.

She didn't answer.

Ronald turned back to her. 'My daughter was eighteen,' he pleaded. 'Eighteen. If you know anything . . .'

She stared at him, defiantly. Suddenly Ronald had an inspiration. He realized the marks on her arm meant she was an addict, and addicts could always use money. He pulled out his wallet and offered her a ten pound note. She laughed. Ronald didn't know the price of Anadin, let alone whatever she injected herself with. He offered her another twenty.

'It's all I've got,' he apologized.

Suddenly she snatched the money away and pulled a small card from her bag. Then she took out a ballpoint pen, scribbled on the back of the card and handed it to him.

He looked at it: *Nefast, Arton Road, Lane End*.

'Where's Lane End?' But she had walked off. One of the truckers leaned down to Ronald's ear.

'I'd go now, mate, if you know what's good for you. We don't like Annie getting upset. Understand?'

Ronald didn't argue.

Five minutes later he was in his car in the underground car park looking through his AA atlas. Lane End turned out to be a village in Cheshire, just off the M6, not more than a dozen miles from where Julie's car had crashed. Progress.

He checked his watch, 11:30 a.m. No time like the present.

Ronald crested a rise a mile north of the village of Lane End and spotted the farm, the only buildings in the valley. It was a strange place to build trucks.

The farm was situated to the left of the road on a wide, dusty track about a hundred yards long. The rest of the valley was hilly, criss-crossed with hedges with only the occasional clump of lonely trees for company. There were no sheep or cattle to be seen and, even allowing for its secluded location, the valley seemed unusually desolate, as if it had been forgotten. As a geography teacher, Ronald should have found it interesting – it bore all the stark features of a Pennine valley rather than Cheshire farmland – but, if he was honest with himself, he had lost what little heart he had for his job long ago.

The road ran straight through the bare valley for half a mile until it disappeared over a hill at the other end. It was a solitary spot, all right, and while the farm offered an ideal location for noisy metalwork to take place, the thought of lorries chugging their way up here for a paint job was faintly absurd.

The woman at the village Post Office had told him where to find the garage. Apparently it had been a customizing operation, doing panel work and spray jobs on standard trucks. Sometimes the work was so extensive they renamed the trucks Nefast. Her son had tried to get work there a year or so back but hadn't landed the job. That's how she knew about the place, and that it had burned down last November. That was not welcome news.

The farm boasted a small old farmhouse and two huge barns: one half-tumbled down and beyond salvaging, the other still sturdy, but very weather-beaten and rusty, the bulk of it painted black but looking large enough to contain a garage workshop. Ronald parked his mustard Allegro and stepped out to look around.

The farmhouse itself was long deserted, only the kitchen containing any furniture. He wondered why it was still abandoned, without even a 'For Sale' sign. Tarted up, it would fetch a pretty penny, even in a depressed market; it was near enough to the M6 to be worth commuting from.

The biggest barn was made from a jumble of materials: corrugated iron, asbestos, tarred wood. It was a mess but, at about forty feet wide, at least a hundred feet long, with twenty-feet-high walls and a roof that gradually inclined to about thirty feet high in the centre, it was also rather imposing. Too big, in fact, for a farm.

Ronald was uneasy. The place gave him the creeps. It was *so* quiet . . . He couldn't even hear any birds; just the wind whistling through the bare boards of the barn. He tried to ignore his foreboding as he reached the doors. A good ten feet high, they were solid and sturdy.

What was he doing? Why was he here? It did nothing to calm his nerves when he reminded himself that he was there to find out about a truck that no one else could see except himself and a junkie!

He tested the doors. They seemed to be held together only by a large rusted bolt which looked almost medieval. Bracing himself, he retracted the latch and hauled the high doors open wide and, as his eyes became accustomed to the gloom in the barn, he saw what was inside.

Nothing. It was a completely empty space. The concrete floor was stained with oil, and a large black hole had consumed half the roof. There wasn't even any rubbish or abandoned tools, just a huge empty space and the sky looming above.

Disappointed as he was, Ronald wanted to step inside but something stopped him. The tension he had been feeling was still building within him. He felt his pulse. His heart was racing. Why? There was nothing here, the place was empty. And it looked like his quest was over before it had started. He slammed one of the doors in disgust and stalked back to his Allegro, climbed in and roared off down the dusty drive.

He sped back to the village, slewing to a halt outside the Post Office and cornering the old woman inside, insisting that she tell him all she knew about the garage. She became flustered and said she knew nothing more than that, it had been run for a couple of years by a father and son called Simmons who kept themselves to themselves, never joining in the village life. Truth was that no one had liked them and the villagers weren't sorry they kept away. After the son was killed, the business went downhill, the father apparently a drunk, and then there was a fire which killed the father and destroyed much of the big barn where all the work was done. Receivers came in, cleared out all the equipment and furniture and the place had been left abandoned ever since.

Satisfied that she had told him all she could, Ronald calmed down and apologized, giving her some guff about his brother's haulage business being left with one of the Nefast lorries. The woman seemed pleased to accept his explanation, particularly when he made it clear that he was leaving.

★ ★ ★

It was a warm afternoon. Ronald was relaxing on a bench outside a cafeteria enjoying the weather, idly scanning the car park. Traffic buzzed in the distance like insects and all was calm and peaceful.

Suddenly a Transit van appeared from nowhere and drew level with Ronald. It slowed almost to a halt as someone tossed something out of the back onto the pavement, then it sped off and out to the exit road. All he could read as it zipped past were the words *Education Committee*. He pondered the scene for a moment then decided to investigate.

There was no one else about as he walked over to the newly dumped item. It was a black bin bag. Bulky, it had been tied at the neck by what appeared to be the ripped-off edges of computer print-outs, light blue with regularly punched holes. Wary at first, curiosity nudged him into action and he untied the neck and peeled the bag back.

It was Julie! She was dressed in a neat school uniform, either asleep or dead, and covered in dust and dirt. Ronald knelt down and delicately brushed the soil away from her face. He was surprised to recognize the uniform as being from his own school – although the motto on her blue jacket pocket had changed from *Ut Severis Seges* to *Semper Nefast*. He checked for a pulse but couldn't find one. He started to panic, tears splashing holes in the grime of her face. Unsure of his own medical abilities, he took a deep breath and forced himself to pull open her eyes.

Two grey, dusty orbs stared up at him. Then as he watched, two windscreen wipers emerged from the girl's lower lids and twin jets of water shot out from her tear ducts onto the eyeballs and the eyes were wiped clean in half a dozen back-and-forth movements by the wipers. And there, revealed to Ronald, were two perfectly blind white eyes without pupils. But even as this latest revelation sank in, the eyes suddenly blazed into life and shone directly into his face, blinding him.

He woke up with a start, rubbing furiously at his eyes. He looked around. He was on the sofa in his lounge, the TV on, sound down, weak light filtering through the drawn curtains. He stood up, his back paining him. The clock showed 6:52 a.m. Oh God, it had been the same dream.

He walked into the kitchen and threw up into the sink. The third time he'd had the same damned nightmare. What was happening to him? He sat down at the table and caught his breath. He was afraid to sleep now. Every time he'd slept since he had come back from that farm he'd had the same sickening nightmare, vivid and brutal.

He looked at the bottle of Bell's in front of him. He'd used it to try and help him sleep; now he wanted it to help him forget. As he took his first sip, the clock in the lounge chimed seven o'clock.

When he woke later, screaming again about the lights, it was, ironically, dark. He had no idea what time it was and cared less. He had dreamed again but this time he had come awake to a single overpowering certainty and, now that he considered it further, propped up against Julie's door, it seemed so obvious he actually laughed out loud. It would solve *everything*. So, armed with his new-found resolve and another bottle of Bell's, he walked outside to his parked Allegro, climbed in and drove off.

It was so simple, really. His thought processes were clear and unbefuddled. He had the answer. Alpha double plus, ten out of fucking ten. He was going to kill himself.

He paid little heed to other road users or traffic signals as he drove through Wilmslow and out into the dark Cheshire country-side. If he had met any cars coming the other way, both vehicles would have been destroyed; he had no way of stopping in time and, more dangerously, no desire. All he saw was the road ahead, all he felt was his hands on the wheel and all he wanted was oblivion.

For what seemed hours he wound his way around the lanes, often clipping hedges or slithering onto the rough verges until, finally, something snapped on in his head, like a blinding white flare. He had no idea where he was or how far he had travelled or even how fast he was driving. Nonetheless, he took his hands off the wheel and, with a heart-felt cry for his lost daughter, let the car leave the road.

But just as he closed his eyes something in his rearview mirror caught his eye. Something white. Not headlights, but something that gave off a sick luminescence. A radiator, grinning down at him. And a word, unmistakable, even in reverse. N E F A S T.

And then he ploughed through the hedge into darkness.

SIX

The new routine in Handland soon had Cally feeling happier than she could remember. She was allowed to sleep in her own room and only twice a week was she required to sleep in the lab. The relaxed atmosphere, her growing friendship with Nurse Bigg, her time with Mark, and Dr Gantry's sympathetic attitude all made for a lifestyle that, while obviously restrictive, allowed her a vital modicum of freedom. Besides, what would she do if she were outside Handland?

Go to school and live in council care, that's what. With her record and at her age there was no way Cally could be fostered. So she would remain in the system until she reached eighteen and was cut loose, uneducated and unskilled, with a psychiatric record to blight her for the rest of her life. With the way the State looked after disadvantaged people these days, homelessness and worse beckoned. No, Handland offered everything she needed, from three square meals a day to companionship she could trust. And, although she hadn't been troubled by her problem for weeks, Dr Gantry was still attempting to resolve it. One night they might effect a cure and then there would be one less problem in her life. Unfortunately, her new-found optimism was to prove premature.

Cally had been sleeping in the lab and, as usual, when they had completed their tests they had wheeled her back to her room and let her finish off her sleep with the help of light sedatives. She woke up around noon feeling groggy and got up and ran a shower. It was as she removed her nightshirt that she felt a pain in her nipple. Carefully removing the garment, she examined her breast more closely. Its tip was red and sore. Looking more closely, she recognized the mark as a hickey. Some creep had been sucking on her tits while she had been asleep.

Her urge to run screaming to Dr Gantry was overcome by her need to wash and for half an hour she soaped every inch of her body, finally convincing herself that the assault hadn't gone any further. Cally was no innocent about sex and, when she had towelled down and put on her dressing gown, she checked the bedclothes, but found nothing. On an impulse she checked the carpet – and there she saw it. A white crusty stain. Dried semen. Some fucker had wanked himself off.

Now she ran to Dr Gantry's office, rushing in past his protesting secretary to find him sitting, talking to another patient. Both looked up at Cally in surprise but when Dr Gantry saw how upset she was he immediately dismissed his patient and asked the distraught girl to sit down.

'What's wrong, my dear?' he asked.

'One of your fucking nurses has been sucking my tits while he jerks off, that's what's fucking wrong!'

Dr Gantry didn't bother to ask her if she was sure. Instead he insisted she have a strong cup of tea and only when she had calmed down did he ask her to explain.

Finally convinced of the veracity of Cally's story, he called in the two nurses who had escorted her back to her room and confronted them both with her allegations. The younger of the two immediately denied responsibility, claiming to have left the older nurse, a middle-aged man called Clements, to sort her out as the younger man had had to use the loo.

To her surprise, Clements confessed.

'I'm sorry, Dr Gantry, but I couldn't help myself . . .'

Dr Gantry was not sympathetic. 'There is only one course of action open to me, Clements. You have betrayed the trust of a patient in your care and, I might add, that of myself. You know the consequences. I am dismissing you as of now. You will receive no further pay and it only remains for Cally to decide whether we should call in the police.'

Cally was taken aback by Dr Gantry's ruthlessness. He had made no attempt to apologize for the man's behaviour; he had sided with her from the first. The man was sacked. Now he was asking *her* if she wanted to take it any further.

'Well, Cally?' asked Dr Gantry.

'No. Let's leave it at that.'

'If you say so, my dear. Right, Clements, clear out your room, collect your cards and leave. Do not expect to receive any references.'

'But how—'

'Perhaps you should consider a different profession.'

'But it's twenty years—'

For the first time, Cally saw Dr Gantry lose his temper. 'Clements, you are not fit to work! For all I know this may not be the first incident. Are you prepared to accept with gratitude this girl's generous offer to let the matter stay out of the hands of the authorities?'

The man stared at Cally, then turned and left the room without a word. Dr Gantry told the other nurse to leave the office.

'There, my dear, I hope that has solved the problem. I realize it must be a shock to—'

'I'll get over it,' said Cally, truthfully. After all, worse had happened to her before. 'I'm just surprised you did that so . . .'

'So quickly? But why? Look, Cally, this is a hospital, you are a patient. Our job, *my* job, is to cure you. Clements's job is to help me in my work. Not only has he assaulted you, but he had also abused the trust I had placed in him. The man is an animal and as such merits no further consideration. Now, is there anything else I can do for you?'

'No. I'll be all right.'

'Might I suggest that you avoid brooding on this. You know how your anger can . . . get out of hand, as it were.'

To her surprise Cally found herself saying, 'No, it's over. I'm just pleased you saw it from my point of view.'

'Indeed,' said Dr Gantry, pressing the intercom. 'Could you locate Nurse Bigg for me? I think a little shopping expedition is called for,' he said to Cally.

'Pardon?'

'I think you and Nurse Bigg should go to town and buy some clothes. You are, after all, a guest. There is no reason why you shouldn't dress as you like.'

'But I've no money.'

Dr Gantry pressed sixty pounds into her hand.

'And Cally, please don't take this as some kind of bribe to make you forget Clements's behaviour.' He handed her the phone. 'Dial nine for an outside line, then call the police. Much as I fear for the reputation of Handland, I would rather protect the integrity of my patients.'

Cally refused the phone but kept the money; as Dr Gantry kept insisting, she wasn't crazy.

SEVEN

The cab dropped Ronald at the Flying Horse just after 2:00 p.m. He had got the address from the card that the woman Annie had handed him at G-Mex. It was a greasy spoon café on the East Lancs Road, set in a large parking area half full with trucks and vans. Inside he found the usual clatter and chatter of a diner, overlaid by steam and cigarette smoke. He walked to the counter through the confusion of cheap furniture and oily-garbed truckers and ordered a fry-up. Finding an empty table he tackled his lunch, surprised at the generous portions and suddenly realizing it was his first full meal since his 'accident'.

Ronald had been cut out of the Allegro and had spent three days in hospital, his worst injury severe abdominal bruising. He had discharged himself, the time he had spent in bed giving him a new and deep resolve: he wanted to find the truck, and to find it he needed to talk again to the woman Annie.

Surveying the café, he saw a counter at one end with a beaded curtain leading to some stairs. At the counter sat a gargantuan woman dressed all in black reading a Mills & Boon. Behind her was a rack of keys and a notice stating that the Flying Horse offered bed and breakfast for £7.50 a night. Setting aside his unfinished meal, Ronald walked over to the woman and showed her the card Annie had given him.

'Yes?' she said without interest, her jowels wobbling with every syllable.

'Annie. I'm looking for her.'

'So are we.'

'What?'

'She left here three days ago, packed up and left.'

'Why?'

The woman looked up, her face impassive. 'No idea. She was

upset about something. Just upped and went.'

'No idea where?'

'M6.'

'Pardon?'

The woman sighed her impatience. 'Annie used to work the M6. Probably went back there.'

'Worked?'

'Annie is on the game, does it to get her smack. When she runs out of cash she works the service areas on the M6, picking up rides with truckers, blowing them, taking cash for fixes. Understand?'

'Oh,' said Ronald, feeling like a lectured first-year.

'Clear?' she sneered, adding for emphasis: 'She works the M6 like some girls work Sackville Street in town, okay?'

He turned to go but, realizing this had been his last chance to find out more about the truck, he forced himself to face the woman again.

'I have to find her. Does she work certain service areas?'

'You've got it bad! Can't get enough of her or what?'

Ronald was about to protest but saw a last possibility of help. 'Yes,' he said, looking sheepish. *Think, Ronald, think.* 'I met her a couple of weeks back. Gave her a lift. We . . . we got on well. She gave me that card, said to look her up if I ever . . . if I—'

'Wanted another blow?'

Ronald blushed with embarrassment. Fat and ugly as she was, he was still discussing sex with a woman; he had never spoken about sex to anyone except Ruth and even then they'd found it difficult to talk about certain of their desires.

'Yes,' he managed before looking away from her.

There was a long silence, Ronald acutely aware that the woman was continuing to stare at him, probably with disgust. Finally she let out a big sigh and closed her book.

'I've no idea which service areas she works. If you're really desperate, there are other girls—'

'No! No, it has to be Annie.'

The woman bristled. 'You're not some psycho perv, are you? A blow's a blow.'

'No, I'm not a psycho. It's . . .' *Think, you idiot.* 'It's . . . she used to know my wife.' *Sorry, Ruth*. 'She died a while back and Annie was the first woman I'd . . .'

'You sad bastard,' she said. Her voice had dropped so he couldn't tell if she was being sympathetic or judgemental.

She dipped down behind the counter and, fumbling in a drawer, pulled out a photograph. It was a model card, showing a young, happy woman: an Annie from a lifetime ago.

'Annie used to earn a living as a cabaret singer. Then things went wrong and, well, you've met her. Flash this about. Someone might know her. All I can do.'

Ronald thanked her and took the photograph, but the woman wouldn't let go. She beckoned him to lean closer.

'And you do her any harm, I'll cut your fucking balls off and fry them on that griddle over there. Clear?'

'Yes,' said Ronald, taken aback by her sudden vehemence. 'I just want to talk to her. Truthfully.'

The woman let go of the picture and Ronald walked away and out of the café, his heart pounding, aware that a lot of the truckers had stopped eating and were looking at him as he wound his way round their tables.

Outside, he gulped in fresh air and steadied himself against the low wall fronting the café entrance. He looked at the photograph.

Her stage name had been Anna Lee. She had been pretty if a bit thin, but at least her eyes showed life. He wondered what exactly had gone wrong; what could turn an attractive woman with a career into a heroin-addicted whore? Given that she had named the truck, he couldn't help reflecting that what had happened to her might not be far removed from what had shown up the devastating emptiness of his own existence. He just hoped he would be able to find her, but on the M6? That was an awful lot of road.

EIGHT

The assault on Cally and Nurse Bigg's sympathetic treatment of her had the effect of bringing the two of them closer together and the nurse soon proved to be more than just another member of staff.

She coaxed Cally into revealing more than she might have to Dr Gantry. Nothing really important, more girl stuff than anything else, but the fact that Gantry never seemed to get to hear what she had told Nurse Bigg led Cally to believe that she really was there to help her and not Gantry. Besides, Nurse Bigg was female – appearances to the contrary – and Cally always felt safer with women than with men, a point she made to her new-found friend as they sat in the sun watching Mark drawing the vegetable garden.

'You know, Elizabeth, Mark here's the first bloke I've been able to talk to for ages.'

'But he's autistic. He never talks.'

'Doesn't mean he can't listen.'

'True, but what's the point if he can't answer?'

'What's the point of talking to Dr Gantry if he can't sort out my problem?'

'But you don't know he can't.'

'How do I know Mark's not got an answer, it's just he can't say it?'

'Touché.'

'What?'

'It's French. Means this argument's going nowhere. So, what do you talk about to Mark?'

Cally took a deep breath. 'What I'd like to happen when I get out of here. The shit I've had to take . . . well, mostly it's about that. The bad stuff. Talking it through helps. Dr Gantry explained that and it's true. Like a confession in church, I suppose.'

'Bad stuff. Have you had a bad time?'

'Ha! Dr Gantry hasn't told you?'

'No. He prefers an unbiased approach. I learn from you, not from his case notes. So, what bad stuff?'

'People who helped fuck me up. Who were supposed to help and didn't. Men, mostly. Like Dr Rogers – the twat who sent me here – the teachers, other psychiatrists, boys, my stupid dad . . . Every man I've met has messed me up in some way.'

'But not Mark. He's not a threat.'

'Obviously not. So I trust him. Pathetic, really. The only man I can trust is a loony.'

'Autism doesn't make people loonies, Cally. Besides, if you think he can hear you, won't he feel insulted?'

'He knows I'm joking.' Cally leaned forward and tapped Mark on the shoulder. 'You know I'm only joking, don't you?'

It took another couple of prompts before Mark let out one of his all-purpose 'fugs'.

Nurse Bigg smiled. 'What about Dr Gantry? Will you trust him?'

'Maybe. He's been pretty friendly so far. Doesn't treat me like a crazy. I like that. I may be fucked up but I've not lost my marbles. I can still think straight. Besides, my problem's under control at the moment, so no worries.'

'And what is your problem?'

'Dr Gantry's not even told you that?'

Nurse Bigg shook her head.

'Really?'

'Really. He's just said you'd had a bad life and you have emotional problems. To be honest, I think he thinks you're lonely here and he wants me to be your friend.'

'Could be. Do you want to be my friend?'

'Yes. I had a daughter . . . she would be about your age now. She died of cancer. Leukaemia. She was seven. Lovely little thing. Tara was her name.'

'Tara. Nice name. Better than Cally.'

'Cally's nice, too. Is it short for something?'

'Yeah. Short for dad was a space cadet.'

'What?'

A bleeper in Nurse Bigg's pocket went off. 'His master's voice. I'll see you later.'

She got up and walked briskly back into the building. As she reached the entrance, she turned and shouted:

'Cally, how about I get a McDonald's tonight?'

'Really? McNuggets. And a strawberry shake and fries!'

'You'll get fat!'

'Good. I need to!'

Nurse Bigg brought back the McDonald's that night, and other treats most nights from then on. They became good friends, Cally slowly letting Nurse Bigg grow into the role of big sister. Most of her time was spent with Nurse Bigg but, when she wanted to be alone the woman would leave her be. It was like having a friend on tap. And the trust between the two reached new heights on one of the Saturdays that Dr Gantry let Cally sleep in her own room.

All week Nurse Bigg had been probing Cally as to her sexual experience and, as close as they had grown, to admit that she considered herself to be gay was a hell of a step for Cally. She had come to terms with her sexual orientation – or as much so as a sixteen-year-old can – but had never had the opportunity or nerve to see if the reality lived up to the fantasy. Nurse Bigg, and another bottle of Martini, had managed to drag the truth from her and on that Saturday night Cally returned to her room to find a woman on her bed.

Attractive, brunette, early twenties and with a welcoming smile, she explained her name was Estelle and that Nurse Bigg had asked her to come in and meet Cally. Cally, not surprisingly, was taken aback. Her first reaction was that it was some kind of joke, or a test, but when she looked up at the video camera, she saw that it had been covered with a bag. Nurse Bigg then popped her head round the door and said she would make sure there were no intruders and that Cally was to go ahead and do what she felt like – adding, with a wink, that she always did.

And, eventually, Cally did.

She awoke the next morning after a long peaceful sleep to find herself alone. She enjoyed a lie-in, idly playing with herself as she

relived the experience of the night before, pleased she'd had the
nerve to ask Estelle to show her everything she knew. It had
taken quite a while. Finally, she got up, showered, dressed and
was about to leave her room when Nurse Bigg came in and closed
the door behind her.

'Hallo, Elizabeth,' said Cally, acutely embarrassed. 'Thank
you . . . thank you for last night. Estelle and every—'

'Shut up, you little slut,' said Nurse Bigg.

'What?'

'Shut up and get on the bed!'

Before Cally could respond, the nurse had pushed her back
onto the bed and, kneeling heavily on her chest, had plunged a
needle into the girl's arm.

Cally tried to rise but fell back limp, as if all the energy had
been drained out of her. Nurse Bigg started removing Cally's
clothes until she was completely naked. Then she pulled a large
black dildo from her pocket.

'Now it's my turn,' said Nurse Bigg.

The drugs stopped Cally screaming but they didn't stop the
pain.

When it was over, Nurse Bigg left Cally with a warning: tell
anyone, including Dr Gantry, and she'd be dead.

Cally was hurting too much to worry about telling anyone and
she stayed in her room complaining of stomach ache. That night,
just as she was falling asleep, Nurse Bigg came into her room
again. This time the big woman didn't touch Cally but showed her
a scalpel and told her to strip and pose. A dozen ignominious
polaroids later and the nurse left, laughing.

The humiliation and the pain were nothing compared to the
huge emotional void that suddenly overwhelmed Cally. She had
been on such a high for so long at Handland, with help and
sympathy at every turn, that to have it stolen from her by the
vicious and sick demands of her so-called nurse was too much for
her to bear. For the first time in a long while she allowed herself
the luxury of tears.

When she had done with her crying, Cally began her planning.
It was clear now that she was on her own again and would have to
depend on her own devices. But what devices! She lay back and
stared at the ceiling, planning Nurse Bigg's demise in intricate

detail. She thought of the trust betrayed, the hopes dashed, and she remembered the agony and the shame and the look of glee as the nurse had forced Cally to recite in explicit detail everything Estelle and she had done, while all the time the black rubber alien had sliced into her virgin body and splashed blood onto her thighs. The traitor would pay and Dr Gantry would miss his chance to witness Cally in action. No wires, no drugs, no lab. Just Cally and Nurse Bigg. *Time to pay, you fucking bitch*! Cally closed her eyes.

Just after 11:30 p.m. on Sunday, Nurse Elizabeth Bigg died, her massive disfiguring injuries necessitating eventual identification through dental records and a ring on one of her severed fingers.

The next evening, after a day spent in a darkened room that mirrored the state of her mind, Cally was visited by Dr Gantry. When he broke the news of Nurse Bigg's death, Cally immediately confessed that she had done it. Instead of surprise or horror or even outright mockery, Dr Gantry merely nodded and said he knew she had, and pointed up at the video camera. The bag was still there.

'Opaque material and night vision,' he said simply.

'When? What . . . what did you see?' asked Cally, confused.

'Nurse Bigg doing as I told her.'

'What?'

'I got her to get you to kill her.'

'What? All that stuff about being my friend—'

'Was all in a day's work for the late Nurse Bigg.'

'Did she know—'

'Of course not. There are only two kinds of nurses, in my opinion. Those that do what they're told and those that don't. Only the former work at Handland. And Nurse Bigg was one of the best. Her job was to befriend you, then betray you. She didn't ask why, she just did it. I'll miss her.'

'But she's *dead*! I killed her!'

'Shame. I only wish I could have been there to watch it happen. All we saw is what the video showed.'

Cally launched herself at him but he side-stepped her attack and shouted. Immediately two male nurses entered the room, including the one Gantry had sacked after his assault on her.

They strapped her to the bed and gagged her.

Gantry pulled a syringe from his pocket, removed its cap and squirted the excess into the air.

'Now, Cally, I don't want to hurt you. This is just a little pepper-upper, to make sure you're bright-eyed and bushy-tailed until we're ready for you in the lab. There's so much to be done and we've only just started.'

Cally thrashed about on the bed but it was no use. She felt herself waking up, her head bursting with colour, her body vibrating. And then they left her, exposed and bare like a live wire waiting to be reconnected. She'd never felt so alive, and she'd never wished so much that she was dead.

NINE

The M6 motorway. Two hundred and thirty-one miles long, running from its Junction 1 link with the M1 near Rugby north to Junction 44 where it joins the A74 near Carlisle. On its journey it passes Birmingham, Coventry, Stafford, Stoke-on-Trent, Manchester, Warrington, Preston, Lancaster, Kendal, Penrith and Carlisle. One of the country's major arterial routes, connecting North with South in six smooth lanes, linking directly to other motorways including the M55, M61, M56, M58, M62, M54, M5, M42, M40 and M1. It is vital in helping the reliable flow of goods and people the length of England west of the Pennines. As such, it is busy every day of the week although it can be brought to a standstill by Bank Holiday traffic, roadworks or accidents. Parts of it are spectacularly beautiful, especially in the Lake District, but mostly it looks like any other motorway. In Birmingham it is elevated, stretching across the city like a badly healed scar. Along its length are ten service areas, from Corley, near Coventry, to the services near Carlisle, including the south-and north-bound access-only services between Lancaster and Kendal. Millions of vehicles use it every day and thousands of them are trucks hauling goods.

Thousands of trucks, forty-nine junctions, ten service areas, one junkie prostitute: Ronald had his work cut out, but it was better than his alternatives.

The day after he had visited the Flying Horse, he had gone to his bank in Wilmslow and emptied both his current and deposit accounts. Then he had closed his Nationwide account. He had gone next to a caravan dealer and bought himself a Volkswagen camper van. Then, parking it outside his home, he had stripped the interior of everything except the two front seats and put in the mattress from his bed, plus bedding, clothes and road maps. By

6:00 p.m. he had finished and gone indoors, run a bath and enjoyed a long soak, probably his last for a few days. That was all he thought it would take to find Annie and learn the secrets of the white truck. Yes, for once in his life he was going to get off his fat, hide-away-from-it-all arse and *do* something.

He joined the motorway at Knutsford and headed south. He travelled at a steady 50 m.p.h. and although he saw lots of white trucks none of them were his quarry, whatever the pounding of his heart told him whenever one hove into view. He stopped at each service area and showed the photograph of Annie to any likely-looking drivers. None recognized her. The day dragged on, and motorway café food soon took its toll and he had to stop for Milk of Magnesia.

At Junction 1 he turned round and headed north. By the time he reached Bamber Bridge it was getting dark. He must have shown Annie's photograph to two hundred drivers, not one of whom registered a flicker of recognition. It was going to be a long job. He called the Flying Horse, but no one had seen her since she left and when he refused to give his name they slammed the phone down on him. Plainly, others were worried about her absence as well.

The next question was when and where to sleep? As soon as the motorway became empty, he turned at Junction 31 and drove back down to the Charnock Richard services, where he parked his van with the coaches and went for a meal. Lingering over his third coffee at 11:30 p.m., he realized that he was too tired to do anything but sleep in his VW.

Unfortunately, with traffic flying past on the motorway, vehicles coming and going and the noise from the cafeterias, he found sleep an elusive partner. Indeed, it wasn't until some time after 4:00 a.m. that he finally succumbed to fatigue and slept. Even then, it was a fitful doze, the same nightmare jabbing him awake two hours later – a sleep pattern that was to repeat itself with distressing regularity, almost as if something didn't want him to find any respite.

Ronald was surprised how quickly the days blurred into one long journey, punctuated only by darkness and the need to stop for rest or enquiries.

If he wasn't driving, then he often found himself outside the entrance to a cafeteria or shop, photograph in hand, stopping customers who looked like truckers. He would first apologize for bothering them, then show them the photograph and ask if they 'had seen this woman recently.' Most would pause, look, then shrug and walk on, a 'Sorry' sometimes offered. Others would shake their heads, or make crude suggestions. Ronald soon learned to refer to Annie as his sister, so as to pre-empt sexist remarks. But whatever his approach, whoever his audience, the final answer was always negative. No one recognized her, no one had seen her.

And so, despite having asked a hundred or so drivers at every service area he had stopped at, Ronald was no nearer a solution. He tried out his truck photographs a couple of times, but he saw a look come into their eyes when they realized there was no truck to be seen, and he soon reverted to his shot of Annie. He also tried shop and restaurant staff, but unless he was buying they weren't interested.

Soon disappointed, and, after that, quickly dismayed, Ronald nonetheless continued his questioning. After all, how else was he to track down the truck if not by tracking down Annie?

Days passed. Service area names like Corley, Hilton Park, Keele, Forton and Burton became landmarks as familiar in Ronald's daily journeys as Watson's News, the Open Later Saver and the Golden Lion pub had been on his way to and from school. And the logos – Granada, Roadchef, Rank, Forte – grew as commonplace to him as the marques of his fellow teachers' cars once were. He soon found himself attuned to the rhythm of the road. Like a living organism, it pulsed according to the time of day, the weather, the day of the week. Fast or slow, busy or quiet, traffic moved up and down the motorway like blood pumped around a body, eventually disgorging him onto a service area like exhausted haemoglobin in search of revitalizing oxygen. But Ronald never found the replenishment he needed; all he found were shaking heads and shrugged shoulders. Yet, despite his lack of progress, he tried to retain some semblance of normality.

Each morning he would wash and shave, then sit down in a cafeteria with a breakfast of cornflakes and coffee and read the

Daily Mail, but he soon gave up the newspaper. The world didn't interest him any more: he had his own world, and his own politics to play by – the politics of revenge.

Lunch would again be cafeteria fare and sandwiches bought from a shop, sometimes eaten on the move. He always tried to stop for tea and cake, then more questions or more motoring, then supper, normally around 8:00 p.m. But soon his urge for routine, a need inculcated from childhood and reinforced by the working patterns rigidly adhered to in school, gave way to a growing alarm at the hopelessness of his task. Four days in, he had spoken to hundreds of drivers and hadn't raised so much as a flicker of recognition.

After the fifth day he stopped shaving.

After seven days he stopped washing in the morning.

Nine days and he stopped washing last thing at night as well, instead just splashing his face when he felt like it.

After ten days Ronald stopped changing his clothes. The VW was a warm, fuggy place and whatever smells it offered (and he himself contributed) his nose had become used to them long since. More and more, all he wanted to see was the road ahead as he drove from one service area to another, ever eager for a positive response, but always to be disillusioned. However, as a man with a mission, he didn't let it get him down: he just cut out distractions.

No more cleaning his teeth. Breakfast could wait until lunch. Only wash his hair when it itched. Change his underpants only when they chafed. He also started economizing on his meals by buying tinned goods – beans, hot-dog sausages, rice puddings – and eating them cold in the van. But even those lost their appeal; food was simply an inconvenience, something that stopped him driving or sleeping or searching. Soon he was down to one meal a day and the occasional drink – non-alcoholic, of course. It all took its toll.

He'd had an attack of diarrhoea and hadn't made it to a service area in time. Instead he had had to stop just off Junction 18, and run behind a hedge. Once he had felt it safe to return to his van, he had had to drive seven miles with the result of his accident before he could fill a bag with other clothes and visit the lavatories at Knutsford Services. Once there he cleaned himself up as best he could, changed, and exited the cubicle, leaving the soiled garments behind. It was 9:00 p.m. and the place was empty so he didn't have to hurry out. He needed to wash his hands and it was as he looked up from the basin that he saw himself for what he had become.

Ronald's face was streaked and dirty, his hair dark, greasy and unkempt. He almost had a beard, the pronounced stubble flecked with grey and the remnants of baked beans. His eyes were puffy and bloodshot, his clothes, though relatively clean, smelled and were badly creased. He looked like a wino, no two ways about it. He was surprised rather than shocked; he was too lost to the new world he had chosen to react with any real emotion. He saw what he had become, it registered but he didn't do anything about it. On an impulse he weighed himself. He had lost thirteen pounds! There was a time he would have had a slap-up meal to celebrate such a hard-won loss but now it meant nothing. Then someone came in and he scurried back to the VW.

Three days later Ronald was in a phone box, calling the Flying Horse from the Granada Southwaite Service Area in Cumbria. He continued to phone regularly in the vain hope that Annie might turn up. After his 'accident' in the van and his realization of how fast he had let things slip, he did clean up his act a little, washing more often and sucking peppermints. Whenever he needed to talk to someone he tried to present a clean appearance. He would shave and comb his hair and put on his relatively clean clothes, but it was like icing on a rotted cake; the decay still seeped through. Maybe it was the smell or his bad teeth or maybe just that hint of desperation in his eyes, like a junkie trying to act calm in order to get hold of cash for a fix.

The Flying Horse people were in an abusive mood and Ronald had cut them off in mid-insult, stepping out of the phone box and walking back to the VW. He had a cold and his head ached and he longed for the comfort of his own bed, flannelette sheets and Radio 4. And Ruth bringing him Lemsip.

Ronald spat phlegm onto the car park, another habit he had once abhorred in others but now practised like a veteran. He climbed into the van and pulled a coat round his shoulders and hugged himself. He missed Ruth's rug. He had taken some

Anadin a couple of hours before and didn't want to risk any more. He checked his watch. 2:16 p.m. He'd been on the road nine hours now. He hadn't been able to sleep the night before – another nightmare – so he'd given it up as a bad job and hit the road. The van's engine had started pinking and needed fixing, but he didn't have the time. Every hour off the road was an hour he might miss Annie.

Ronald switched on the radio. Pop drivel. He flipped to Radio 2. Middle of the Road drivel. It wasn't so much the music as the patronizing tone of the presenters that annoyed him. Still, it gave him something with which to occupy his mind; something to shout at as he drove up and down the motorway.

There was a traffic announcement. A crash on the M6 was causing delays five miles away. He set off, praying he would be there in time. He had a theory that the white truck might have continued to cause accidents and that if he reached a 'fresh' accident he might find some evidence of its activity. However, after six such accidents he had seen nothing.

The scene that the motorway police waved him by was terrible. Two cars were buried under an overturned milk tanker, the motorway awash in white liquid lending the carnage an aspect of purity that was surreal. It was a fatal accident, that much was plain to see, the cars crushed down to a matter of inches. It blocked two lanes of the motorway but traffic was light enough that it could be funnelled past on the hard shoulder.

Ronald slowed and stared at the remains. Had 'his' truck had anything to do with it? He passed a police car with a shocked man in overalls sitting in the passenger seat, his legs outside the car, his head in his hands. He was probably the tanker driver. Had the truck made him swerve? Suddenly the immediacy of the event and the unproductiveness of the last fortnight combined to snap Ronald's hold on logic. In a second he convinced himself it had been caused by the white truck. There was no other explanation. None.

He threaded the van through some cones, slid to a halt and jumped out and was running to the man before any policeman could stop him. Side-stepping an alarmed sergeant talking into his radio, he confronted the tanker driver.

'What happened?'

The man looked at him, plainly in shock.

'What happened?' pleaded Ronald. 'Was it a white truck?'

The man looked through him, reliving the accident again and again, aware that whatever actions he had taken, however unavoidable the collision, human beings had been killed by 'his' vehicle.

The sergeant grabbed Ronald's arm and heaved it up his back. Ronald let out a yelp, but would not be deterred.

'Was it a white truck?'

The driver continued to stare up at him, his face blank.

Too soon Ronald was dragged away, the sergeant yelling obscenities into his ear and hurling him into the arms of another equally disgusted traffic cop who marched Ronald over to his VW, telling him that unless he drove off immediately, he was in a world of shit; they didn't have time to waste on ghouls like him. Ronald decided it was better to agree. He climbed into his van and drove off, the cop flagging down traffic to let him enter the stream. He saw the man spit after the van as he accelerated away.

However, Ronald couldn't help himself. At the first exit, Junction 15, he crossed back over the motorway and made his way along the southbound carriageway, slowing to a crawl as he viewed the dead carcass of the tanker lying broken over the opposite carriageway, its unmarked cab propped up on the central barriers as if dropped there by some giant.

It was the eleventh crash Ronald had seen on his mission and the first time he had actually been able to talk to one of the victims, but it had yielded no more information than the others. Noticing a policeman waving him on, he drove by, regret making his head ache even more. This could have been the one: the one where he got to see his truck.

Ronald pulled off into the service station five miles further on and parked, then sat back rubbing his head. He needed some proper rest to shift his cold, so he climbed into the back of the van and lay down, trying to get comfortable, but the van was cold, the bedding damp. Nights without the heating were taking their toll. He stared up at the ceiling, listening to the hum of the motorway and the *zing* of heavier vehicles flying past. Over two weeks of this and he was no nearer his goal. There would have to be a time when he gave up, when he admitted defeat, but he knew now he would only ever do that when it was physically impossible to continue. If he had no transport or money, or his health became so bad that he couldn't carry on, only then would he give up, and then possibly only to recoup his strength and resources before setting out again like some modern-day Don Quixote tilting at trucks. Or was it more a case of hunting the Holy Grail? Maybe that was more fitting.

All Ronald had ever cared about in his life had been his wife and daughter. Now they were gone he had to replace them with something else, some goal that gave him a reason to carry on. Teaching and the pub and TV, they weren't nearly enough to keep his spirit alive. No, he needed to hunt down that which had snuffed out the last remaining light in his life. That truck had killed Julie; he was going to kill the truck.

But first sleep, the shadowland where Julie could still live and his life ran on a different road.

TEN

Anger is a negative tool. It blinds a person to their true intent, fudges plans, destroys reason. In the days following Nurse Bigg's murder, Cally had time to work her anger through, to dissect her hatred, to compartmentalize it and file it away for future use. It was easier than she thought.

After her initial rage Cally had tried desperately to do to Gantry what she had done to Nurse Bigg, but the medication stopped her. Gantry kept her in her room for four days and nights, pumping her full of drugs to ensure that she would remain awake and alert, clearly intent that, when she came down and sleep claimed her aching mind, he would be able to mould it to his will. And that, Cally decided, was where the old bastard had made his mistake.

As soon as she had decided that everyone was worthless, that every man and, now, every woman – everyone *else* – was her enemy and out to destroy her in some way, then she was able to take her rage and control it. Nothing anyone could do to her, no amount of abuse would make her unsheath it until the time was right. Gantry was in for a frustrating time. He might have the power of night and day over her mind, but she controlled her anger. Cally had the power.

On the Friday afternoon, she was moved up to the sleep lab, stripped naked and strapped to the bed, wires attached to her head, neck and chest, a catheter and rectal thermometer inserted, and six cameras and two microphones trained on her. The room was warmed to a pleasant temperature, the light lowered to a soothing level and the sounds of heartbeats in the womb, waves on sand and wind in trees mixed through speakers. And then everyone waited.

'Let's see what the Sandman brings, shall we, Cally?' were

Gantry's only words as one of his assistants injected something into her arm.

Cally came down from her precisely prescribed high as predicted and within thirty minutes had fallen into a deep, contented slumber. Time enough for her to relax her mind and drift off on dreams of warm sunny afternoons spent with naked lovers who were gentle and sharing.

When she was woken up it was dark outside and Gantry was not happy.

'Holding out on me, Cally?' he said and slapped her across the face. 'Next time . . .'

She was taken back to her room, injected, and left strapped to the bed, the TV locked onto Sky One.

On Saturday night Cally was taken back to the lab and the same procedure was repeated. However, this time, she refused to sleep. Gantry almost injected her but decided against it and returned her to her room. There, despite the constant babbling of the television, she lost herself in mind games, remembering the good things in her life, banishing the bad.

On Sunday afternoon she was injected again, taken to the lab and prepped as before. This time she succumbed to fatigue and drifted off, dreaming of a cold winter's night and a lover wrapped in warm white fur that needed to be unwrapped slowly.

Cally was wakened by being thrown onto her bed in her room where two nurses strapped her down, each threatening sexual torture when Gantry went off to London the next day.

She acted terrified but as soon as they had left, their promises like poisonous insects awaiting the opportunity to strike, she relaxed. Cally knew now that everything that happened to her was at Gantry's bidding; he had told her too much too soon about his techniques. As long as she kept calm, he would never get what he wanted. The only worry then was, what would he do when he realized he was losing the war? Unfortunately, the next day she found out.

'Cally, my dear, come in, sit down,' said Gantry – who obviously hadn't gone to London – as she was brought into his oak-panelled study.

Despite the large window behind his desk, it was a gloomy room, dominated as it was by heavy masculine furniture and walled with books. One of the male nurses sat her down in a chair across from Gantry's desk and left her. Cally was too tired to protest but not so weary that she could sleep. Part of the process, she presumed.

'How are we today?'

'We're fine,' she said, determined not to be antagonized.

Gantry slowly spun round in his leather wing chair and stared out onto the lawn a floor below.

'Cally, we are locked in a war of nerves. I know it, you know it. I want you to show me your murderous ability, you want to frustrate me. Just what I might expect from a teenager.' His laugh was every bit as unconvincing as his smile. 'And I'll tolerate it for some time yet. To you it is a matter of dignity, of personal pride. To me, on the other hand, it is a life's work. I'm sixty-one, I have something of a reputation with the more enlightened members of my profession, but I have yet to prove myself to *all* my fellow scientists. You hold the key to that acceptance. You, Cally, will make my name, one way or another.

'You are in Handland for as long as I and Dr Rogers say so. You are committed as insane because of your insistence on taking the blame for certain deaths. You will never leave until we say you are cured, do you understand? You have been waging your private little war against me for about a week. How will you feel in another week, a month, a year?'

Gantry turned round and stood up, fingering a green and yellow Tiffany lamp on his desk.

'I could order you into confinement now. Lock you away in the dark on a minimal diet, no human contact for months.'

'Pin down?' said Cally. 'Been there.'

'I know. I have your records. You seemed to take to it like a duck to water. So, we shall have to think of something worse.'

'Torture?' she offered. 'Red hot needles? Bamboo shoots? "Take That And Party"?'

'Tempting, my dear, but I would rather you co-operated more willingly. No, I was thinking of something a little more subtle. A bit less personal.'

Gantry pressed a button on his intercom. The door behind Cally opened and he gestured her to look.

She twisted in the chair, her limbs slow to respond, and looked into the outer office. There stood Mark, the blank gaze fixed as ever on his broad face. Suddenly one of the nurses punched him full in the stomach and he collapsed to his knees, coughing and spluttering onto the floor. Soon he was vomiting. The door closed.

'Mark is here permanently. He is of little value to me but his family pay extortionate amounts of money to let him stay. The last time he was visited by *anyone* was two years ago and then only by the family solicitor to ascertain if he was still alive. He is mine to do with as I wish. And what I do is up to you.'

Cally tried to rise but it was pointless. 'You bastard.'

'That's it, girl. Use it. We both know that's the key. Hatred. Anger. Revenge.'

'You're playing a dangerous game . . .' she managed.

'On the contrary, my dear, it is *you* who are playing with fire.' Gantry walked round the desk and stood in front of her, cupping her face in his right hand. He raised his left hand as if to strike her and she flinched. He smiled and instead merely patted her hair.

'Fire, Cally, fire. You're not my only interesting case. I have a pyromaniac who can sometimes combust material just by looking at it. I have several lunatics capable of telekinesis, though their results are undependable. Then there's the madman who can project his own image onto unexposed film. Difficult to harness but exceedingly interesting to work with. I even have identical twin simpletons who say the same thing at the same time, even when apart. All of them fascinating and all of them on the fringe of current knowledge. But you, Cally, *you* are in a different league.

'So far I only have your word for Nurse Bigg's death and the evidence Dr Rogers has offered – but that is only a tape and his hysteria. I want proof. I want facts. I want to see you at work, my dear. And I will, because if you don't come across soon, your friend Mark will pay the price, and if your stubbornness extends even to allowing the innocent to suffer for your behaviour, I could call a halt and terminate the experiment altogether . . . and you along with it.'

Gantry pushed his face to within an inch of Cally's, his bad breath caressing her mouth like the whispers of a rapist.

'We all have limited patience, girl. You are patiently frustrating me, I am patiently enduring it, but one day one of us will
snap. If it is you, then I'll be a happy man. If it is me, you will be
a dead girl.'

He leaned back on his desk. 'I have already altered your case
notes, incorporating conversations we have never had. They
make it plain that you are suicidal, blaming yourself for the
deaths of various people you couldn't possibly have killed. Guilt
is eating you up, you are balanced on a knife edge. One incident,
one we might never understand, could topple you over and we'd
find you hanging from sheets in your shower, or slumped in bed,
blue of face, head in the plastic bag from a jigsaw . . . the list is
endless but it reads the same way: little girl lost who, despite the
best efforts of the staff, could not face reality as she saw it and
took her own life. Meanwhile, we'll carry on our little game, shall
we? Johnson!'

The door opened and Cally turned to see Mark being held
upright by a nurse standing behind him. The nurse was pulling
Mark's head back by the hair. Mark was still breathing raggedly
and was obviously in a lot of pain. His face also betrayed his
confusion. Upon seeing Cally he let out a strangled 'fug'.

The other nurse looked questioningly at Gantry, who nodded.
The nurse kneed Mark in the testicles, not once, but twice, and
then bundled the crying man away. They might as well have
kicked an innocent babe.

Gantry spun Cally round again. 'I am a scientist. I want results,
I need data. You are just another experiment. Get that? Not a
patient, not a responsibility: an *experiment*. Co-operate and we'll
all be happy, including your friend. Fuck me about and the pain
will spread. Think about it.'

He walked back to his desk and sat down, ignoring Cally as a
nurse came in and pulled her out of the room.

'I'll get you, Gantry, I'll get you, you evil fuck!'

'I very much hope so, my dear,' he said without looking up.

The nurse walked Cally back to her room and locked her in.
She hadn't the strength to do anything other than slump on her
bed and cry. How she wanted to sleep! But she knew she
wouldn't be able to until Gantry let her. What she would do then
she didn't know. She couldn't let Mark suffer, but what if Gantry

learned her secret, was able to harness it, to use it? What then? And what of her? She had to do something, otherwise she and Mark would really start to suffer.

So she did. Two days later Gantry took her down to the sleep laboratory and Cally gave him exactly what he wanted.

ELEVEN

One hand on the wheel, one hand on the Polaroid camera, Ronald edged past the wreckage and took four shots, *click-whirr, click-whirr, click-whirr, click-whirr*, letting the pictures drop onto his lap. Then he saw the policeman looking straight at him, his face expressing utter dismay. Ronald dropped the camera and accelerated, edging into the inside lane behind a large Pickfords pantechnicon, and waited a couple of minutes. Then he picked up the shots.

The first two were full-on shots of the burnt-out car, corpses still visible in the back. Ronald nearly threw up, the enormity of the intrusion of his photography devastatingly clear. But even as he had been taking the shots with his autofocus camera, he had remembered that it was the environs of the crash he was shooting, not the remains themselves. So the next two shots had been taken aiming over the wrecked car. And there it was, the white truck!

Involuntarily Ronald slammed on his brakes, a horn shrieking at his rear. He slipped the van onto the hard shoulder and waved apologetically at the coach that drove past.

He picked up the last two shots. The truck was there all right, parked on the hard shoulder on the opposite carriageway, but he could have sworn he hadn't seen it as he passed. There was only one way to find out.

Unfortunately the next southbound exit, Junction 32, was ten minutes away in the slow-moving traffic that was even slower on the way back because of the accident. So it was nearly twenty-five minutes before he reached the scene of the crash again. By now the ambulances had ferried away the injured and the firemen were freeing charred corpses by cutting the cars up with powered saws and acetylene torches. Ronald took three more shots and found himself looking at the same policeman as before. He obviously recognized the van and made to run at it, but traffic intervened and Ronald lost him.

The new shots revealed the truck again, this time parked on the other side of the road. Ronald knew for certain that he hadn't seen it there for himself, so why did it register on the film?

He was tempted to turn round and drive past the wreck a third time but decided not to push his luck. The truck had been there, but so had that policeman; all the cop needed to do was radio in the VW's licence plate and Ronald could be pulled over any time they wanted. And if they looked inside the van . . . So he drove on to the next service area and parked out of the way. Then, stepping into the back of the van, he stuck his new pictures up with his others.

Ronald had a gallery of eight accidents now, gleaned over the two weeks since he had bought the camera. He had been lucky, if that was the word, to be on the scene of most of them within minutes of their occurrence. With the rest, the emergency services had been still in the process of cleaning up. On each occasion the truck had been there, lurking in the background like those old women at the guillotinings during the French Revolution. It was always parked, its doors and windows closed. Whether it had caused the accidents or was just there, Ronald didn't know. He had never seen an accident actually happen and didn't want to.

He lay back and stared at the shots. He had kept newspaper articles about the various crashes, too. Ten people had been killed altogether and as many injured. In most cases no cause was given, though one was put down to a burst tyre at high speed. No mention of a mysterious white truck from any survivors, though. Just plain, everyday motorway pile-ups.

Ronald had also plotted the crashes by location and time on a large map of the motorway he had made by sellotaping together several pages of an AA atlas. There was no pattern. The accidents happened in different places in different times with no apparent connection. From a three-car smash at the M42 turn-off to a fourteen-vehicle pile-up near Knutsford; from a head-on smash between two trucks at Gravelly Hill to a minibus clipping a bridge support at Kendal; from an aquaplaning multiple shunt at the M61 junction at Bamber Bridge to two joyriders killed by an

express coach when they misjudged a contraflow on the Thelwall
Viaduct. The only connection, in fact, was that Ronald had
passed these crashes, taken shots and discovered the truck was
there. So what did that tell him? He had racked his brains over
the last couple of weeks trying to understand it. And he would
have to find out soon because he was running out of money.

Ronald was averaging three hundred miles or more a day and
that alone was costing him over fifteen pounds a day in fuel. Then
there was his food and drink. His credit cards were drained and
closed and all the money he had left was stuffed in an old sock
inside the rim of the van's spare wheel. He needed to start finding
answers – and quickly.

He had tried showing the accident shots to people at service
areas, but most looked at him as though he was offering them a
swig of methylated spirits and marched away. Quite a few
suspected the shots were pornographic and got uptight. But when
they saw what the photos really were, some people actually
became violent. This creep was carrying around pictures of car
wrecks and dead bodies, for God's sake!

Shunned and reviled, Ronald was slowly cutting down his
sources of clues. No one would talk to him, so what was he to do?
He looked at the shots for the thousandth time, the truck
omnipresent, taunting him. Did it cause the crashes or did it just
show up to gloat? What did it want, who drove it and why?
Unable to come up with any answer, Ronald forced himself to
leave the van and go to the service area shop and buy a Pepsi. It
was as he was deciding what to buy that the rack of soft porn
magazines caught his eye.

Ronald had never been particularly interested in sex, even as a
young man. He enjoyed it, certainly, did it quite often in the early
years of his marriage – having married as a virgin – but it had
never been an obsession. No strange habits, no affairs. To
Ronald, sex was like a good meal or a wine; you enjoyed them
when you could, but they weren't the only things in life. A cuddle
on a cold night with his darling Ruth while the wind rattled the
windows was more to his liking than all that humping and
grunting – and Ruth agreed – but looking at those *Escorts* and
Penthouses with their naked models framed by promises of
ecstasy made him pause.

It was three years since he'd had sex. As Ruth had got sicker Ronald had occasionally relieved himself, but the guilt he felt at his lone pleasure while she lay upstairs waiting for death was too much. But now, perhaps, the old fires could be rekindled. It would at least signal some semblance of humanity amid his obsessive pursuit of the truck.

The irony of this desire for apparent normalcy was lost on Ronald as he purchased one of the magazines, walked up to the cafeteria and sat with his coffee, flipping through the pages. His reading material soon drew looks of consternation from nearby tables, though it could as easily have been his odour that produced the effect. Yet, despite page after page of big breasts and pubic hair and 0898 scenarios, all he could think about was how cold Ruth's hand had been when she had slipped into her drug-induced coma before finally dying. Such a warm woman rendered so frail and pained for no reason other than that her body had decided to eat itself. So damn cold, as cold as Julie when he had brushed her face in the coffin . . .

Ronald turned a page and found a girl called Julie spreading her arse and inviting readers to fill her up. He hurled the magazine aside in disgust: disgust at himself and disgust at the women who allowed themselves to be shown so demeaningly, daughters every one.

He sipped at his coffee oblivious of the mounting hysteria behind him as a party of infants fought for a view of the magazine's centre spread. However, Ronald soon felt hands gripping him under his arms and around his collar as he was unceremoniously bundled out of the cafeteria.

As he was hustled downstairs, he protested but knew it was pointless, especially when he caught sight of himself in a window and saw how scruffy he looked: unwashed, unshaven, his coat stained with mud and bird droppings.

He tried to go to the Gents to clean up, but two security men blocked his way and ordered him off the premises. He meekly obeyed, much as any vagrant would, to avoid trouble.

Back in his van Ronald lay his head on the steering wheel and wept. He wasn't even fit to be in normal company. Discarding that magazine as carelessly as he had went against every principle he had employed in his teaching. If ever he had found dirty pictures or books, he used to punish the culprit severely, including burning the offending material. Yet here he was, tossing it into the laps of seven-year-olds. How much further could he sink?

Ronald wiped his eyes, switched on the ignition and drove off. Time for another patrol. There truly was nothing else in his life now. No sex, no home, no family, no dignity, no self-respect. Only that damn truck.

TWELVE

It was a Wednesday night when Cally finally gave Gantry the firsthand demonstration he had been waiting for. It was incredibly hard to keep control once she had let the rage take her, but it had been worth it just to see the destruction and Gantry's clear horror.

The damage included the laboratory's smashed equipment, shattered windows – and everyone's underwear. Knowing that the great Gantry had actually shit his pants when she had let rip was deeply satisfying for Cally. She herself had had an accident but she didn't care. The look on the man's face when he saw what he had been waiting for all these weeks, the way his eyes opened wide, his mouth dropped and the colour drained away from his face! It was just what Cally needed to focus on to keep her rage under check. And when it was all over, and people started breathing again, she had lain there like a queen while they unstrapped her, Gantry babbling her praises and his amazement, and let them carry her back to her room. There they showered her and put her to bed, a final injection ensuring continued wakefulness.

The next day, Cally realized that letting Gantry see her power for himself was a mixed blessing. True, she'd had the pleasure of seeing him soil his trousers, and she noticed one of the male nurses wasn't around any more. Probably too scared to come in. Ha! And Gantry had left Mark alone, apparently believing Cally's claim that he could threaten all he liked, but he would have to wait for the next time, it couldn't be rushed. He seemed eager to believe her so, while the pressure was off Mark, it was back to the usual monotonous routine for Cally. Days awake, her mind buzzing with life, then back to the lab and the experiments.

Cally's plan, such as it was, depended on various unconnected elements coming together. There was Mark, Gantry, the door, the ward, nurses, her drugs, the hospital . . .

It was Friday morning when things started to fall into place. Cally had been returned to her room a little after 7:00 a.m. following another fruitless night in the sleep lab. Gantry hadn't been best pleased but neither had he resorted to threats. She had overheard an assistant mention Kirkby. Apparently Gantry was visiting another hospital there to check out a 'promising young boy'. God knows what he had in store for the poor Scouse bastard, but at least it meant he would be away for the day and, if everything ran to form, Cally would be locked up in her room the entire day. And that's exactly what they had done.

At about 11:00 a.m. she spotted Mark on a bench sketching the view towards the vegetable garden. Good. As usual, he was unsupervised. Night could fall, snow blow and the hospital burn down and he would continue to draw.

Cally went to her shower and removed one of the metal rings from its curtains, straightened it, then slipped it into the mortice lock on her door. With practised twiddling the lock sprang open. The things one picks up in council care.

She carefully edged the door open and peeked into the hallway. Although she was on a secure ward, her room was actually outside the main dormitory area. This meant one less barrier to circumvent, but she still needed to get past the nurses' station and the outer door to the main building.

Cally edged her way along the wall, careful that her trainers didn't squeak on the highly polished floor, until she could see into the nurses' station.

There were two in there, a male and a female, neither of whom she recognized. Once she was locked up, Gantry's assistants must go elsewhere, confident she was out of harm's way – at least until the next time they came for her.

Cally could sneak past the office on her hands and knees, but there was always the risk that someone on the ward or coming through the security doors would spot her. She decided the time was wrong and carefully retraced her steps to her room, there to await the right opportunity.

Every five minutes or so she would pop her head around the door and check. The door to the ward was spring-loaded but, if she remembered rightly, the door to the landing wasn't; she could always hope someone would leave it open.

At noon a cleaner arrived. He propped the main door open and retreated, presumably to collect cleaning equipment. It was likely to be her only chance, so she took it.

Cally walked purposefully towards the open door, her eye on the nurses' station. Only one person inside this time, a female nurse she didn't recognize. Not surprisingly really, it was over three weeks since Cally had been allowed to associate on the open ward. She was ten yards from the door when the cleaner appeared, pulling a mop in a wheeled metal bucket. He looked at Cally and stopped, his mouth opening to speak. Cally froze, fearing the worst. She had seen him before and they had never spoken, but he was a member of Handland's staff; it would be his duty to shout a warning. But he didn't. Instead he edged to one side and held the door open, putting his broad dungareed back to the station window.

Cally walked up level with him and stopped, convinced he was about to shout but he simply waved her through. He was in his fifties, big and rough, with fingers like bananas matched in ruddiness by an open, dim face. Of course, thought Cally, he wasn't on staff; he was an inmate. A trusty. He nodded at the open door, his eyes pointing the way. She put her hand on his chest and smiled at him. He smiled toothlessly back, plainly nervous. She walked briskly through the door and turned left onto the corridor outside.

It was only as Cally made her way towards the main stairs that she remembered where she had met the trusty. He had cleaned the ward when she used to sit with Mark. Sometimes he would stop and watch them; he must have appreciated Cally having time for Mark when everyone else ignored him – much as he was probably ignored, of value only as free labour. Poor sod.

Cally reached the stairs and paused. Two flights down its broad steps and she would be able to leave the building through the main entrance, but she needed drugs. There would be little point in taking Mark with her if she were to fall asleep. She had seen the Pharmacy from outside the hospital, behind a window with bars, wire mesh and an extractor fan. So she strode purposefully down the main staircase, ignoring anyone she met.

At the bottom in the main entrance hall, Cally turned left and walked down another corridor to find the Pharmacy located on the west corner of the building. Good. Now all she needed was a weapon. A secretary's office door was open. She nipped inside and surveyed the desk. Aha.

Armed, Cally returned to the Pharmacy and burst through the door. She found herself in a small anteroom with a counter, behind which stood a door with a frosted glass window. The anteroom was empty but she could see a figure approaching through the glass. She bounded over the counter and stood to one side of the door. As it opened, she jumped into sight and pushed the woman who stood there back the full length of the Pharmacy, past rows of high shelves stacked with bottles and packs until the woman slammed up against the window looking out onto the gardens.

The middle-aged, white-uniformed nurse was about to scream when Cally held up the scissors.

'One word, bitch, and I'll cut your fucking tits off!' Cally had long ago learned that people are as much intimidated by attitude as they are by actions.

The woman started to struggle, plainly believing she had right as well as size on her side. Cally immediately stabbed the scissors into the woman's skirt with as much strength as she could muster. The nurse stopped dead and stared down in between her thighs where Cally's hand was bunched, the scissors no longer visible.

'Have we got the message, you stupid fat bitch?' hissed Cally, throwing the woman one of her best mad stares.

The nurse nodded dumbly, her face registering terror at her predicament. From then on she was as obedient as a butler. Five minutes later Cally had the drugs she needed – thanks to the patient records held under her name on the Pharmacy's computer and the nurse's knowledge of their effect – and the woman was tied with rolls of Elastoplast to a chair in the furthest corner of the storeroom. Then Cally gagged and blindfolded her.

Slipping out of the Pharmacy, Cally worked her way along the corridor until she found herself back in the main entrance, Tesco carrier bag of drugs swinging gaily from her hand. Something so ordinary and in plain view couldn't possibly contain anything sinister, could it?

Apparently not. She left the building unchallenged and ambled slowly round to where she had seen Mark. It *was* a nice day; she'd forgotten what they could be like. He was still there. A short conversation ensued of which he appeared to understand not a word but managed a 'fug' when prompted. Then Cally took his pad and pens and led him round the building to the central courtyard.

Although they were overlooked by more than a hundred windows, most of the staff had offices on the outside of the building; here the view was reserved for patients.

Cally checked the cars like the professional she had almost become while in care. She selected a Vauxhall Cavalier L, J reg. No alarms, no Krooklok, but the radio had been removed. Sensible. Chances were thieves would go for that rather than the car itself. Okay, Cally, let's see if we've still got it.

A coathanger from the Pharmacy cupboard was quickly inserted into the gap between the driver's door and window and the lock pulled. Inside, she kicked at the steering column covering until it came loose, then prised it off. Fifteen seconds later – getting rusty, girl, she thought – the car fired up. Revving it a couple of times to stabilize the engine, she stepped out of the car and carefully showed Mark into the back seat, strapped him up, then locked the back door, climbed into the driver's seat and set off.

Two minutes later and Cally was approaching the entrance to the hospital. She had never seen this and was annoyed to find that there was an automatic barrier on the left of a small booth containing another guard who checked people coming into the hospital. She could try and talk her way through – *very* chancy – or she could ram it. It looked a bit hefty, though, and it was at windscreen height. Could end up killing herself! There was just one last chance.

She pulled open the glove box and rummaged inside. Nothing. The door? No. The visor? She flipped it down and there it was, slipped into the band. A pass card. She wound down her window and drove up to the barrier and, keeping her head back out of sight, she slipped the card into the machine and smiled as the barrier raised. She extracted the card and drove through, avoiding the eyes of the guard. Reaching the main road she turned left and accelerated away.

Well done, girl. Plan A had worked! Now she was on the run with a kidnapped autistic man fifteen years her senior, in a stolen car, with no money, and only drugs to make sure she would stay awake. How long did that give her? And what would happen if Gantry caught them?

She switched on the radio. The Fun Boy Three's 'The Lunatics Have Taken Over The Asylum' blared out. For the first time in weeks she allowed herself a genuine laugh.

THIRTEEN

Rain. Lots of it. Ronald watched two drips racing down his steamed-up windscreen and bet £5 the left drop would reach the bottom first. After an agonizing detour around some leaf debris, he won. That made him £45 up on himself after – he checked his watch – four hours and ten minutes. What a waste. He looked out of his side window and scanned the M6 below the bridge.

Tuesday afternoon. Traffic was heavy. Cars, vans, trucks, buses, they streamed by underneath him northwards and southwards like six multi-coloured snakes. The only problem was that the poison fangs of his white truck never showed. Occasionally he would experience a frisson of expectation as a large white trailer loomed into sight and made its way towards him, only for it to reveal itself as Connor Carriers or Hotpoint Appliances.

Four hours, eleven minutes. He was cold (he couldn't afford to keep the engine running), he was tired and dirty but duty called. He'd give it another hour then he'd drive on to the nearest service area and sit out the night, watching the endless procession of trucks easing in for a refill or a rest, hoping against hope that his white truck would be one of them – or one of them would be carrying Annie.

There was a tap on the window, startling him. He refocused to his left and saw a stern-looking woman in a raincoat and hat staring in at him through the quarterlight.

She motioned him to wind down his window.

'What are you waiting for?' she said gruffly.

'Pardon?' said Ronald, rain dabbing at his face and making him blink.

'Why are you parked here?' she demanded, her face flushed with cold, and possibly anger.

'I—' Ronald was lost for an answer.

The woman, large and middle-aged and armed with self-righteousness the way muggers are armed with knives, pointed ahead of the van.

'We know you're waiting for the school to get out. We've been watching you and we've called the police.'

Ronald peered into the gloom through the streaky windscreen. Sure enough, bundles of mothers were hovering by the gates of a primary school a hundred yards the other side of the bridge, not a few of them staring in his direction.

Not again, thought Ronald. Why hadn't he noticed the sign?

He turned back to the woman to protest his innocence, but she had stepped away and was waving at her fellow mothers, mission accomplished.

What choice had he? Stay and explain why he had parked outside a school for four hours in the rain in a van with a mattress in the back. Or simply drive off, his fate to be a topic for dissection at a dozen dinner tables that night?

He switched on, checked his fogged mirrors and despite being unable to see anything in them, wheeled the van round and drove off in the opposite direction, turning down the sliproad onto the motorway and joining the anonymous streams of southbound traffic as quickly as he could.

It was the fifth time Ronald had been questioned about his long-stay parking on motorway bridges, but it was a risk he had to take. How else would he spot the truck? He thought of what the women would be saying now, huddling over their children like protective mother hens, clucking them home, fear tainting their hearts. There was a time he'd have been the one doing the asking of the lurking stranger. Once, back in the Sixties when the horror of the Moors Murders was dominating the headlines, he and a fellow teacher had sneaked up on a Cresta parked near their school and kicked in the headlights. The man had never returned. Had he been a genuine pervert or just a victim of their paranoia? They'd never known, yet here Ronald was playing the same role, unable to explain himself, branded a menace and yet trying to save lives, to *protect* children, not molest them.

He realised he needed to pee, but as he was on a stretch of motorway with service stations twenty miles apart and was midway between the two, he took the first exit ramp at Junction

37 and followed the road until he reached a parking lay-by.

It was long but empty and Ronald eased the van to a stop, locked it and trotted up the steep verge until he reached a wooden fence. Climbing over it he walked twenty yards to the cover of some trees and bushes. Once there he found himself in need of more than a pee so, trousers down, he crouched out of sight and relieved himself. He hadn't brought his toilet roll with him so he carefully pulled up his trousers and underpants, promising himself that he would clean up properly the first chance he got.

He kicked some leaves over the evidence, then made his way back along the edge of the field, now aware that anyone passing would know what he had been doing. But, Ronald realized with genuine surprise, he no longer cared. People pissed, people shitted, people vomited and fucked and cried and bled and died. He used to worry what people thought of him. Yes, he had been fat and bald and middle-aged, but at least he had been intelligent and smart and didn't smell and held informed opinions on subjects that mattered. But now . . . take away his van and he'd pass for homeless or senile.

Senile. Now there was a thought. What if he was going off his head? Stress, trauma, brain cell decay . . . One of his aunts had gone mad, ended up in a home after the war. Though it was obvious now that she had been suffering from Alzheimer's, to the young Ronald she was held up as the fate that awaited him if he masturbated or was cruel to animals.

Ronald had been a lively, cheery lad but his father had done his best to grind him down, to plane him into his own image. To some extent he had succeeded: teaching and its predictable routine – the hours, the terms, the curriculum – had all appealed to Ronald eventually, and as the years went by his sense of vocation, his calling, had seemed just another wild dream of youth.

At one time he was going to become a cartographer – the name had a ring to it – and map unknown territories (there were still plenty of them, even in the 1950s). He had also dreamed of becoming a professional racing driver like Stirling Moss, but he'd never had the opportunity to test his mettle. Besides, any expression of ambition outside the hallowed halls of academe would be greeted with a pleading look from his mother and an ominous rustle of the ever-present *Daily Telegraph* from his father's chair. So perhaps now his life of denial – of fitting in, doing what was best – had finally come home to roost: his mind paying him back for all the hoops he had made it leap through over the last thirty-five years in his denial of his own potential and his setting of easy goals for himself. Aim your sights low enough and even mediocrity becomes an achievement.

Ronald stopped walking and stared into the field, watching crows stalking through the stubble, their *caawing* scratching at the afternoon calm. Was that it? Had he spent so many years thinking up excuses for his stultifying existence that his mind had finally stopped trying and was now wandering where it wanted? Had Julie's death so soon after the death of Ruth finally made him fixate on some truck as his nemesis?

Ronald stood and stared for a long time, not seeing, just letting his mind sift over the possibilities. And finally it dawned on him that it didn't matter. Mad or sane, he was hunting the truck and, mad or sane, he was going to find it and deal with it. He walked back to his van but, as he stepped up onto the fence, he heard a hiss. Looking down at the VW he saw something that made him lose his footing and bang his jaw on the top of the fence.

The truck was parked nose to nose with his van, waiting.

Ronald dived for cover, ignoring the blood on his lip and the pain in his chin. For several minutes he lay there, face down, breathing raggedly, his heart racing almost as fast as his mind. The truck! It was here. Now. In daylight. And he was alone.

Finally he edged towards the fence and, parting the grass, looked down at the lay-by. The truck was still there, white and gleaming against the dull strip of road. What did it want, and what was he to do? Watch it. So he did. For two hours.

Cars came by, another truck stopped but soon drove off. Hitchhikers ambled past, ignoring it. The sky clouded over, rain speckled Ronald's back, then fell out of the skies and drenched him, but he didn't care, didn't even move. For two hours he lay in the wet field and stared down at the truck while it did nothing. No window wound down, no door opened; it just sat and waited.

Ronald's initial fear was replaced by a curiosity that, as the afternoon wore wearily on, gave way to irritation. He wanted to get up and run down and yank at the truck's door, to see who was driving it and ask him . . . what? Exactly! What would he ask? Who would he find inside the cab? Inside a truck that no one else could see, that killed people and vanished?

So he waited and watched until, without warning, it started up and drove off, just like any other truck after its driver had enjoyed a nap during a long haul. Thirty seconds later and it was out of sight.

It was another twenty minutes before Ronald clambered over the fence and edged his way down to his van, and another ten before he was sure the road was safe and he could get in and drive off – straight to the crowded motorway, naturally. But in those ten minutes, he couldn't help noticing the fresh rust on the bumper and the bleached paint on the front of the VW, the two spots closest to where the truck had parked. Nor the hundreds of dead flies that covered its windscreen.

Once inside, Ronald fumbled the van into life and used the washer to clear the insects off the windscreen before screeching a U-turn over the dual carriageway's central reservation and, foot down, driving back onto the southbound side of the M6.

It was two days later, a Thursday, when the fog came down. There was no warning, no ominous blanket draped across the carriageway ahead, just a sudden whiteness that enveloped Ronald's VW and every vehicle within his sight in a matter of seconds – and at fifty miles per hour, it was devastatingly disorientating.

Ronald's instinctive reaction was to slow, but he was aware that others behind him might rear-end him. On the other hand, he had every chance of running into cars in front of him who *did* slow down. What made it worse was that he had been cruising in the middle lane and was tempted to pull into the inside, but his rearview mirrors were useless, visibility down to feet; he couldn't even *see* the lefthand lane.

Ronald lifted his foot off the accelerator and wound down his window, straining his ears to hear anything other than road-roar. But what he actually heard was the screeching of tyres, a distant *crump* of metal and desperate horn blasts, though where they were from he couldn't tell. Suddenly he became very frightened;

no matter what he did – slowed, speeded up, turned right or left –
he was inviting disaster.

He strained to look in the offside lane to see if it was clear but
found himself wandering over white lines that zipped out of the
grey. A large car blared its horn as it zoomed past, a white blur in
a blurred white world. What speed was the maniac doing? Ronald
checked his speedometer. Forty. He had to slow down; better
yet, get right off the motorway.

He started sweating, despite the cold that was rapidly invading
the van's interior. He was *blind*, and couldn't even rely on the
intelligence of other drivers to save the situation. He'd seen
enough stupid behaviour in rain over the past weeks to know that
temporary blindness was no impediment to the rushing salesman
or speeding trucker.

Down to thirty miles per hour, Ronald still hadn't seen any
lights ahead of him. Lights! He only then remembered his own
and flicked on his headlights and foglamps, but he might as well
have shone a torch on a whitewashed wall for all it revealed.

He listened some more. Something had crashed and there was
a stream of thumps receding into the distance as cars tailgated
each other. Ronald leaned out of his window, his speed down to
twenty, and tried to see ahead. Useless. The fog stroked at his
face like wet ribbons, the cold beads it laced on his face mating
with the sweat of fear already there, its starchy blandness
reaching into his lungs and smearing the back of his throat. And
all around, through the dead stillness, he could hear the sound of
panic as tyres squealed, people shouted and metal slammed and
crunched together. Occasionally a vehicle would pass by but he
sat frozen to the wheel, unable to make any decision. Then he
heard a dull explosion somewhere off to his right, and saw a dim
yellow glow. Panic seized him and he edged the van onto the hard
shoulder, slammed on the brake, jumped to the ground and ran
round the front of the van and onto the slick grass slope, where he
fought to gain a foothold as he clawed at tufts of grass in a
desperate attempt to climb.

Every so often Ronald lost his footing and slipped back, all the
time convinced he would roll right down onto the motorway and
be crushed, while behind he heard the continuing sounds of
collisions and screeching tyres and now, Oh God, he smelled

smoke, burning fuel and rubber, the stink of road carnage.

Finally he crested the top of the verge and slammed face down in some dirt. He rolled over, sat up and nearly shouted in amazement. Just below his feet bubbled a sea of white, crossing the hundred yards of the valley of the motorway cutting. Like a river of milk it sat silent, obscuring everything underneath it. Ronald stood up, careful to mind his footing, and stared into the deep. He could see nothing, but could hear rending metal and the cries of the injured as their cars and companions disassembled about them.

He looked up and across the road he saw, standing above the mere of mist, another figure, dressed in yellow. Squinting, he made out a woman in a mac, her head swathed in a blue scarf, her hands to her ears as she shrieked silently at the horror beneath her feet.

Ronald tried to shout to her, but his words barely registered in his own ears. He waved at her, what for he didn't know, but, stranded above the clammy pool that obscured so much terror and death, he needed to reach out to another human. But it was no use. Then he noticed something familiar about her. Tall, slim, but her shoulders hunched, like she was embarrassed by her height . . . Julie? What? No. But that yellow mac. It couldn't be . . . Oh God, it was!

'Julie! Julie! It's me! Dad! I'm—'

Suddenly she dived forward, as if the fog had momentarily parted and she had spotted someone she knew. Then she was gone, swallowed up, screams and all.

Ronald slumped to his knees, then fell onto his backside and wept. Silence now brooded beneath him, a lack of sound all the more frightening for the subdued cacophony of disaster that had preceded it.

He waited for a couple of minutes, a man alone – perhaps the only man in the world – then decided to walk back down to the muted motorway and see . . . and see what? See hell? If he could help? If his van was still in one piece? But, as he walked down the steep slope, the fog began to thin, soon becoming a mist then just an overcast day . . . and then he saw exactly what had happened on the motorway while he had been hiding like a whimpering child on top of the slope.

Nothing. It was a normal mid-morning on the M6 near Shap. Traffic was medium to light in both directions, but there were no wrecks, no burning cars, no bodies, no debris, nothing out of the norm. Nothing except his VW van parked on the hard shoulder and behind it, just pulling out into the inside lane and accelerating away, a large white truck.

Ronald stopped and stared as it disappeared northwards, then he walked numbly to his van. That was when he saw, burned in reverse into the black paint of his van, the legend NEFAST.

Had he the strength Ronald would have run, but he didn't. Instead he slumped to the ground and, leaning back against the defaced rear door, laughed mirthlessly. His grip on reality was as close to snapping as it had been at any time over the last few weeks. One more incident and he might well steer the van into a bridge support and end it all.

FOURTEEN

How had she got herself into this mess? Cally wondered as she stirred baked beans in the dark. She looked out of the kitchen window at the darkened fields beyond the cottage and imagined what unseen terrors might lurk there watching her. They didn't frighten her. Even the chilling shriek of a fox didn't make her jump. The horrors she knew lay within herself were far worse than anything the Cheshire countryside could offer.

Satisfied the beans were warm enough, she carried the pan into the sitting room, shut the door to the kitchen, then turned on the lamp. Mark was sitting there and he started drawing as soon as the light came on. He was studying the fireplace and its burned wood.

Cally poured Mark's portion of the beans into a bowl, sprinkled broken salt and vinegar crisps on the top and led him to the table where she sat him down and handed him a spoon. He started to eat, hunger spurring his mind into action. There was little point asking him if he enjoyed it; he always said the same thing, but this was the fourth meal in a row with beans. She would have to get something else soon.

Cally sat down with her own bowl and, not for the first time, couldn't be bothered to eat. Instead she swigged on a can of Vimto and watched Mark devour his food. They had been in the cottage for three days and could stay here almost as long as they liked as long as they had food. The place was up for sale and had been for quite a while judging by the damp and the smell. She had switched on the power and the water and had found the place bare but fairly cosy, and a lot better than some of the squats she had been in. (At least this one didn't come with smackheads who thought she should pay rent by lying down whenever they could get it up.) The cottage was also off the road so no one could see them but, just to be sure, they stayed at the rear of the house and she tacked heavy blankets to the windows so light wouldn't escape at night.

Cally wasn't sure how Gantry would deal with their escape. The shit he had put them both through made it unlikely he would involve the police because of what she could tell them. Nonetheless, they *had* stolen someone's car and the Handland security people would probably have reported it before Gantry's return so Cally and Mark had to find some other wheels.

Cally had found a large car park outside a Tesco's and parked next to a rickety-looking Mk4 Cortina. Two minutes later she and Mark were driving out in a Ford.

Next problem had been money. She'd had to resort to her old ways. Parking in a side street, she had handed Mark his pad and pens, then pointed him at a church beside the car and immediately he had begun scribbling away. It would have been endearing if it hadn't been so sad. He was almost old enough to be her father.

They had needed cash so theft was their main hope. Cally was surprised at her dexterity, having been so long out of practice. Two wallets and two purses later and she'd purloined a grand total of eighty-five pounds in notes and a handful of loose change. She had spent seventy pounds on tinned and packet foods, then carried the heavy bags back to the Ford and driven off to their cottage.

Having put away the food, she had ensconced Mark in an upright chair, given him his gear and let him draw away to his heart's content. At least one of them was happy.

By nightfall she had realized they were missing one or two essentials, like a radio and toilet paper and bedding, and she had vowed to sort them out the next day.

Cally had been grateful to find out that Mark could use the toilet unaided, though his 'fug' on emerging had underlined their need for toilet paper. But otherwise he seemed happy enough. She had then managed to get him to sleep on curtains she had torn down from upstairs.

Two days on and she was again watching him fall asleep and allowing herself the luxury of tears. All she had done was delay the inevitable. Perhaps the best thing to do would be to give themselves up at a police station and plead that Gantry was evil.

But where was the proof? One look at Cally's record and the police would *post* her to Gantry, just to get her out of their hair. As for Mark, well, she'd kidnapped the poor sod. What for? Because Gantry, a leading and respected psychiatrist had let his nurses beat him up in order to make her sleep in his lab? Yes, sure, whatever you say, *girl*. And what if she told them why she was in Handland in the first place?

Let's face it, you shithead, Cally thought, idly kicking at the table leg, you're fucked. She pulled up the carrier bag of drugs. That was another nail in her coffin. Stealing drugs. She was a junkie. Who would trust her word? She read the labels in the half light from the lamp: Nitrazepam and Temazepam to get her asleep fast and deep; Methylyphenidate and Dexamphetamine to keep her awake. They worked but as her tolerance to them was growing, their effects were diminishing, and then what . . .? She wanted to sleep but knew it would be dangerous, not only for Mark but maybe even for herself. That last time in the lab the rage had been so intense that only by focusing as hard as she could had she been able to control it. Drift off here with no controls, no limits, and she could kiss goodbye to her reason. Maybe even her life. No, she needed to stay alert, if only because some time in the future she might figure a way out of her predicament.

Cally found the bottle she needed. Pills this time, thank God. She took two tablets and swilled them down with Vimto. Staying awake wasn't so much the problem as finding something to do to occupy her mind while she was. There was no TV or radio, nothing to read. If there had been a working phone she could have rung a chatline or a musicline but the one in the cottage was dead. So she settled herself down on the only easy chair in the place and tried to work out what to do next.

She was grateful when dawn broke and she was able to walk freely in the garden of the cottage without fear of being seen. The dew on the grass, the birds in the trees, the crisp air promising sunshine and high temperatures: it felt like freedom, it even smelled like freedom, but it wasn't real. Cally was as much a prisoner here as ever she had been at Handland and, thinking of the drugs on the table and the child-man sleeping innocently nearby, she had been a lot safer inside Handland, whatever Gantry's ultimate ambitions.

FIFTEEN

Ronald felt good. It was a bright if cold day, perfect for driving. He had just cleared a slow contraflow north of Birmingham and the traffic was beginning to speed up. He was passing a convoy of four transporters carrying Escorts. It was as he drew level with the first truck that he saw a shape dart out from the verge. He couldn't be sure what it was but it looked larger than a dog. A child? The truck didn't react and nothing crossed into his lane, so Ronald ignored it, even as his heart started pounding with fear.

A minute later he saw another figure. This time there was no mistaking the young boy in blue blazer and light grey trousers. Ronald slammed on his brakes but watched in horror as the truck ran the boy over and, instead of slowing, carried on as if the driver hadn't even seen him. A blast of an air horn and flashing lights told Ronald the transporter that had pulled out behind him didn't appreciate his slowing and he had no choice but to take his foot off the brake and carry on.

He tried to accelerate until he was level with the truck cab, perhaps to flag it down, but as he increased speed so did the truck. Shit. Then another figure ran out onto the motorway. This time it was a girl, dressed in a white blouse and blue skirt. Again he slammed on his brakes as the girl was smashed underneath the transporter and again the truck behind him merely registered its protest.

Ronald was beside himself with horror. Two children had died and the truck hadn't stopped. He had to do something. He checked his mirror. The bulk of the transporter behind him filled his vision. He couldn't argue with its momentum; best get out into the outside lane and see what he could do there. But as he signalled to move out, a coach bore down on him on his right at an amazing rate and in seconds he was boxed in on three sides.

He pressed his foot to the floor but all three vehicles kept pace with him. Ronald was trapped.

He saw another child run onto the motorway, this time reaching his lane. But even as he braked, the transporter behind him nudged his VW in the rear and the child skipped to the right to be obliterated by the coach. Ronald took his foot off the brake again and stared up at the coach.

A row of children's faces stared down at him, each grinning maliciously, eyes bright and blue and full of delight at what had just happened. Ronald stared back and they laughed all the more, each face contorted with evil knowledge. Ronald couldn't help swerving away from them and then he caught sight of one of the Escorts on the transporter to his left. It was full of equally gleeful kids, their faces pressed to the glass, all straining to look for the next victim. And sure enough, as Ronald turned to look ahead, there were two more children waving at him as he bore relentlessly down on them.

A violent thud. Snapshots from hell. A girl's smiling face splitting in two from top to bottom. Teeth flying like scattering marbles. Blood and brain splashing against his windscreen. Fingers sliced off by his wing mirror. Ronald let go of the steering wheel and covered his face with his hands and screamed, only to pull them down some moments later and find two truckers staring at him across a car park. It had been another nightmare.

Ronald ignored the truckers. Christ, what was happening to him? Almost every time he slept he would dream something horrible, usually involving children dying and cars crashing and . . . and those damn blue eyes. He looked at his shaking hands and realized he couldn't stop them fluttering. The nightmares had seeped into his muscles and nerves, taking root, taking over. God help me, he thought, as he fumbled the door open and made his way over to the brightly-lit ground-floor cafeteria, purposely ignoring the truckers still peering after him.

As Ronald reached the broad swathe of the cafeteria window he paused, catching sight of his reflected white face and plastered-down greasy hair. Disgust made him refocus on the customers on the other side of the glass. They might as well have been on the other side of a brick wall for all they had to do with him now, all of them just so many strangers taking a break from a journey to the rest of their lives; a life Ronald had long left behind. Just so many faces . . . But then one face registered and held his attention and then his heart banged in his chest. It couldn't be, not after all . . .

Annie! Ronald had found her! By accident, true, but what did that matter? He had been looking for her for two months, and no one had recognized her and the Flying Horse had only ever offered the vaguest notion of her whereabouts – and then only when they weren't quick enough to recognize his voice. Yet here she was, sitting barely ten feet from him, her hands fiddling aimlessly with a napkin as she chain-smoked Regals over a coffee and brace of doughnuts.

Before he could stop himself, Ronald was hammering on the window, startling Annie into dropping her cigarette. She turned to look at him and took a full ten seconds to recognize him.

Ronald was too excited by his discovery to think of the effect of his sudden appearance on the woman who, after all, had literally been on the run since he had shown her his photograph of the truck.

He signalled that he would come in and join her, but by the time he reached her table she had gone. Looking around the crowded cafeteria he spotted another exit and dashed through it into the coach park, just in time to see her disappearing behind a Wallace Arnold double-decker. Jogging to its front he met her as she reached the driver's door.

'Hey, calm down,' he said. 'I'm not going to hurt you.'

Annie's panic seemed to have muffled her mind and she didn't know what to say. Instead she kept looking around as if surrounded by other Ronalds, all intent on doing her harm. Her fear was palpable and for a moment Ronald considered backing off, but then the urgency of his own needs and the wasted weeks he had spent tracking her down gave him the impetus he needed to persuade her.

'Look, I know this is a shock,' he said. 'Christ, it is for me – you don't know how long I've been looking for you.'

'I do,' Annie said, her eyes wide, her hands clutching tight to her large black handbag. She was dressed all in black and her vicious make-up and undernourishment made her look like an old crone hugging a bag of hexes. Looking closer, Ronald could see her hair was in rats' tails, her clothes creased, her legs bare and scratched. One sleeve had risen half way to her elbow and Ronald could see scabs on the inside of her arm.

'Would you like something to eat? Money? I haven't got much but . . . A lift? What do you want – and don't tell me to go, I need to talk to you.'

Annie pushed him away weakly and leaned against the coach, as if the decision was too much for her body to bear. Finally she nodded. 'Lift,' she said quietly. 'Give us a lift and I'll talk to you.'

Doubtful that she would follow, Ronald nonetheless led the way to his van and, opening the door for her, was surprised to see her climb in. He walked round to his own door, got in and set off.

After they had joined the northbound traffic, Ronald looked at Annie again. She was crying and her make-up had run. He still didn't know what to say, so he passed her a toilet roll. She stared at it then, realizing his intent, ripped off some sheets and wiped her face.

'Ready to talk?' he said.

'What about?'

'That truck.'

'What truck?'

Ronald looked at her. She seemed genuinely puzzled.

'The truck in the photograph I showed you.'

'What?'

'At G-Mex. You gave me a card with its name. Nefast.' Ronald looked at her again. Something had clicked, but Annie didn't speak.

'Well, what do you know?' he insisted, his anger rising.

'Nothing.'

He was about to swear when he felt her hands round his neck. He slammed on the brake as one hand started scratching at his eyes as she shrieked incoherently. Tyres screeched and horns blasted past his window as he slithered along the hard shoulder, fighting to avoiding bouncing off the verge.

As the VW finally stuttered to a halt, the madwoman crashed headfirst onto the fascia between the two seats, but the impact did nothing to lessen her fury. Stabbing out with her hands and feet she caught Ronald in the face, chest, balls and shins. Soon his screaming was as loud as hers and all thought of gaining information was forgotten as he struggled simply to escape the howling harridan.

Ronald hurled himself across her – her head was against the windscreen, her feet between the seats – and pushed open the passenger door. Then, head down, he shouldered her out of the van. He leaned over to grab the door handle but Annie was already up and biting at his hand. He pulled back, slammed the van into gear and lurched forward out of harm's way, the door just missing her hand as it banged shut. But as Ronald considered his next move, he saw in his right mirror a police car, lights flashing, about half a mile back. He then saw Annie scrambling up the slight incline of the verge away from the motorway. He had no option. He checked the inside lane and slowly pulled out, desperate to avoid drawing attention to himself. He slowly accelerated up to forty, then kept it at that speed, his attention focused on the police car that was gaining on him.

Within twenty seconds it was alongside him, but then the car passed and carried on. With relief Ronald checked his mirror, but Annie had disappeared over the fence.

Five minutes later he was parked on the hard shoulder studying a map. From what he could see, there was nothing between the motorway and the Samson Retail Park but fields for a distance of about a mile. If he took the next exit and doubled back he could be at the Park in fifteen minutes. If Annie had headed that way he might be able to intercept her, if he was in the right place at the right time, and if she hadn't passed out in some ditch, and if she hadn't hitched another ride and if, if, if . . .

Ronald finally found Annie hiding behind a rubbish skip at 11:00 p.m. She was dirty, her clothes soaked from recent rain, her hair greasy and straggly: it hung over her face but failed to hide her frightened eyes.

He had arrived at the Retail Park as it got dark and had spent the first hour combing the slowly emptying car parks for any sign of Annie, then had broadened his search to the perimeter fence bounding the empty fields that led to the motorway. Finally admitting defeat, Ronald had decided on one last search before returning to the motorway. Then he had come across her at the back of a discount furniture warehouse in an alley leading to the larger of the two car parks, now empty of all vehicles except his VW van parked on the other side by the fields.

Ronald leant down and touched Annie's shoulder. She started, then looked at him. It took a few moments, but finally she recognized him and the real panic started. Wailing, like that of a lost child, was accompanied by a frantic crabbing backwards until she was stopped by the wall of the building. There she rose slightly, as if trying to climb up and away from Ronald, but she was weak and soon gave up the struggle.

'Don't be frightened, Annie. I just want to talk.'

'No. No talking. Go away. *Go away!*'

'No, Annie. I'm not going anywhere, not until you tell me about the truck.'

'No!' she screeched, but the energy required seemed to exhaust her and she slumped forward, her hands limp on her thighs, and started sobbing.

Ronald sat down beside her, ignoring the stink from the rubbish strewn about the skip. The ground was wet and oily. The woman was in danger of contracting pneumonia and he vowed to get her to a hospital, but only after she told him what she knew and why she was so terrified. He put his arm around her shoulder. She didn't react.

'Annie, I don't mean to harm you or frighten you. I've been looking for you for weeks. Months. I need to know about the truck. I keep seeing it, at accidents. Who's driving it? What's he up to? *Is it real?*'

Annie stopped sobbing and lifted her head up until her eyes bored into his. He could almost feel the contempt.

'Of course it's not real, you bastard! Why'd you think only me and you can see it?'

Suddenly she punched him in the face and scrabbled away, pulling herself erect by holding onto the edge of the skip.

'You think I want to be like this? You think I want a habit? To be hiding all the time?' she shouted.

'No, of course not,' said Ronald rubbing his cheek. She still had some strength. 'It's the truck?'

'God, you catch on quick, you fuckhead. Course it's the fucking truck!'

'What did it do?'

'Killed. Killed my daughter, my husband. Right there in front
of my fucking eyes. Just ran them off the road. No one believed
me. Said I'd been drinking. But I saw it, remember it like it was
yesterday. See it over and over in my head. In my dreams. That
fucking white monster. It's out there now, waiting to get me. Get
you. Get anyone it can.'

'But how? Why?'

'How? How the fuck should I know. The bastard's dead. Why?
That's Simmons's way. Always was. Should have known.'

Ronald had been looking for answers and suddenly they were
coming too fast. 'Simmons. Who's Simmons?' He had heard the
name somewhere else but . . .

Suddenly the alley exploded into light, taking their vision
away. Ronald spun round but could see nothing but white, his
head pounding at the unexpected rape of his eyesight. He heard
Annie scream but her cry was lost as an engine roared and air
brakes hissed like wild cats.

Still unable to focus, Ronald backed away, only to find himself
tumbling over Annie. He grabbed her by the arm and hauled her
to her feet. She was shaking and, close to, he could hear her
babbling incoherently, her mind dislocated. Behind him he heard
the truck roar nearer. It was after them. The alley was fifty yards
long and only wide enough for the truck and Ronald couldn't
remember any doorways. They would have to run.

Hugging Annie round the waist he started running away from
the headlights, surprised at how light the woman was. Thank-
fully, she offered no resistance and he cantered as fast as he
could, but all the while the truck was coming nearer and nearer.
He could hear the gears jarring as it speeded up, smell the
coppery odour of its exhaust, taste the rancid oil that smoothed
its motion, and feel the dead heat of the blazing headlights as it
targeted them.

Ronald thought of weaving but it was pointless. The truck
would hit them wherever they were in the alley, either crunching
them under its bumper, or smearing them across a wall. No, his
only hope was to run.

Ten yards from the end of the alley, where it opened out into
the car park, he heard the truck's engine growl louder and then
felt the beast lunge at him.

Something hit Ronald square in the back and he started to tumble. His momentum carried him three or four steps but there was to be no stopping his fall. He pulled his arm up under Annie's armpit and, as he crashed to the ground, he hurled her away from him. As his knees and then his chest and face scraped on the wet tarmac, he saw Annie rolling in front of him, eventually coming to rest a couple of feet beyond the end of the alley's walls.

'Run, Annie, run!' he shouted, unable even to hear himself as the truck rose above him.

Ronald's shout turned to a scream as he plastered himself face down onto the floor and waited for the truck's wheels to begin crushing him. But, even as he squeezed his eyes shut, there was a tearing of metal and the roaring of the engine increased then died. The engine gunned again and again, but came no nearer. Ronald rolled over and looked at the truck towering above him, barely inches from his feet. He could see the whole cab shaking as if with frustration, then realized it was jammed. *Jammed!*

He edged backwards until he could confirm the fact. Yes! The fucker was too wide for the alley. There was a slight step in one of the walls. Six inches maybe, but it was enough to wedge the truck fast.

Ronald stood up and faced his tormentor. The white seamless body, the black nothingness of its windows staring back, the engine reverberating angrily.

You're stuck, you bastard, stuck!

Ronald didn't waste time with insults or cries of victory. Instead he turned and ran, scooping up Annie as he did so, dragging her on her knees into the car park.

The truck let out one final roar of anger, followed by a grinding of metal and Ronald glanced back to see the nightmarish vehicle reversing. He didn't wait to see if it was renewing its charge or seeking another route.

Their only chance would be to get to his van and lose the truck in other narrow alleyways, but it was a hundred yards to the VW, and now Ronald began to feel the strain of his flight. His breath was hurting, his legs were weak. They weren't going to make it. He had to find another—

There was a wrenching crash and the truck shot out of the

alley, whipping through its gears, aiming itself squarely at the pair of them.

Annie suddenly flopped from Ronald's arms and fell on the floor. He tripped over her head and fell heavily. The truck was bearing down on them, seconds from crushing them both. Ronald rolled over and tried to get onto his knees, but something wouldn't work and he remained on his stomach.

Annie finally did something for herself, but all she managed was to stand up and stumble backwards in a daze, not even seeing the truck, just staring at Ronald as if he was a curiously-shaped piece of litter. He shouted to her but she couldn't hear and all he could do was try and roll out of the way.

The truck roared between them and Annie disappeared from view. Ronald screamed at her as he rose, but dust filled his mouth and he spun away, hacking. As the truck continued on into the car park, Ronald hobbled across to see what had happened to her. He found her at the base of some steps leading down to an exit, her head twisted hideously, her limbs spastic and unnatural. She was obviously dead. Whether she had fallen or the truck had hit her he didn't know but he was damned if he was going to die as well. He turned to run but knew he had little strength left. After a few faltering steps towards his VW, he knew it was pointless and instead backed towards the high wall of the building on his left that faced the open arena of the car park.

The truck was now facing him again and accelerating. He knew his only chance was to sidestep the behemoth before it reached him, but that was easier said than done. Trained stuntmen had screwed up simpler manoeuvres: what hope had Ronald? Better that chance, however, than the alternative of surrender.

'Come on, you bastard!' he shouted. 'Come and get me!'

It hurtled towards him, halving the distance in a couple of seconds. He shouted at it some more, comforting himself with the fact that if it did hit him it would all be over very quickly.

Its radiator grinned savagely. Ten yards. With its split black windscreen, it looked like a giant albino fly hauling a coffin.

Now! He dived to his left, landed hard on his shoulder and started a roll.

Too late, the truck's bumper caught his left foot and sent him thudding into the wall, upside down and face first. As his world turned red, he felt rather than heard a tremendous thud as the truck made head-on contact with the brick building at forty miles per hour.

Ronald forced himself to remain conscious, aware that by some miracle he had been granted another chance. He looked at the truck. It had buried three feet of its snout in the building and was now silent. He wiped the blood from his face and began the long, long journey to his van.

After a full minute of hobbling, clutching at his chest against the pain in his overworked lungs, he was only half way. He could hear the truck behind slowly disengaging itself from the wall, its engine howling in anger, tyres squealing and smoking, their rubbery stench drifting across the bare car park.

Ronald continued his slow, painful journey, his energy reserves almost exhausted. He had fixed his mind on the VW and that was all he saw, its squat shape as appealing as a mother's arms, a haven from all that was evil in the night.

Another thirty seconds and he was only ten paces away from potential safety. But suddenly the grinding and screeching stopped and so did Ronald. He turned to see the truck reversing in an arc. Its trailer punched over a lamppost, causing the light to stutter and then disintegrate as it smashed against the wall. Then he watched in horror as the truck's cab, at right angles to the trailer, slowly turned its wheels to stare directly at Ronald.

It was battered and misshapen, but it had lost none of its whiteness; there was no bare metal showing, no brick stains, no scratches. Then, to his horror, the dents and dints filled out, and the cab regained its perfect appearance, as if it was a plastic container being inflated. Despite the danger, Ronald was transfixed, his terrified eyes drinking in every detail of the truck like a suicidal man contemplating the barrel of his gun.

The truck was white, a pure unnatural white, its front and sides untarnished by anything as everyday as a company name or logo. The cab sat high up, its windows dark, shielding its occupant. On top, the aerofoil was on a level with the top of the trailer. Below, the deep radiator was marked by wide dagger-shaped bars that plunged to twin white fat bumpers. The radiator also curved up at the edges to accommodate twin headlights at the corners, giving the truck a huge evil grin that was now so obvious and

threatening. Nowhere on the cab could chrome be discerned –
around the windows, on the radiator, the headlight surrounds,
even the bumpers themselves: all were white – and whereas
trucks can be seen to be made up of panels and wings and engine
covers, this truck looked to have been moulded in one piece.
The headlights seemed to have grown like eyes, to have been
formed rather than added as a means of illumination. Only the
trafficators looked out of place, the ugly orange blobs clinging
to the cab like dayglo parasites on a giant maggot. And then
the beast started wheeling round, dragging its corpulent trailer
behind it.

The movement snapped the spell and Ronald dashed for his
VW and dragged his weary frame into the driving seat. Thankful
that he had left the keys in the ignition, he was even more
relieved when the van fired up first time. He shifted into first, but
let the clutch out too soon and felt the van stall.

The truck was accelerating, already halfway to ramming him.
Ronald switched the VW's engine back on, stamped on the
accelerator and let go the clutch. With inches to spare the van
found grip on the damp ground and pulled away as the truck
ploughed into the chain link fence that separated car park from
field.

Ronald aimed the van straight for the black alley, noting the
truck's approach in his mirror but ignoring the threat; he had only
one chance and he was going to take it. Sooner than he thought
he had angled the VW into the alley and was sending litter
scurrying for cover.

As he reached the bend, he slammed on the brakes and turned
the wheel, aware that the van would slide sideways into the
building that blocked the alley's straight path, but even as
bone-juddering contact was made and the passenger window
blew in, he was looking up the alley towards his tormentor.
Would his plan work?

It did! The truck hadn't straightened up in time and slammed
into the left hand wall, then jack-knifed so that its cab turned
inwards and its trailer smashed into the building on the right. It
was trapped, wedged tight. Ronald put the VW in gear and drove
off.

He took a random route, turning corners at the last minute,

desperate to put as much distance between himself and the truck as he could. He took the first turn-off he came to, barely managing to get the battered VW round the bend as it sliced into the verge on the opposite side of the road. It was a winding lane, high hedgerows on either side blocking off darkened fields and farms. In places the road narrowed sufficiently to make passing another car a delicate operation. Luckily he met nothing coming the other way but he didn't care. Panic had consumed him as tree limbs batted at the van roof and branches slapped at the windscreen and sides as the van careered on into the darkness, his single headlight showing only half his route ahead. He didn't care. Ahead was all he needed; ahead and away from that monster.

A signpost loomed out of the dark like a thin spectre and Ronald spun the van left and found himself on a larger road, open fields on both sides. Feeling newly exposed, his panic began to reach new heights; the longer the truck was out of sight, the more inevitable it seemed that it would appear until, half a mile further on, he glimpsed headlights in the distance. He considered turning round but caught sight of lights behind him as well. Of course, they couldn't both be the truck, but which to trust and which to fear? He continued, his foot hard down, his mind undecided. The lights ahead scattered as curves and hedgerows intervened, but they continued to come nearer just as the lights in his mirrors grew. He had to act.

Suddenly he saw an entrance and spun the VW into it, a sign flashing by on his left, a darkened lane dancing as his headlight bounced on the uneven surface. Then, as he turned another corner, there was a car and he tugged the wheel to the left but too late: he smashed into its rear, shunting it to the right, his van sliding left and then down, nose-first into a ditch. As the van came to a jarring halt, he was thrown into the windscreen, then darkness.

SIXTEEN

Time passed oddly for Ronald. There were moments of lucidity when he appreciated his surroundings and understood his circumstances, but others when a warm shroud seemed to envelop him and he would drift off. Sometimes it was sleep, at other times just staring into space. There was pain, occasionally, but only when he had to get up to go to the toilet or if he lay in the same position for too long, but in any case he didn't care; his body had given up the fight and his enforced idleness was being exploited to the utmost by his weary limbs.

He didn't remember the crash but he was told that he had driven into the driveway of a house, hit the back of a parked car and slid into a ditch. Whilst this had written off the van – both axles were broken – it had also hidden the van from the road. Ronald had been taken into the house and been put to bed on some blankets. Someone had then cleaned his cuts and applied antiseptic and bandages.

He kept drifting in and out of consciousness for three days, nightmares sometimes jabbing him awake. He was fed soups, baked beans, eggs, but he didn't care. His nurse didn't speak much, particularly after he insisted on calling her Julie and giving in to a bout of crying.

Finally, despite aching all over, Ronald found himself fully awake and sitting up and, for the first time, taking in his surroundings.

He was in an empty house, the floorboards bare, most of the furniture removed. From his position on the floor underneath a window covered in a blanket he could make out a table, a couple of chairs and a large fireplace containing some half-burned logs. Sunlight streamed through chinks in the window coverings, and he could see dust motes sparkling as the sunbeams lanced across the room to light up dark red flock wallpaper and patches on the wall where horse brasses must have hung for some time. The room was large and low, giving it age, and the floorboards were rough and obviously used to being carpeted. In the far left of the room was a doorway to a kitchen and, in the opposite corner, a staircase – beyond which, presumably, lay a door to a hallway or the front door. The place smelled musty rather than damp, and was surprisingly warm considering how much sun had been shut out. It was as his eyes adjusted to the gloom that he caught sight of a pair of feet clad in trainers next to the table.

Following the blue jeans that covered the owner's legs upwards Ronald found he couldn't see who was sitting in the chair, as their torso and face were rendered invisible by a shaft of light. He pulled himself upright and coughed to gain attention. The figure shifted, then walked out of his vision, returning a few seconds later with a tin which he took, the light hiding the person from him still. But he saw the hand. It was female, the nails badly bitten.

Ronald leaned back against the blanket covering the window, took a spoonful of the food and tasted it. Cold rice pudding. It was delicious. He devoured half the can without pausing, then belched and let it rest on his lap.

'Where am I?' he asked.

The woman had sat down again, her dirty shoes his only reference point.

'Here,' said a female voice.

'Yes, but where's here?'

'You came here, you should know.'

True, but he couldn't remember. Too long chasing and being chased . . .

'Did you get anything from my van?' he said, starting in on the rice pudding again.

'Only the creeps,' said the female.

'The pictures?'

'And the rest.'

He laughed weakly. 'You wouldn't understand.'

'Maybe not, but you're going to tell me.'

'Oh?'

'Got no choice, have you, Ron?'

'You know my name?'

She leaned forward and he saw his wallet being waved.

'You a teacher, then?' she said.

'Yes. Well, was. How'd you—?'

She pulled out his ragged NUT membership card. She then pulled everything else out of his wallet. There wasn't a lot. Finally she held out a shot of himself, Ruth and a twelve-year-old Julie.

Ronald snatched at it and she pulled it out of the way, then retreated back behind the screen of sunlight. It was like an interrogation scene from some Sixties spy movie. If he hadn't been so tired, he might have protested but some small perverse portion of what remained of his personality was taking pleasure in the attention: at last, there was someone who would listen to him – if only they would talk about the right things.

'Wife and daughter?' she asked of the photograph.

He didn't answer. *That* wasn't one of the right things; his family was precious, and private.·

'Wife and daughter . . . so, only one kid. Pretty. Bad clothes or it's a few years back. You were fatter then.'

'Lost weight recently.'

'And your marbles, judging by your van. Let me guess. They died.'

'How'd you – what's it got to do with you?'

'Nothing, but you wrecked our car, fucked up our plans. You were in a mess and I fixed you up. You owe me.'

Ronald twisted himself upright and noticed he was wearing only his underpants.

'You undressed me?'

'No, the fairies did, ran off with your dirty togs. Course I did. Blood, piss, shit, puke, mud – even Daz Ultra wouldn't have shifted that lot.'

'Where are they?'

'Binned them.'

'So what do I—'

'Where you got to go?'

Nowhere. Outside was the world and Ronald had had more than enough of that for the time being.

'*Our* car?' he said.

'You haven't met him.'

'Boyfriend?'

'No.'

'Your name?'

She paused, as if unsure if he could be trusted. 'Cally,' she finally said.

'Odd name.'

'Thanks.'

'Sorry, I didn't mean . . . Cally? What's it short for?'

'Later.'

He stretched and groaned, his body still aching. He checked his head. A plaster over his right eye. A sore spot on his right cheek. Cracked lips. He looked at his arms. A plaster on his left forearm, a bandage round his knuckles. He pushed aside the blanket. His chest was deeply bruised, visible even in the half-light, and he had a forest of plasters on his right shin.

'That was the worst,' she said. 'Your leg. Wouldn't stop bleeding.'

'You did this?'

Cally tossed him a pair of jeans and he slipped them on carefully, pleased they were a good fit. He checked the label. Forty inches. He *had* lost weight.

'Didn't know what else to do. Me and Mark are . . . well, on the run, I suppose. Until we knew you who you were or why you crashed we didn't want to take any risks.'

'What if I'd been badly injured?'

'Don't know. Sorry. But you're not.'

'You're very young to—'

'Hey, not so much of the "very", eh, Ron.'

'Okay. And it's Ronald.'

'Yeah, whatever, Ron.'

'Where'd you get the clothes?'

'Oxfam. Got your size from your old stuff.'

'Where is the infamous Mark?'

'He's busy. Don't worry about that poor sod.'

'Why?'

'Another time, okay. Now, what are you doing, piling into our car like that?'

Ronald debated whether to tell her the truth but then decided he didn't care. 'I thought I was being chased.'

'By who? Fuzz? Gangsters?'

'A white truck.'

'A white truck.'

'Yes, a big white truck. I . . . I believe it killed my daughter and I've been trying to track it down and it . . . it came after me.'

'Who's driving it?'

'Don't know.'

'How do you know it killed your daughter.'

'I don't. I . . . have you looked in my van? The pictures?'

'Those crashes? Bloody weird, Ron.'

'Did you see a white truck in any of them?'

She thought for a while. 'Can't say I did. Just mangled cars and bodies.'

'No point in continuing, then.'

'Why?'

'I can see a truck in those pictures and I saw it in pictures of my daughter before she died, in a car crash. But, like you, no one else can see it. Except a woman, Annie, and she . . . she got killed by it just before I ended up here.' He shivered at the memory of her death.

Cally didn't comment on his story. What could she say? A half-crazed, middle-aged man crashes in their front yard and Cally has to decide whether to help the bleeding fool or run for it. So she drags him inside, makes sure his van and their car can't be spotted from the road and does her best to patch him up. From her time in hospital and helping out the nurse at her council home she knew a little about first aid and, as best she could tell, he hadn't broken anything and wasn't bleeding from the mouth so she'd fixed his cuts and hoped he got better. Luckily, he'd been delirious for a couple of days and she and Mark had continued to be safe. And if, when the guy came round, he caused trouble, she could always whack him one and she and Mark could run for it. Again. After all, it was she who'd done the fat guy a favour; he owed her. Though what he could give her God alone knew; after seeing the inside of his van she suspected he was one fucked-up dude – and their conversation was doing nothing to allay her fears.

Cally handed Ronald a pair of new socks.

'Anyway, I'm probably mad,' he said, trying to smile.

'Join the club,' said Cally.

'What club?'

'Mark and me, we're on the run from Handland Hospital.'

'Hospital. Why should you run—'

'Mental hospital, Ron.'

'Handland? Never heard of it. Is it near here?'

'About forty miles.'

'So why are you running?'

'You wouldn't believe me. But you're safe, don't worry. We're harmless, leastways Mark is.'

'You're not?'

'As long as I'm awake, you're fine.'

'What does that mean?'

'Never mind. Shoes?'

They were a size too large but Ronald was grateful for dry footwear; his own shoes had been leaking for the last couple of weeks. He stood up and walked about, Cally watched him warily, toying with what Ronald could now see was a bread knife on the table, its blade flashing in the sunlight. He understood her unease.

He could smell himself and he felt grimy and greasy. Mind you, the girl was no picture. Thin and scruffy, her badly-dyed blonde hair hung like string over a sallow face that looked as if it had never seen daylight. An image of a vampire girl hiding out in a deserted farmhouse and slowly sucking the lifeblood from a captive adult flashed in his mind. Ronald dismissed it, but the central theme of captor and captive stubbornly remained. And why not, he thought, eyeing the knife. How old was she? Seventeen? Eighteen at most. And what could he do if she decided to stab him? Nothing. He was old and fat and tired and she was young and desperate with a lot more to lose. Best to keep on her right side until he knew he could trust her – and she knew she could trust him.

'Don't worry,' he said. 'I may be mad but I'm not stupid. In here I'm safe and I need the rest. I'm in no rush to leave and I'm certainly not going to report you.'

Cally seemed relieved but she didn't believe him. Why should she believe anyone any more? Especially some creep who liked taking snaps of car crashes.

'Where's this Mark you keep telling me about?' Ronald finally asked.

'Drawing.'

'Drawing?'

'It's all he does. He's autistic.'

'Oh. Is he your brother?'

'No, why'd you ask?'

'Why else would you take him from Handland?'

'Oh, there's a good reason.'

'And that is?'

'Let's go find him.'

It didn't take long. Mark was sitting on the kitchen doorstep of the cottage sketching the small garden, beyond which, like a yellow paint spill on a green carpet, lay a wide field of rape. Ronald said hallo but the man ignored him.

'He's not a great talker,' said Cally, rubbing Mark's head.

'He's a damn good artist, though,' said Ronald leafing through some sketches Mark had finished. 'Autistic, you say? Must be sauvage.'

'Talented, you mean? Yes, he's that all right, poor sod.'

'Shouldn't feel sorry for him. He's happy.'

'Yeah, well, some people try to stop that.'

'How?'

'Oh, it's a long story.'

'We're going somewhere?'

They sat in silence, one either side of Mark, and watched him draw. Cally managed to elicit a 'fug' from the man when she persuaded him to accept a can of Fanta.

'Where do you get your money from?' said Ronald, nodding at the can.

'Steal it,' she said matter-of-factly.

'Oh,' said Ronald. There wasn't much else he could say.

'Well, I ain't no heiress, Ron.'

'It's Ronald. I didn't think you were.'

'Get the picture, Ron. Me and Mark are on the run from Handland Hospital. Neither of us has anything except each other and he's not much use to me. Sorry, Mark,' she said, patting him on the head. 'But it's true. We've been here a week and things are okay. They won't last but for now they'll do.

I've lifted a few purses and wallets and spent the cash and used the credit cards. So far I haven't been caught. We've got food for a few days, and other stuff so, as long as no one bothers us, we'll be okay.'

'Then what?'

'Find somewhere else.'

'Then somewhere else, I suppose?'

'Yes, Ron.'

'It's Ronald.'

'Who gives a fuck, Ron? God, you're getting on my tits. Wish I hadn't got you out of that van . . .'

'Look, my life's as big a mess as yours, so I'm not one to judge—'

'But you are, aren't you? You're a teacher and a parent; you think you've got every right to judge, that's all you've ever done. Order kids about, make them do this, do that.'

'You've got a problem with authority, haven't you, Cally?'

She laughed; it was cold and empty. 'Authority? Only authority I've ever known is the authority to fuck things up for me. Plenty of people in a position to do that. Plenty.'

A cool breeze blew across the garden, rustling the papers on Mark's pad but he didn't seem to notice. Ronald shivered. 'Nippy,' he said. 'Can we go in?'

Cally nodded and followed him in. Mark, as ever, stayed exactly where he was. They sat next to the fireplace.

'Smoke,' said Ronald, nodding at the ashes in the grate. 'Wouldn't it show from an empty house?'

'Only light it at night,' she said. 'Place is pretty way out of town, can't see it from the road and it's a dump.'

'There's some money in the van if you—'

'Spare wheel? Found it. You can have it back.'

'Why'd you look there?'

'You looked like you'd been on the road a while. Got to stash your cash somewhere. It was either there or the lining of the seat or in that mattress. That's one weird van, Ron.'

'Ronald. There's a reason. Much as I presume there's a reason for you being here with Mark and stealing.'

'Oh, don't get so high and mighty, Ron. I do what I've got to do. Just as I *presume* you do what you've got to do.'

'Yes,' he sighed. 'Something like that. So how do you, you know, steal?'

'Interested?'

'Curious.'

'Nosy.'

'Yes.' They both smiled.

'Besides,' Ronald said, stretching his aching legs. 'There isn't much else to do. I don't suppose you stole a TV.'

Cally then proceeded to explain in great detail how to steal money, be it cash or credit cards; where to find a man's wallet – usually the top inside left jacket pocket; how to forge signatures, or distract shop assistants while you copied one; how to sell on goods bought with stolen credit cards; and how to deal with being discovered in the process of stealing – if it was a wallet, throw it where the man can see it so he'll go after his money rather than the thief and, if it's a handbag, just forget it and leg it.

'You sound like a pro,' said Ronald, taken aback by the girl's straightforward approach to crime.

'Yes.' She didn't take it as the insult Ronald intended. 'I had a good teacher.'

Both fell silent, Cally surprised at how candid she had been with a man she hadn't really spoken to until an hour before; Ronald amazed that he seemed to have fallen in with Fagin's great-granddaughter. What amazed him even more was that she wasn't cocky about it; she needed money, so she stole it. No pride, no guilt. She could have been Julie describing how she changed nappies when she was babysitting.

Cally yawned and it proved infectious and he also yawned. He looked at the girl. She seemed to have fallen asleep. He remembered her saying something about that being dangerous.

'Cally?'

'Yes, Ron,' she said without a movement.

'You said something about a problem if you sleep.'

'Yes.'

'Why? Are you epileptic?'

She laughed. 'God, if only that was all it was, Ron!'

'Well, what is it? And could you do me a favour?'

'What?'

'Don't call me Ron. It's Ronald.'

'Anything you say, Ron.'

'Ronald!'

'It's only a name.'

'It's *my* name.'

'It's still just a name.'

'But it's mine!' His reaction was out of all proportion to her annoying habit, but he couldn't stop himself.

She shot up and stood in front of him, glaring down at him. 'Tough tit, Ron. My name's Cally. I hate the fucking name but I don't change it. People call it me, it stuck. Fuck it. If I want to call you Ron, does it really matter?'

'Does it really matter that you call me Ronald?'

'Because I don't fucking want to.'

'Aha!'

' "Aha" what?'

'If I'd said call me Ron, you'd call me Ronald, wouldn't you? Just to keep the upper hand.'

'Don't talk shite. I like Ron. It's short. Friendly.'

'But it's not friendly! What if I called you Cal?'

'So what?'

Ronald could see they were having an argument because they needed one, not because they had anything worth arguing about. But he didn't care! He had so much pent-up rage and frustration that he needed an outlet and this cheeky young girl was teeing him off as much as any of his pupils ever had.

'Right,' he said. 'Right, Cal. I'm Ron, you're Cal.'

'Right.'

'Right.' He sank back in his chair, slightly out of breath, and looked at the girl standing in front of him, hands on hips, jaw jutting petulantly, determined to prove she was in charge. Sod it, *she was*! He could hardly walk, he had no money, no van and no way of continuing his mission to find the truck. He held out his hand and she looked at it warily.

'Cally, it's Ron. Okay. You win. Call me Ron.'

She didn't know what to do but finally she touched his hand as if anything more committed would signal some kind of defeat. Then she sat down.

'Fancy a drink?' he said.

'Tea. All the stuff's in the kitchen. Boil water in a pan on the electric cooker. No kettle.'

Ronald went into the kitchen and made tea. He made a cup for Mark and placed it down by the man and showed it to him. He doubted it would get drunk so he decided to come back later when it was cooler and help him.

He and Cally sat in front of the dead fire in the quiet of the afternoon for all the world like a farmer and his daughter after a hard morning's graft. His aching body certainly felt as if it had worked overtime.

'There's an explanation. It's not as bad as it seems . . .' He thought over the last couple of months. 'Then again, maybe it is. But I need to tell someone.'

'Go ahead. Telly's lousy, anyway,' she said, nodding at the empty corner.

'Make me a promise, though. If you want me to leave when you know what I've done, just tell me and I'll go.'

She raised her hands in mock horror. 'Oh my . . . Okay, you go first, Ronald, and then I'll tell you mine and the deal's the same: if you think I'm just a nutter, or you think staying's too dangerous, then you can still fuck off.'

Ronald winced at the girl's profanity, but agreed.

SEVENTEEN

Two hours later Ronald had finished his story. He hadn't spared her any details. Julie, her photographs, hunting for Annie, the van, the questions, the crashes, the polaroids, the police, the truck, the madness . . . once he had started he forgot he was talking to a teenage girl younger than his own daughter; she was a priest, a confessor, someone to help him cleanse his sorry soul and, he hoped, comfort him in his insanity.

There was a long silence as the two of them thought over his tale. It was getting dark outside and the unilluminated room was all the more gloomy.

'Well, Ron, that's a story and a half.'

'Yes, I suppose it is. But do you believe it?'

'Do you?'

'Yes, of course I do. I lived it.'

'But you said yourself you never touched the truck and it's never touched you. You said it was like a ghost; others couldn't see it, only you and that woman.'

'Annie.'

'Yeah, Annie. I know weird shit happens – believe me, I know – so I've no reason to doubt you.'

'You believe in the truck?'

'If you do, yes.'

'What's that mean? You're not being patronizing, are you? "Loony in the room, let's all keep calm." '

She laughed loudly. 'If you only knew, Ron. Look, either the truck is real or it isn't and even if it isn't, it exists for you. One thing Dr Gantry—'

'Who?'

'The fucker in charge at Handland. One thing he taught me was you have to accept what a patient goes through is real before you

can start to deal with it. Accept that some poor fucker can see
giant rats eating his toes, then try and calm him and see what'll
get rid of them. Maybe talk, maybe drugs, but until you accept
what they're scared of, then you'll get nowhere. He believed my
story – too right the fucker believed it – so you have to accept
yours and then start dealing with it.'

'Meaning?'

'Meaning if you want to get rid of the truck you've got to
believe it does what you say, then deal with it.'

Ronald mulled the girl's words over. She had accepted his story
too glibly; he had been talking for two hours about carnage and
murder and death and she took it as if he was arguing about
parking privileges.

'No,' he said. 'You've accepted what I've said too easily. Any
normal person would have barricaded themselves in the kitchen
now and be screaming for help knowing how my mind was
working.'

'Exactly, Ron. But who said I was normal?'

Cally got up and walked over to the back door and helped
Mark into the house, shutting the door behind him. She showed
Ronald his latest sketch; it could have been a photograph of the
back yard. She sat the man down on the blankets that were
Ronald's bed and gave him back his pad.

'Tea time,' she said. 'What'll it be?'

'Anything.'

'Corned beef and beans it is.'

Later, as they sat eating their food, Ronald restarted their
conversation: 'You're not normal?'

'No. You've never heard of Handland, have you? But you've
heard of Rampton and Broadmoor? Handland's the same. A
secure psychiatric unit for the criminally insane.'

Ronald looked over his shoulder at Mark as he slowly edged a
spoon of beans to his mouth.

Cally shook her head. 'Okay, Handland isn't quite the same.
Gantry told me about it one time, when he was feeling extra
friendly.'

'A mental hospital's a mental hospital, secure or otherwise,
isn't it?'

'Not when Dr Taylor Gantry is in charge, it isn't. Gantry tells you it is and pretends to the outside world it is and most of it is run as a hospital, but meantime some of us are guinea pigs in his experiments. That's why I was there.'

'And Mark?'

'Money. His relatives dumped him and paid a lot to keep him there, poor sod. He's completely harmless, shouldn't even be locked up.'

Just then Mark farted and Ronald and Cally looked at each other.

'Well, not that harmless,' she said, before they both burst out laughing.

'What do you do for washing here?'

'Nothing. Well, there's cold water so we've washed our faces but . . .'

'And you've been here a week?'

'Hey, Ron, you ain't exactly a perfume ad yourself.'

'True. Well, is there a bath?'

'Yes, but no hot water.'

'There's the stove.'

'Boil up pans? Be at it forever.'

'And you have a pressing engagement elsewhere? Lukewarm is better than cold. We could all do with a bath. Even if it takes half the night, it'll be worth it.'

'Okay. I didn't want to say anything . . .'

'Who goes first?'

'You,' she said. 'You're the whiffiest.'

'You could have said.'

'Well, I have now. What about Mark?'

'Oh, well, I can wash him, I suppose.'

Cally let out a sigh of relief. 'Another reason I haven't bothered,' she admitted.

'But he's only a child.'

'You haven't seen him taking a piss. Mark's not, um, all child . . .'

'I do believe the girl's embarrassed.'

'So?' she bristled.

'So, nothing,' said Ronald. 'Let's get boiling, shall we?'

It took the best part of an hour to boil sufficient water to make up a usable bath.

Ronald took the first dip and was appalled to find how dirty he was and that the grime was ingrained everywhere. It took fifteen minutes of serious soaping and hard scrubbing with a nailbrush they had found to shift it all. The bathwater turned almost black, like the water in Ruth's old twin tub after she had washed black jeans. In fact, the water was so disgusting, he let out the plug as he towelled himself dry with a blanket. Nonetheless, he was pleased to feel clean and refreshed – almost reborn – before he dressed again and went downstairs to apologize for using all the water.

'Black, was it?' asked Cally as she stood at the stove, already boiling up more pans of water.

They both laughed, and Ronald went to warm himself by the low fire that crackled in the grate in the lounge.

Another forty-five minutes and it was Cally's turn. She only took five minutes and it was agreed that, as the water wasn't too grey, rather than waste another forty-five minutes boiling yet more water, Ronald would help Mark to bathe in Cally's bathwater.

Mark was as compliant as ever, showing no objection either to undressing in front of Ronald or getting into the bath.

'Mark? I want you to wash yourself, can you do that?' asked Ronald, eyeing the well-built young man in the tub.

Five minutes of gentle coaxing got Mark to run the soap up and down his arms and over his chest but it was left to Ronald to ensure his genitals were clean. Mark, again, didn't mind and, to Ronald's relief, didn't become excited by his attentions. It was only when Ronald came to wash Mark's hair that he found the scar. Anxious not to confuse Mark, he delicately finished the shampooing – he had to do it twice because of the colour of water that coursed down the man's back – and carefully flushed all the soap away.

'Was that nice?' he asked.

'Fug,' said Mark, touching his hair. It had probably been itchy and he enjoyed the relief the wash had given him.

Ronald lifted the thick hair from above the man's ear and sifted his way through the strands until he could see quite clearly a semi-circular scar running from just behind the hairline about an inch above Mark's right ear for almost six inches down towards the back of his head. The scar was neat and skilfully done but wasn't very old.

Checking the rest of Mark's head – which Mark seemed to enjoy, judging by the blissful 'fugs' that he let out – Ronald found another smaller scar on his upper right temple, again successfully hidden by long hair. Had he been given a short haircut, both scars would have been plain to see.

'Mark, feel these,' said Ronald, holding Mark's hand to white raised ridges. 'Do you remember when you got them?'

Mark let Ronald run his fingers the length of the scar and back again. Ronald let go but Mark kept his hand pressed to the scar.

'Do you remember?' asked Ronald.

Mark started to cry. Soon his sobs were loud enough to attract Cally and she burst in.

'What's wrong, what's up with Mark?'

'His head. Look for yourself. He remembers but . . .'

'It's okay, Mark,' said Cally, hugging the naked man. 'Come on, it's okay, don't worry.'

She gently took his hand from his head and modestly placed it over his penis which floated limply on the dirty water, then she examined the scar.

'Fucking hell,' she said. 'What would that be there for?'

'An accident?'

'God knows. Could that have fucked him up?' she asked.

'You said he was autistic,' said Ronald.

'Gantry said. So did Elizabeth . . . Jesus, no.'

'What?'

'Suppose he is autistic and you're Dr "Fuck With Your Head" Gantry, wouldn't you want a root around the poor bastard's head, see why it wasn't ticking right?'

'You mean an exploratory operation?'

'No. I mean a fucking experiment. That bastard, *that fucking bastard*!'

Her anger worried Mark and he started sobbing again. Ronald grabbed the girl by the shoulder and ushered her out of the bathroom, then he comforted Mark and got him out of the bath and dried him off. Next he took him into one of the empty bedrooms and made him dress himself. Mark could pull on his shirt and trousers but couldn't understand buttons. Ronald

helped him, then combed the other man's still wet hair into some
semblance of order, and slipped his shoes on.

'Okay now, Mark? No more crying, okay?'

Mark was staring down at his shoes, but he still managed a 'fug'
and Ronald patted his hand.

'Let's get you drawing some more. Cally and I need to have a
serious talk about your Dr Gantry and Handland bloody Hospital.'

EIGHTEEN

'I've never told anyone the full story before, except Dr Gantry and another psychiatrist,' said Cally. 'So I might be forgetting some bits, but I'll try and get it in the right order. It started, oh, seven years ago, when I was nine . . .

'Mum and Dad were never able to have a little brother or a sister for me. Mum's insides weren't up to it, so until I was eight I was on my own, but then Mum and Dad adopted a little baby girl. Chloë, she was called. Must have been about two and a half. Pretty little kid. Dad gave me a talking to just before they brought her home, told me not to be jealous. She was going to be my little sister and they wanted me to be big and grown up about it. Fine by me, I said. Then they wheeled in the kid and she was really cute. A pretty little blonde girl. All of us are dark so she stood out like a sore thumb, but who cared.' Cally stopped.

Ronald was looking at her hair.

'Oh, for God's sake, Ron. It's dyed!'

Ronald offered an exaggerated smile. Cally continued:

'Chloë was almost deaf. She would have to have some operations when she got older to get her hearing up to the mark, but otherwise she was great. She was bright, too, despite her hearing. And a giggler. Lovely kid . . .'

Cally went quiet, her affection for her adopted sister obvious. Ronald waited until she carried on.

'We lived in a three-bed semi, so Chloë got her own room, but because she'd been used to being with other kids, that first night on her own she freaked. So they moved her into my room and that seemed to quiet her. I could have resented her but I didn't. All she had to do was smile and you'd do anything for her. Honest. She was like a pretty little doll.

'She came in the summer so school was out, and as Mum didn't

work she used to take us for walks. Down to the front most days.
I didn't know it then but we weren't well-off. Dad had a steady
job but it barely paid the bills. He used to be a bit of a hippy.
Actually he was a pop star. Had two top ten hits, in '66 I think.
Bass player with The Crawlers. It went to his head. None of them
could play, especially him; they were just lucky. He did a couple
of tours, including one in the States and that's where he got into
all that peace and love crap. But then the group dumped him and,
as he was always telling us, he couldn't get another "gig". Said it
was a vendetta or something, but listening to him play, it was
obvious he had no talent. I loved him and all – he was my dad –
but he was a lousy guitarist. Couldn't sing either. So, after
messing about for a few years living his hippy dream, he settled
down in Blackpool of all places, met Mum, got married, and had
me. Got a job, too. He hadn't got rid of his dreams of San
Francisco, though, so he called me California. Cally. Stupid
name.'

'Oh, I don't know,' said Ronald. 'He could have called you
Monty after Montana. Or Tex after Texas.'

'Yeah, or Louise after Louisiana or Georgia after Georgia. But
no, it was Cally. Man was a twat. Now, can I carry on?'

'A couple of nights after Chloë came I heard him and Mum
having a row about Chloë's name. Dad wanted to re-christen her
Summer. Can you believe that? Daft sod. I think he might have
taken too many drugs in the Sixties. Anyway, he ended up
working in a factory, on a lathe, I think. Pretty basic stuff but he
wasn't trained for anything else. His group made it big when he
was seventeen so he'd never had a real job before and no
qualifications. He was lucky he had been left the house by his
parents the year before I was born.

'We didn't have a car. We used to have to cart Chloë
everywhere by bus. Most days I'd be down on the beach building
big castles, keeping an eye on the kid while Mum snoozed or read
her Agatha Christies. Sometimes she worked in shops and stuff,
but I think she had a problem dealing with people. So she was
more or less a full-time housewife.

'I liked Mum. Most nights Chloë would wake up crying 'cause
of her ears and Mum would be the one that came in to soothe her
back to sleep. Most nights she'd bring me in a drink to keep me

quiet, too. I didn't mind. I felt sorry for the little beauty. I never could see the point in getting upset with a kid who was hurting. I overheard Mum and Dad arguing about her. Dad hadn't wanted a "defective kid" as he called her. Git. Hypocrite, too, given the way he'd cocked up his own life. And ours, I suppose. Dad never did come into her that I remember . . . Some nights, to let Mum have a rest, I would sneak over to Chloë's cot and pick her up and rock her to sleep. I'm not sure it was always her ears. I think she just needed comforting sometimes. Reassurance. With no real Mum or Dad, moving around all the time – we were the third family she'd stayed with – she must have been lost. I loved that kid, I suppose, as much as if she *had* been my sister.'

Cally fell silent and sipped some more of her tepid coffee. Ronald could see the girl's hands were shaking.

'What happened to her?' he said, guessing what was coming.

'She got killed.'

'Killed? How?'

'Train. A bloody steam train, would you believe? I read one of the newspapers at the time. She was the only person to have been killed by a steam train in seven years. Mum and me and the kid went out for the day to a local railway place where they had steam rides at the weekends. Mum's brother, Uncle Larry, was one of the drivers and he got us in for free and let us up on the engine's platform when it was in the station. Real steam train, it was, big bastard. Scared me to death. See, all I'd known were diesel and electric, but this thing didn't hum or growl; it hissed and dribbled and whooshed. It was like it was *alive* and at nine that's a hell of a thing to come across without warning. Mum asked Uncle Larry to let me stay on the footplate while he did one of his trips. I didn't want to. I was convinced the thing would blow up with all that steam and the noises it was making. I begged not to go but bloody Uncle Larry thought I was fooling and Mum called me a big baby so I had to stand there for half an hour as the thing ran through the country. I actually pissed myself, I was so scared. Cried all the way. Uncle Larry either didn't notice or maybe he got a kick out of seeing me crying, the bastard.

'When we got back to the station I hopped off and ran and hid behind the station, bawling my eyes out. And when Mum came looking for me, she lost Chloë. Just for a minute. Then the train was loaded up and Uncle Larry set off. They didn't find Chloë for over three hours. I was terrified, convinced it was all my fault. Mum was hysterical, weeping all over the place. The police came and the St John's Ambulance came and Dad got brought by the police. He hit Mum in front of everyone and the police took him away. Funny thing, though, Dad seemed more upset about being dragged out of work rather than that Chloë was missing.

'It was after seven when they found her. They'd closed down the train ride and someone was working the track on one of those trolley things where the handle goes up and down. He found Chloë or what was left of her. They reckon she'd climbed up on a buffer or the steps and when the train had set off she couldn't get off. After a mile she must have fallen and been dragged . . . oh God, poor little Chloë.'

Cally broke off and ran to the kitchen. Ronald listened to her being sick. She might like to come on as a street smart punk but it was obviously only a veneer hiding what was clearly a vulnerable young girl. For the first time Ronald felt sorry for her.

She eventually emerged, red in the face, mumbling an apology. She looked her age now; a sad, frightened sixteen-year-old.

'We had the funeral,' Cally continued. 'And life sort of went on. I used to wake up at night screaming and crying about that fucking train . . . sorry. I had nightmares most nights. I even slept with Mum and Dad for a while. They also got rid of Chloë's bed and all her toys but it didn't help. There was some inquiry or other and while it was decided the whole thing was a dreadful accident, Mum and Dad weren't allowed to foster any more kids. For Mum that was the final straw. That, and Dad's drinking.

'Maybe he'd been a drinker all along, but it was after Chloë died I started noticing it. Most nights, and weekend lunchtimes, he'd be out at the pub, then come home drunk, stinking of booze. He wasn't violent or anything, it seemed to quiet him down. He always was a moody git but there were times now and then when we had fun together, when he was almost a friend. We'd go out for walks or go to the Pleasure Beach. For a while he had a thing about photography and he got me interested in taking pictures. It didn't last but at least he'd shown some interest in me. But after Chloë died he seemed depressed all the time, and with Mum throwing moodies too it wasn't the happiest of places to be, specially at ten years old.

'I remember him coming into me late some nights, smelling of drink. Sometimes he was dressed, sometimes not. He'd start rambling on about how he loved me and was doing his best. Sometimes he'd hug me so tight, shaking and crying. And sometimes he'd . . . touch me.'

'You mean he . . .' Now it was Ronald's turn to feel sick.

'Maybe.'

'Maybe? Surely if he—'

'I was ten, Ron! He didn't rape me, I know that, but I'm in bed naked and he's only got a vest on and he's touching me, he might have done it for the wrong reasons. I know one time his hand slipped . . . I started crying and he stopped. Maybe . . . but he was my *dad*. I *have* to think he didn't try it on, okay? *Okay*?'

Ronald nodded at her demand.

'Anyway, what with him coming in some nights and me waking up every night and losing sleep I was just knackered all the time. At school I used to fall asleep in lessons. Sometimes I got away with it but other times I used to wake up screaming about the train . . .

'So, I was having nightmares. I kept hearing train whistles, seeing steam in the room and it was hot. One night I swear I looked out the window – I was wide awake, cross my heart – and I saw a horrible train standing in the street! I pissed my nightie right there by the window. I screamed and Mum came in – Dad had finished bothering – and she found me crying in bed. I can't remember getting back into it. She rocked me back to sleep. It was probably shock more than anything else. But in the morning I found a damp spot by the window. Now whether there had been a train outside our house or not, I'd certainly taken a leak by the window.

'I suppose both Mum and Dad had switched off about Chloë's death; their way of coping with it. But I still felt guilty. Remember, it was me running off made Mum lose her. Which meant that life in our house had become pretty shitty. And at school things went from bad to worse.

'I never was much good at anything but I tried my best, but being so shagged out I couldn't work much and soon I was in Mr

Hancock's bad books. He never had taken to me – I used to muck
about too much for his liking. Now with me coming in tired he got
on my back, then got onto Mum and Dad, but with Dad pissed
most of the time, and Mum on Valium I think, what were they
going to do?

'Just around this time – maybe three months after Chloë died –
Dad lost his job. For obvious reasons. Mum showed her first bit
of emotion since the funeral by throwing his dinner at him. I was
scared shitless and hid in my room most of the night. Mum didn't
come to comfort me and Dad went down the boozer. I cried
myself to sleep that night, as much worried about Mum and Dad's
shouting as terrified about Mr Hancock at school. He had said I
would be in trouble the next day if I didn't get decent marks in his
test. He said it would affect my whole future if I didn't do well.
How, God knows, but I believed him then and who was to tell me
otherwise? I'd never had many friends and those I did were
warned off me by their parents once they saw how Mum and Dad
were. Bastards, parents, sometimes. Sorry, Ron . . .

'Anyway, that night I fell asleep dreaming of Mr Hancock. I
still remember it. I was in his classroom on my own and he was
standing at the front pointing at some words on the blackboard. I
was shaking my head; I couldn't answer his questions. He started
to walk towards me with the big plastic ruler he used to thwack
the desk with. If you were really bad, he'd clip you on the back of
the hands with it. He seemed to enjoy doing that . . . So there he
was, in my dream, walking towards me, this ruler a yard long in
his hand, and then I heard that train whistle, screaming really
loud. Mr Hancock heard it in my dream, too. He turned to look
at the door. I was shaking all over, as terrified of the train as of
him. The whistle stopped and Mr Hancock turned to look back at
me. He looked just like that actor who played Dracula in that
black and white film. And that's when I noticed the steam around
his feet. And he saw it too, looking down real puzzled like. And
then the train came.

'It crashed through the door of the classroom. I remember it
managed to fit in the space of the door, yet when it was in the
room it was as big as it would have been in real life. Mr Hancock
got smashed by it and carried right across the classroom and
through the other wall. The whole fucking train just ran right

through the classroom and over Old Widow Twanky Hancock. That's when I woke up.

'Well, next morning I remembered the dream – it had really frightened me – but I knew it was just a dream and I went to school expecting Mr Hancock to pick on me again, but he wasn't there. A substitute teacher came and took us for the day and it was only when I got home that Mum showed me something in the evening paper about Mr Hancock.

'He had been out walking his dog near his house at about ten-thirty and he'd been knocked down by a hit and run driver. Police were baffled about how a car could have hit him and leave without anyone seeing it. I don't really remember if I made the connection then but I *do* remember feeling guilty about hating him. So now I felt guilty about two people dying!

'I started having the nightmares *every* time I went to sleep. I always woke up when the train whistle blew. During the day any sudden noise – a car horn, kids shouting, even a kettle whistling – made me jump. In the end I got stomach cramps and was taking so much time off school, even Mum got worried a little. Not Dad, though. He didn't care – Mum and me saw less and less of him. He'd sleep in till lunch, go down the club, come back for tea, then go out for the evening. Mum managed to do the shopping now and then and cook us meals but otherwise she just watched TV all day and evening. I might as well not have been there.

'When Mum was out Dad would sometimes walk round undressed. You know, everything on show. Didn't seem to notice I was there. One time he started playing with himself, right there on the couch while I watched Scooby-doo. I ran out of the room and hid in the bathroom until Mum came back.'

'And you still give him the benefit of the doubt?' Ronald had found on too many occasions that pupils who were badly behaved or too often absent turned out to be abused in one way or another at home. It had always upset him and Cally's story stirred the same anger.

'You weren't there, Ron! It was like he was in another world. If he asked me to do something or if he'd started undressing me, yes, I'd say he was a pervert, but he just . . . did it. After that I wouldn't go near him those few times he did turn up. And I

started getting scared of other men. If Dad was what was
supposed to be normal . . .

'Came a time my school head had had enough and he and a
social worker carted me off to a psychiatrist. I told him everything; I had nothing to hide. More than that, I had this stupid
hope he could get rid of my nightmares.'

'Did he?' asked Ronald.

'No chance. He told me to pull my socks up. Chloë's death
wasn't my fault. He gave Mum some pills to help me sleep. They
did – for a while – but the dreams came back.

'I still visited the psychiatrist, Dr Loon – what a name – once a
week but I began to realize something was wrong. You might
laugh but I really thought I had to take my skirt off for a doctor,
any doctor, even a psychiatrist.'

'You what?' said Ronald, aghast.

'Dr Loon was a regular little pervy. How on earth a child
doctor can get the hots for little kids, I don't know. He tried it
on with me a couple of times. Hands on my legs, asking me to
show him my "thingy", to see if I was normal. He even showed
me some pictures of men and women with their clothes off.
Asked if I was interested in that sort of thing yet. I was ten!
And I was scared, especially after the way Dad had behaved.
And these pictures had hard-ons in them. I'd run out of the
room before Dad got that far, and there I was forced to look at
pictures of men with their clothes off with these big things
sticking up like rolls of anaglypta! I thought they were
deformed, and here was the doctor telling me I should want to
play with things like that!'

Cally was visibly upset by the memory.

Ronald was appalled. 'Did he ever . . .?'

'No! No. To cut a long story short, Dr Pervy Loon got killed,
along with a schoolboy who was fourteen, I think. They were in
some bushes and they got run over too. I read it all in the papers
'cause I knew him and had started to hate him. Police couldn't
understand how the two bodies could have got where they did if
they were hit by a car. The bodies were there a couple of days
before they were found. And of course, the day they'd died I had
dreamed of a train running over the doctor.'

'You're saying you killed them with your dream?'

'You catch on quick, Ron.' Cally got up to make herself another coffee.

Ronald joined her. He said, 'Cally, sorry, but it doesn't wash. Just because you have nightmares about people you hate and *by coincidence* a couple of them die . . .'

'I know it sounds silly, stupid and impossible. But it happened. I didn't want it to, it just did. All I've ever wanted was a good night's sleep! Now, do you want the rest?'

Ronald nodded.

'*Thank you.* So, a teacher I hated was dead. And a doctor who was trying to get into my knickers instead of helping me was dead, along with some poor chickenhawk. By now I—'

'Chickenhawk?' asked Ronald, sitting down.

'Yeah. A male prossie. A rent boy. The kid was well known to the police for "going with men". Okay?'

Ronald nodded, vaguely embarrassed at his ignorance. After all, here he was with someone young enough to be his daughter and he was asking questions about male prostitution. Where had he gone wrong?

'As I was saying, I was just about to twig a connection. I was only ten, remember. I was more concerned with answering the questions on Saturday Superstore than sorting out my brain. One thing in the story of Dr Hansbacker's death that did catch my eye was someone who lived nearby saying they distinctly heard a train whistle about the time he died. But that was absurd, they'd gone on to say; the nearest steam train was miles away and they didn't run at night.

'I kept on sleeping badly. Occasionally I would dream of the train, but it seemed to be going away. Maybe my guilt over Chloë's death had gotten less. Dr Loon had been some use after all, I suppose. School got a little better but I was still pretty much the dunce of the class.

'A year passed. Things improved. The train came into my dreams maybe once a week, usually when I was upset about something. Going to the dentist or Dad having a bad turn or something. Mum and Dad's marriage must have been pretty much over by then. There weren't many fights or that. Just a lot of silence. He stopped bothering me, too. Went out of his way to avoid me, actually. We were like three strangers. Mum cooked the meals and we ate them and that was about it. Dad had no luck getting jobs and just seemed to drink more.

'One day the police called round. Dad had been caught stealing stuff and had gone berserk and smashed up a couple of grands' worth of electrical gear and a shop window. He couldn't pay the fine so they put him away for a month. That month was very little different from any other. He might as well have been down the boozer or crashed out in bed as in the nick. Mum visited him the first week but didn't bother again. Couldn't really afford it, she said.

'Dad came out and carried on the same. Within a week he was done for nicking a car when he was drunk. Three months this time. Mum filed for divorce. I don't blame her. He wasn't going to get better. Even I knew Dad was losing it. We lost the house about this time, too. Couldn't pay the mortgage, Mum said. We sold it in a hurry and moved into a flat. Only later did I find out that Mum had sold the house behind Dad's back and gone into hiding. The house had been in her name – a condition of the will, apparently: even his own parents didn't trust Dad. Poor sod.

'He came round a couple of months later and had a scene with Mum. The one thing I'll give him is he never got violent. He'd shout and threaten and wreck things outside but I never once saw him raise his hand to Mum or damage our own property. Very considerate that way, he was. Anyway, Mum told him to get lost. The house had been in her name and that was it. She gave him a few quid and he left.

'Two days later the police were round again. He'd fallen or jumped off the pier and drowned. Now he had never been a great dad or anything, but your dad's your dad and it hit me hard. I freaked, but Mum was too upset about Dad and the funeral and all to pay me any attention. What else could I do? Luckily I found the funeral so upsetting – my *dad* had gone forever and I was never going to see him again – and tiring that I collapsed.'

'What's lucky about that?' said Ronald.

'They called a doctor and he put me on some medicine again. Kept me calm for a couple of weeks. I liked it, being dopey and tired and all. It stopped me fretting about anything. But eventually the doctor had to stop it and both Mum and me had to come back down to earth.

'For a few days everything was all right, but it didn't last long. Mum just wasn't *there* any more. She'd forget to make meals, stay in bed till the afternoon, or sit watching TV till close-down. I might as well not have existed. Even at that age I knew it was only a matter of time before the tension got to me and my dreams started again. And I was frantic not to let that happen. I started acting like someone in a bloody comedy film.

'Black coffee keeps you awake – we hope – so one night I sneaked the kettle upstairs with some coffee after mum had finally gone to bed and made myself some very black coffee. I also made myself sick. The bitterest thing I'd ever had was Vimto! God, was I sick. What a mess! It kept me awake that night, though. Next day I remember was a Saturday, so I didn't have to worry about falling asleep at school. Instead I fell asleep watching TV. The dream came. I woke up.

'Saturday night I dreamed again. Woke up in time. Sunday I was a bundle of nerves and drove Mum mad so I went to the beach and spent the entire day by myself alone. Was I ever miserable. Came home, had tea and fell asleep on the couch.

'I woke up about midnight, Mum shaking me hard.

' "Did you hear that?" she said.

' "What?" I said, knowing exactly what she meant.

' "That whistle. That train whistle. Where would a train be this time of night?" she said.

'I stopped the conversation by shitting myself. Crapped my knickers right there in our living room. Mum started having hysterics – eleven-year-olds don't shit their pants without reason and here *she* was looking for reassurance – but the mess and my misery gave her something to do. After she had cleaned up and we went to bed together and fell asleep. No more train that night.

'Monday the evening paper was full of stuff about a ghost train. A lot of different people had heard this strange whistle in the night in our part of Blackpool. The paper made a real meal of it. Even got on News at Ten. One of their reporters had actually heard it himself while covering one of the Party conferences. Mum was glad she hadn't imagined it and it gave her something to talk to the neighbours about during the day. She didn't make the connection with me and I didn't want to make it for her. Having had a restful night of it I thought it would be over.

'It wasn't. That night I dreamed again. I woke up and went to her room. Now I may have been terrified something was going to happen, but she wasn't and I caught her at a bad moment. I crept in hoping not to wake her, but she was already awake and, well . . . she was stark naked and . . . using a vibrator. Legs all over the place, moaning, the full monty. She went bananas! Clouted me for the first time I could ever remember, in fact. Now, she had never told me the facts of life; I had no close friends and it wasn't on the school timetable till the next term. I hadn't the *faintest* idea what she was up to and now I was even more scared. Of course, she chucked me out of her room, calling me a dirty little tyke. I'd wanted some comfort, I was frightened, and here I was being called all the names under the sun! So I went back to my room and cried myself to sleep.'

Cally sat back and started sobbing again.

'Oh God, no,' said Ronald.

'That's right, Ron. I fell asleep and this time I couldn't wake myself up. Not when I heard the whistle or saw the steam or smelled the smoke. Not when I saw Mum in my dream tied to the tracks like in one of those silent films. I could see her arms and ankles tied and she was looking down the line screaming but the . . . *the vibrator was stuffed in her mouth* which meant I couldn't hear and she was thrashing about trying to get off the tracks but it was no good, and the train appeared out of nowhere, big and black, and ran straight over her, slicing her into three pieces, her blood splashing over the sleepers and up the front of the train . . .' She hid her face in her hands and wept pitifully.

Ronald got up and checked on Mark. He was asleep on Ronald's blankets, curled up in a ball. Ronald felt a pang of jealousy. Some found it so easy to escape . . . He then went to the kitchen and made two cups of coffee, liberally dosing both with sugar, then offered the sweet concoction to Cally who gladly accepted it. She seemed to have calmed herself, like a squall which had blown itself out. For his part, Ronald was tired, frightened and, he found to his surprise, shaking like a leaf. What this girl had done or thought she had done had affected her every bit as much as his obsession with the truck and, despite her scorning his role as a parent and teacher, it affected him. A child was suffering and he could do nothing to help.

After a couple of sips, accompanied by a grimace – it must have been their fourth cup – Cally continued her story.

'I knew Mum was dead when I woke up. I remember looking at my clock. It was four thirty-three. I didn't dare move. I lay there in the dark and watched every single minute tick off until seven thirty-five when the postman always came. Then, when I heard him outside, I jumped out of bed and ran out of the flat – not even looking at Mum's door – and downstairs to the front door of the house and I opened it in time to see him walk past without any letters for us! That wasn't part of the plan but I needed him, so I ran after him and grabbed him by the arm and shouted that my mum needed help.

' "Where is she?" he said, really worried.

' "Upstairs in her bedroom. Could you go and look? Please?"

'He could tell I was frightened so he went upstairs. He was worried but he was a nice man and he knew I was serious.

'That was the first time I ever heard a man scream. He must have been fifty or so; had big hard hands, I remember, red rough face . . . And he screamed like a little girl. Like me. Then he came running downstairs, fell at the bottom, got up and ran past me into the street, yelling and screaming. I ran after him to ask him what had happened even though I already knew and didn't want to find out anyway!

'It must have looked like he was attacking me because when I caught up with him and grabbed his arm, he turned on me and started pushing me away, shouting. To someone just walking past us it would have sounded like he was trying to kidnap me and it was *me* who was doing all the screaming. Anyway, a couple of blokes floored him and only let him go when I shouted he hadn't done anything and it was my mum who needed help. One of them went up, while the other stayed with the postman just in case.

'The man who went in came down white. I remember that; he looked like he'd seen a ghost. He looked really ill, wobbly actually, but he didn't faint, just swore a lot then went next door and called the police and an ambulance.

'The postman and him and me needed the ambulance. They needed plastic bags for Mum.

'I was eleven. Dad had drowned. Mum had been murdered in her bedroom next to mine. And I knew that a teacher and a psychiatrist had also died because of my dream and 'cause I hated them. What else could I do but go bonkers?'

Cally took some more sups from her drink, but it wasn't so much as if she was thirsty, just a way of giving herself time to gather her thoughts. Finally, she stood up and carried a blanket over to the fireplace and there, having stoked the burning logs, she lay down on the floor, closed her eyes and continued. The similarity of this new position to that of a patient on a psychiatrist's couch wasn't lost on Ronald.

'I got locked up in a home. For the first year I was on Largactil and Dartalin and Orap and other anti-psychotics, Phenothiazines, they're called, designed to stop my "delusions". When you're on medication for a long time, Ron, you get to know what they're giving you. I spent a whole year of my life in a grey fog. Can't remember a minute of it. I may have dreamed about my train, I don't know. My whole fucking life was like a dream anyway, and I didn't give a monkey's. I do know that whenever they let up on the dosage and I came back into the real world, I would rant and rave about the train and how it had come and killed Mum and all the others. I was a certified lunatic.

'I didn't know it at the time but they thought I had hacked Mum to pieces. Never proved it, though. I might even have got to believe it myself – even to an eleven-year-old it made more sense that you could go loopy and do your mum in than dream a train had run her over in her own bedroom. But . . . but I would have been covered in blood if I *had* done it. Dr Gantry – when I finally ended up in Handland – told me that the oddest thing was that there wasn't a single spot of blood outside her bedroom, and that was what more or less convinced the police that it wasn't me. Where did I clean up if I had done it? And where were my bloodstained clothes? But, as I said, I was too far out of it to care, anyway.

'So whenever I did start freaking out about trains and murdering people in my dreams, they would pump me full of shit and I'd be back in gagaland. It must have been that I was too blitzed to care about anything so I didn't hate anyone so the train didn't come.

'A year or so later they started dropping the dose as I had finally calmed down. I think what happened was my brain was so zonked for so long that my dream went into retirement. You know, the train went to the old scrapyard. Couldn't take the competition from the pills and injections.

'After eighteen months or so I was pronounced cured and put in a council home and offered for fostering. Well, as you can imagine, a thirteen-year-old ex-loony with dead bodies in the background was top of the list when the mums and dads came round. So I became a permanent resident of the home and spent a year learning to be a criminal.'

'What?' said Ronald.

'Who do you think ends up in children's homes? Middle-class kids? The rich? No, it's the bottom end of the market, and those who stay in the longest are usually the least likeable ones and the least likeable members of society are the loopy ones – like me – and the criminals. I learnt all about drugs and sex and crime. Stealing cars and shoplifting and burglary, the lot. I took it all in, sometimes did a bit of nicking myself – even had a spell on the old Evostick but got off it quick when one of my mates walked through a glass door and bloody near sliced her head off! I watched and listened and kidded on I was with them but I wasn't really into it at all. I'm an *honest* kid, whatever you may think. I was forced to be dishonest. And, of course, if I hadn't gone along with them, I'd have been bopped, so I just went with the crowd. The home helped as well.

'One of their bright ideas was to put those kids with a thing for cars – joyriders mostly and they included me – into a scheme where we got to drive old bangers in demolition derbies. Fucking ace it was. Got rid of all your aggro and anger. Perfect. But it also taught us all how to be good drivers. By the time they stopped the scheme we could outdrive anyone, including the cops, even though most of us were years away from a licence. That's how I got me and Mark away from Handland: a car. Do-gooders: sometimes I wonder if they've got any brains at all . . .

'I also got into the routine of the place, knew what to do and when to do it, knew how much I could get away with and so on. That helped me a lot, I think. After a couple of years of not knowing whether I was coming or going, to find myself knowing *exactly* what I was supposed to do at any time of the day was a relief. I wasn't violent, but I didn't take any shit so I was pretty much left alone. Some of the kids were real hard bastards just waiting until they could be sent to prison for something. Even then you could tell they were doomed, poor sods.'

'Poor sods? Thugs that—'

Cally sat up with a start. 'It was a kids' home Ron. *Kids*. You should understand that, being a teacher and all. Not their fault they had parents who fucked them or beat them up or threw them out the house. Not their fault they had to learn to survive like fucking animals from the day they were born because their parents were such cunts! Sorry, sorry, sorry.' She calmed down. 'Yes, some of them were born bad, no question, but most of them were kids like me who, through no fault of their own, had been abandoned and were just doing their best to keep up with a world full of arseholes and bastards out to screw them one way or another. Some of them thought it was neat that my mum had been murdered and that suspicious fingers pointed at me. A killer at eleven? Wow, top. And some of them were scared of me for the same reason. Kids like me, Ron, but I couldn't get near them.'

She stood up and started pacing the room. 'They used to get us up at seven, we'd get washed, do some PT, have breakfast, tidy the dorm, then go to lessons. Basic stuff – English, maths, history, geography. Bored me shitless. Quite a few of the kids didn't do well in class but, talking to them, you knew they had it in them. They either didn't give a toss or the teachers were useless. After six months they enrolled me in a local comprehensive and, whilst I was keen to fit in, the kids at the school knew where I came from so I got picked on a lot. Bloody kids, I'll never understand them.'

She sat back down on the bed. Whatever else she looked like, this was a very old sixteen-year-old.

'I let myself be bullied, I suppose. I knew that if I started to hate any of them they'd end up underneath my train. That actually gave me a kind of weird satisfaction, you know. The older girls could push my head down the bog or chuck my books in the dirt or push me around and I could take it 'cause I knew the alternative would be them dying. After a while they got bored with it. They could see they weren't going to get me all worked up and it's boring picking on someone who isn't scared of you. No feeling of power, you see. Worse. I think they got *scared*, found me creepy. They knew I wasn't one of those queer types who likes being picked on and beaten up, who gets a kick out of being kicked about. But the fact that I would just take it, that scared them, I think. Maybe they could hear a train whistle in the back of their minds and they took the warning, I don't know. So . . . they left me alone and I settled in. Started doing well, too.

'But as no one would foster me, at nights and weekends I went back to the home and fell in with the routine. But what the hell? I had no choice, did I? I realized with my rep and my age I wasn't going to be adopted, so I set my sights on getting to sixteen and getting out into the world. I fancied being a cook or a chef. They let me help out in the kitchen at the home. I think I'm quite good. I was determined.'

'What happened?' asked Ronald.

'What do you mean?'

'Come on, Cally. We both know you fell into bad ways recently. Studying for English O Level doesn't include stealing wallets and credit cards. What went wrong?'

'Sex.'

'Sex?'

'Yeah. I woke up one day and found out what my fanny was for. Sorry.'

'Puberty?'

'Yes, Ron,' Cally said with a sigh, sounding just like Ronald did when he got tired with some of the simpletons he had to teach in 4Y. The comparison was not lost on Ronald who did all but squirm in his seat.

'Puberty,' continued Cally with an exaggerated smile. 'I suddenly realized *why* boys are a different shape and what periods were all about. Soon all I could think of was sex, but I had a problem: all I could look at was girls; all I dreamed of was girls.' She laughed. 'At least it was better than thinking of trains!

'Now, there were boys at the home but they were kept apart from us girls most of the time. We got to mingle now and again but I had a thing for a girl. Noreen her name was, of all things. Noreen? Sounds like a fruit loaf! Fifteen she was. She was tall, blonde, not really pretty, just nice, and I fancied her like crazy. Her parents had abandoned her when she was a kid and she had been in and out of homes all her life. She was a born thief. Brilliant. She could charm the trousers off a cop and he wouldn't have noticed. Trouble was, she always hung around with dickheads who got caught and shopped her as she was always the oldest. Her nickname was Miss Fagin. Something to do with Oliver Twist.

'Anyway, I wangled my way onto a swimming trip with her and we got talking. We got on like a house on fire. Everything we ate she nicked and a whole new world opened up. Seeing *Bonnie and Clyde* on the telly that night didn't help. What she saw in me I don't know. Probably brains. I don't think she was a, you know, a . . . er,' she took a deep breath. 'A lessie. I wanted to . . . anyway, I wasn't stupid like a lot of the kids in there and that's what she liked. So we decided to run off. And we did.

'Normally one or other of us legging it wouldn't have been so bad. Someone skipped every week. They usually got caught, though Johnny Hayes was always held up as a warning. He got murdered by some queers in London, but as Noreen and I weren't on the game and weren't heading up the Smoke we weren't worried. But the two of us running away together and the others blabbing about us hanging around together all the time made them turn it into some big sex deal but there wasn't anything like that, I swear. I loved her and admired her and wouldn't lay a finger on her without her say-so, but as she wasn't interested in sex at all, I never got so much as a peep at her bra strap. Still, the local papers played up our escape. They seemed sympathetic in a way; went on about my "unfortunate and tragic childhood" and played down the fact that Noreen could have planned the Great Train Robbery and got away with it.

'We stayed in Blackpool – we both knew the place. We both dyed our hair and cut it different – and as we skipped with about fifty quid, we got some secondhand clothes and got into a squat. The hippies there helped us out for a while but then started looking at us both in a dirty way and hinting that the food we'd been eating had to be paid for somehow. We left that night. Slept rough on the beach for a while – it was summer and I thought it was kind of romantic. I loved her, you see. It wasn't just a crush or puppy love or whatever anyone wants to call it. I *loved* Noreen.'

Ronald was vaguely disgusted. 'Are you . . . were you sure you were, you know, gay? I mean, you were only . . . you *are* only sixteen. Isn't it a bit soon to throw away—'

Cally turned on him, her eyes blazing. 'You bloody sexist pig! Who the hell are you to tell me what I should feel? If I'm gay I'm gay. It isn't something you choose. For all you know Julie could have been—'

'*She wasn't!*' Ronald was outraged. Julie was perfect. 'No daughter of mine would turn out like, like *that.*'

Cally was equally angry. 'It's not a fucking disease, Ron! Do you think it's easy listening to girls your own age going on about men and what they've got between their legs while all the time you want to hold a girl? I don't want to be a lesbian but I am. I like girls. I want girls. I'm not interested in boys. It's just the way I am. I can just imagine what it would have been like if Julie had been gay. God, you'd have gone through the roof.'

'I wouldn't!' he insisted. 'I wouldn't . . .' But it set him thinking. Julie was eighteen, pretty, bright, but she had never had a boyfriend.

'I'm sorry. I apologize,' Ronald said. He didn't want to think any further about the subject. His Julie couldn't have been . . . no, not his daughter. Preposterous! But she never *had* brought a boy home for tea, had she? Stop it, Ronald! And she *had* gone on holiday with Caroline . . . no, leave it. And there were only posters of girl singers on her wall . . . *stop it stop it stop it*!

'You all right, Ron? You look . . .'

'Yes, yes, sorry. Carry on.'

'All right . . . Noreen taught me all the tricks in nicking wallets and using credit cards when you could get away with it – we both looked older than our years. She also knew some guys who would buy stuff off us. Cards, jewellery, anything we lifted. We were making about a hundred, hundred and fifty a week, eating well, enjoying the sun. We looked like tourists. We even decided to move into a bed-and-breakfast for a week, see what it was like. It was great. So what we did from then on, right through the summer, was book into a different hotel every week, pretend to be sisters. We could pass for seventeen. Two good meals a day, a bed at night, no sex. I was getting pretty frustrated but I put up with it. Noreen avoided the subject whenever I brought it up. I suppose she was either scared or simply not gay, though she never showed any interest in boys. I . . . never mind. We stayed in hotels for weeks. Nick something in the morning, spend the rest of the day on the beach or swimming. Great, it was. Never got bothered by the fuzz, either. All the stuff about "the runaways" disappeared. They must have figured we had lost ourselves in London, so they didn't bother.

'That was until our landlady shopped us. Someone had nicked her handbag – it wasn't us – but she had searched everyone's rooms and found two wallets in ours. We came back to find a police car outside the house. We ran off, left all our stuff behind. Really screwed up our plans. We hitched out to the Lake District and set up camp in some woods. We bagged a couple more wallets and a purse and got enough money to buy a tent and some sleeping bags. The weather was good and for a couple of days we thought it was even better than being in town. Then it started raining and we got soaked and didn't dry out for three days.

'We both got colds and were really sick. Then Noreen got caught nicking some Lemsips and we both got chased all over some village. Bloody well nearly killed me. We got away, but it totally fucked up Noreen. She got pneumonia or something but refused to go to a hospital. I agreed with her even though I was frantic about how ill she was getting, so I waited until she was too ill to argue, then I carried her to the main road from our hideout and flagged down a car.'

Cally stopped. She looked on the verge of crying again. She said it all in a rush:

'Of all the fucking cars I could have flagged down, I chose that one. Three total bastards! All sympathetic to start with, they let us in the back, all concerned they were. Then they started making jokes. Comments like "She must have done some serious shagging" and "Share and share alike" and then before I could stop them – I was pretty ill myself – they'd pulled off the road, beaten me up and dragged Noreen off and raped her. They came back laughing, kicked me some more, then they drove off. I remember the last thing I saw was the number plate of their car.

'I don't know when I woke up but it was still dark. Must have taken me half an hour to find Noreen, feeling around in the dark, shouting her name. It was a cold night, dry but bloody cold. I found her . . . she had been stripped naked and her hands had been tied to a fallen tree. They must have done everything to her. There was blood everywhere, most of it between her legs. I had hysterics. I couldn't undo the string around her arms and she wouldn't wake up. I couldn't even tell if she was still breathing. I didn't know what to do, so I took off my jumper – I couldn't find *any* of her clothes – and covered her up as best I could, then ran back to the road and waited for a vehicle I could trust to come past. I was convinced the whole world was mad and out to get us. Even that those three fuckers would come back and finish me off. So I waited maybe half an hour until a tour bus came past full of Germans or Belgies, and I stood in the road. The driver had to slide into a ditch to avoid me. He came out all set to beat me shitless but I started babbling something about rape and pointed into the woods. He got the message and took a dozen of these Krauts to find Noreen.

'We found her, untied her and got her onto the bus. I remember the driver driving like a maniac and half the women on the bus crying.

'We got her to hospital. She died the next afternoon. Aggravated something. Shock and pneumonia, stuff like that. The police came and interviewed me. I gave them as accurate a description as I could of the men and the car, but I didn't give them the car number. I was saving that.'

'Your train?' said Ronald, surprised to find himself so caught up in her story.

'Yeah. They kept me in hospital a couple of days. Second night I went to sleep thinking of my train and that number plate. I remember it clearer than anything. The hospital room was very warm, the heating full on, for my benefit. Everyone was very sympathetic, including the fuzz. Apparently this had happened to a couple of other girls in recent months and I was the first one who had been able to supply a description. About ten the nurse put out my light, then I lay on my back, the blankets up to my shoulders, and I crossed my arms over my eyes and pictured that car and its number plate and my train. And as I fell asleep I heard a whistle, long and loud outside the hospital. Funny thing was, next day the nurses mentioned it to me. All the night staff had heard this whistle. Some of them got quite spooked. There wasn't a steam train within thirty miles.'

'And?'

'I dreamed the car was on a motorway. Out in the country. There were no lights, just their car and a couple of other cars, way, way off. They were laughing. The one driving was weaving the car from side to side. I could smell booze. They were swigging from a bottle. They had the radio on, playing Z Z Top really loud. Booming out, it was. So loud they couldn't hear the whistle, or the steam, or the rumble of the train's wheels on the tarmac. They didn't see anything until the last second when the train roared over them from behind. I remember being excited and pissed off at the same time; pleased they had been crushed, but angry they hadn't seen what was coming. They hadn't had time to be scared, you see. Killing them instantly seemed too good. I'd wanted them to suffer. I wanted to hear them scream and shout and beg, like they made me and Noreen beg.

'Next morning the police came and told me they'd traced the rapists' car. It had been involved in an accident on the M61. They'd found bottles – they must have been drunk. No other cars were involved. It had gone straight into a bridge. Totally destroyed. The copper said it couldn't have happened to a nicer trio – they all had records – and the case was going to be closed. Some of Noreen's clothing was in the boot, along with clothes from other rape victims.

'But now the train was back, I got frightened. Could I switch it off again? The answer was no and I knew I needed drugs to keep it away so I acted ape-shit and they got me to another psychiatrist pretty quick. And a hospital. With all that had happened, it was no wonder I went loopy.'

'But you didn't, did you?' said Ronald.

'No I didn't. Very perceptive, Ron. No, I was as sober and sane as a judge. Well, some judges. What happened was he got my confidence, this psychiatrist, a Dr Rogers. He took it easy, recommended minimum dose sedatives and sleeping stuff so I was "relaxed and unruffled", as he put it. That way I calmed down and began to trust him. I was in a hospital psychiatric unit but was kept away from the real nutters. And he talked to me every day, first at the hospital, then at his home where he had consulting rooms. He was very friendly, used to pick me up, or send one of his nurses.

'After he had got my trust. I told him about the train, which of course he didn't believe for one minute. But when I told him the whole story – remember, this was over a couple of hours a day for a month – he was sort of, well, if not convinced, then certainly interested in finding the truth. The fact that my story was identical in every detail no matter how many times I told it seemed to convince him. After all, that's what would happen if I *was* telling the truth wouldn't it? So, he hypnotized me.'

'Oh God, he didn't . . . he didn't make . . .' said Ronald.

'Yes. He first, what's the word? regressed me, like they do on those TV shows – "You are now two years old," all that stuff – to see if my childhood had been as good or bad as I said it was. Then he took me through Mum's "murder" and Noreen's murder. He was convinced I was telling the truth. The fifth time he tried to get the train. As he explained it to me, he wanted to find out why I "manifested my hate and my guilt in the same imaginary object". I think he believed I was genuinely responsible for Chloë's being on that train when she died; that I had put her there for a joke and the train had gone off before I could get her back. I told him it wasn't so, and under hypnosis I confirmed it, so he had to "explore other avenues", as he called it. He put me under and started asking me who I hated and why I hated them and what I wanted to do to them. I was under for about twenty minutes. I came out of it all right but he seemed a bit upset.

' "Well?" I asked.

' "Well," he said. "I believe you about the train. Not that it kills anyone, but that you *believe* it kills people. You wish certain people dead, and when they die, purely by coincidence, you say your train did it. And then you feel guilty, as any honest person would. You feel doubly guilty about the death of your mother because even though she was clearly upset that you found her masturbating, and was upset with you as a result, you went to bed hating her and when she committed suicide, you blamed yourself and your train."

' "So what did I say?" I asked.

' "Very well," he said. "Listen." He had taped all our sessions and he played back the tape for this session.

'It was the usual stuff. He put me under, asked me some simple questions, then got onto asking me who I hated. I gave him a list, all of them people who were dead. And it didn't include Mum. Then, just when he asked me how they died and I said my train, there was a loud whistle on the tape. A train whistle. I remember he looked really frightened.

'He ran over to the cassette player, stopped it and played the same part back. Train whistle. Loud, but still a way away. It was as big a surprise to him as it was to me, but while I realized what it was and wasn't all that bothered – it was my train, after all, and it proved I wasn't lying – he looked about ready to shit himself. Obviously he hadn't heard it when he was talking to me. He let the tape play on. Every half minute or so, the whistle would blow for a couple of seconds, each time nearer and each time blotting out whatever else was on the tape. It was just like his office was next to a railway station. Then you could hear the steam and hear the train chuffing. It was slow and long and very deep. I was frightened now – I had never heard my train other than in my dreams – but Dr Rogers's reaction was even more frightening. He turned *white*. No kidding. He was terrified. The train kept coming nearer and nearer on the tape. Now you couldn't hear anything either of us was saying. It sounded so loud, like it was actually outside the door about to crash through. That's when he reached over and switched the tape recorder off. What happened next made us both shit our pants.

'He had switched the tape off but the train kept coming nearer and nearer! He was frantic, banging on the controls, trying to stop it, but we could both see the tape had stopped. In fact, he hit the eject button and the bloody cassette flew out of the machine onto his desk! And *still* the train was roaring and hissing outside the door. He then pulled the lead out of the recorder, but the train was still there so, finally, he threw the bloody thing at the door! It bounced off, but it also knocked the door open . . .

'It came into the room and stood there. Big and black and steaming. It was maybe ten feet away from us, reaching up through the ceiling. It was unbelievable. It had to be the ugliest, dirtiest train in the whole bloody world. And even though it was a lot taller than the room, it didn't damage the ceiling at all. Oh, it went through the plaster and I suppose up into the room above, but it didn't leave a mark. Only the door was damaged; even then the train must have been five or six times as wide but it fitted through it somehow. I could also see every detail. Later on, Dr Gantry got me a book on trains and I found one that looked like it. Everything was there: the square buffers, the funny-shaped boiler, the little cab, the six wheels. If I remember it right, it's called a Hunslet Austerity O-6-OST. A lot were built for collieries and power stations. Ugly little bastard. Why my train should be like that I don't know.'

'What was the train that killed Chloë like?' asked Ronald.

'I don't know. I know what you're getting at. It might have been one of them. I've always thought it was much bigger, but I was nine and I was scared to death. And I've never been back.

'Anyway, the train stood there for I don't know how long. A minute? It looked like it was watching us, waiting for something, all the time its boiler sounding like it was rolling over and over like a giant . . . like a giant washing machine, I suppose. Like breathing, maybe. Yeah, breathing. *Huff huff huff.* Then suddenly it gave out an unbelievably loud scream with its whistle. Felt like our ears would explode. And all the glass in the room shattered – the windows, the bookcase fronts, his glass desktop, the coffee table. I turned and watched his aquarium blow up and his pretty little fishes fly all over his desk. That's when I screamed, and Dr Rogers freaked. When I looked back the train had gone and a male nurse was rushing into the room to see what all the noise was about.

'Well, there you are, you're a nurse, and you see the room's wrecked, the doctor's on the floor – dead for all you know – and Loony Tunes is stood there screaming her arse off. Whack. I'm out cold in one punch.'

'Very professional,' said Ronald.

Cally shrugged her shoulders in resignation. 'But effective. I think what happened next was that Dr Rogers panicked. He couldn't cope with what had happened, so he had me sedated and shipped out to Handland, said he knew Gantry was interested in the more unusual kinds of mental problems. At the time I didn't give a shit. All I wanted was to be rid of that train.'

She then told Ronald of her time in Handland, how Gantry had tried to gain her trust, how he had introduced her to Nurse Biggs, the sleep lab, the little indulgences, and how everything seemed to be going fine until Elizabeth had messed her up and then died. And then how Gantry had been over the moon about her killing the nurse and how his patience had run out again and he had tortured Mark.

'What else could I do? So I spent the evening staring at books of old steam trains Gantry had bought me and reliving all the experiences that had led to the people I hated dying – even Mum's death: that's how determined I was to get Gantry off my back. I went through everything that had happened since Chloë died, and then I went to bed thinking of Dr Gantry and my train.

'He was there behind the glass screen watching the dials and monitors. I went to sleep: some drug he fed into me intravenously each night. Supposed to allow me to dream. It did. Shit, did it ever. I dreamed that train right into his fucking control room! I tried to hold it back, too, as if it was waiting at a station. Yes, that was the image I had. It was at a station, waiting to go, and Gantry was standing beside it, looking up at it, pissing himself.'

'And?' said Ronald.

'And he pumped something else into me and I woke up. The control room was wrecked, Gantry was having kittens, and the place was full of steam. The train had come and done exactly what I had told it to as I fell asleep. That was two weeks ago. Since then, despite Gantry doing everything he could, I've never dreamed the train again. I know I can destroy Gantry as easily as taking a nap, but I've chosen not to hate and not to let it loose. But the effort of keeping it away is costing me.

'I'm really tired now, despite the sleep I do get. One night I'm not going to be able to stop it coming and then I don't know where it'll go. Or who it'll kill. Maybe it'll go for anyone I happen to think of. Anyone. It came when Dr Rogers was with me, and I certainly never wanted him hurt. *That's* why I had to escape, to get away from Gantry. I don't think he knows what he's doing so, when I do lose control, he's not going to be any use in helping me stop it. I'm also scared that if that does happen – and I'm on some bloody machine pumping me full of shit – I might overdose and never come out of it. Might even die.

'I brought Mark with me because I wasn't going to leave him there with that bastard. God knows what he would get up to with him. You've already seen those scars on his head. And that's why I can't go back; not only for what Gantry might do to me, but also for what he might do to Mark as punishment. I'd have to do anything he said otherwise Mark would suffer, and now Gantry's seen my train, there'll be no stopping him! He wants to get inside my head and get the train out and he doesn't care what happens to me.'

'But if you turn yourself in to the police, explain what Gantry's up to?'

'Oh, come on, you dick, haven't you heard anything I've been saying? I kill people by dreaming up a fucking train! That's going to look real good on a police statement, isn't it? Add to that my record for absconding, past psychiatric care, stealing cards, whatever shit Gantry's put in my notes, taking away a retard like Mark . . . put all that up against one of the country's most respect psychiatrists and he'll have them *posting* me back to his loving care! Don't you see, whether I tell the truth or shut up, I'm fucked. I'm a loony sixteen-year-old girl and he's the expert; he'll decide what happens to me, and only him.'

Cally kicked at the grate of the fire and a log dislodged itself in a shower of sparks. 'Fuck it!' she cried, then ran into the kitchen.

Ronald followed her and found her leaning over the sink, kicking at the cupboard.

'So what's your alternative?' he asked helplessly.

'Stay out of his hands. I've got the drugs, they'll do. But I'm running out. I've been dosed so much in the past they don't have as much effect as they used to. One of the problems with amphetamines and barbiturates: they're addictive and the more you get used to them the less use they are.'

'Like heroin,' offered Ronald, thinking of Annie. 'Pretty soon you're just trying to stop the come down rather than get the high?'

'Yeah. Unless I get something stronger, I'm going to fall asleep and I don't know what'll happen.'

Ronald slipped his hand around her shoulder and she turned into him and hugged him, crying on his chest. Between her sobs, she spoke with a trembling voice.

'There's something else, worse than just the train coming. Each time I see the train it's from a different angle. It's nearer too, like it's drawing me towards it, asking me to get on board. I think the time I dream I'm *in* its cab, driving the thing, *that's* when I'll be lost. I'll get killed or die or go mad or it might stay permanently. I just don't know and I don't want to find out.'

He looked down at the little girl lost crying in his arms. 'And that's why you have to keep awake?'

'Yes, at least until I can get something to knock me out so deep I don't start dreaming. Last time I fell asleep here I heard that whistle . . .'

'But where are you going to get them?' said Ronald.

'Steal them from a chemist's.'

'Pretty unlikely. Neither of us are burglars.'

'Us?'

'You need help; I'm offering. If you can trust me.'

'If a loony can't trust a loony who can she trust?' Cally smiled.

He eased her away and ran water over a paper towel and wiped her tears, just like he used to do for Julie when she scraped her knee.

'But robbing a chemist isn't on. They'll have an alarm, we don't know what we're looking for . . .'

'Will you stop thinking of problems! I haven't slept in three bloody days, Ron! I need something soon and what's left from Handland isn't strong enough. Chances are it'll only set me dreaming which is just what I don't want!' She walked back into the lounge and stopped next to the sleeping Mark. 'And what about him?'

Ronald didn't have an answer, so he went to the bathroom. After he had peed, he looked at himself in the dirty cabinet's cracked mirror. God, he looked old. Too old. And Cally was too young; too young to be on the run with Mark and too young for all she'd been through. Or at least *said* she'd been through.

Ronald rubbed his face. Whatever the veracity of her tale, the detail she had included and her emotions, particularly when speaking of Chloë and Noreen, seemed so real. Yet the Freudian implications were blatantly obvious. He'd never had much time for psychology, but even he knew trains were phallic symbols.

Trains. The girl had gone through puberty traumatized by an

abusive father, an inadequate mother, the deaths of her adopted sister, her parents, a teacher and a doctor she feared, life in a children's home, the rape and tragic death of her best friend . . . and all the figures she resented, all the people she thought she had been responsible for killing, they were all men. And here she was, a self-confessed – or would it be self-*proclaimed* – lesbian, exacting revenge on men with the biggest phallic symbol of them all.

Ronald doubted that Cally was clever enough to deliberately choose a train as her symbolic weapon, so the choice had to be subconscious. But that didn't make it true. Besides, she also claimed her train had killed her nurse: a woman. That didn't sit with his amateur psychological theory, unless . . .

He went back downstairs. Cally had pulled her upright chair towards the fire and was leaning forwards, staring into the dying flames. She looked so vulnerable. He was reluctant to interrupt but his curiosity would not be denied.

'Cally, what did Nurse Biggs do to you that was so bad?' he said.

'Why?'

'Why not?'

Cally shrugged as if it didn't matter what he knew. 'She fucked me. With a big dildo. I bled. A lot.'

'Oh, I'm sorry. Sorry . . .' he mumbled with embarrassment. Then it struck him: *even the nurse had had a . . .*

No, it was preposterous, *insane*. But it also had a logic beyond the girl's ken – and she *believed* it. But all the same, an avenging *train*? A steam engine from hell? Come on, Given the cod psychology it suggested, she might as well have conjured up a psychotic Ken doll, or a rabid Little Pony! She really had escaped from a mental hospital. But Ronald didn't want to debate with her, not now, anyway. Apart from anything else, he was shattered. His body ached and his head throbbed and he needed rest.

'You do believe me,' Cally said, without looking at him.

'Yes,' he said quietly, as if lack of volume minimised his commitment.

'Sure,' she yawned, leaning back and stretching.

Ronald wanted to stay up with her, to help her through to the next day but he could hardly walk. He sat down at the table and rested his head on his hands, staring at the girl as she studied the flames. But even as he tried to fight the urge to close his eyes, the pleasant warmth of the fire and the gentle crackle of the burning wood lulled him into a doze where, despite a couple of twitching awakenings, he soon surrendered to the inevitable.

NINETEEN

The truck was coming. Ronald knew it instinctively. That white horror was still after him, hunting him like an animal, desperate for his blood, his soul. He stared ahead.

He was on a clear stretch of road, it was dark, and there was no street lighting. All he could discern was the triangle of road lit up by his headlights and the myriad pinprick stars above in a canopy so wide and high it looked like a giant curtain. He pressed harder on the accelerator, only to find it already floored. He looked in his mirrors. He thought for a moment that he might be dreaming again – he had a distant memory of a house, a safe haven, scratching somewhere deep within the darkness that had enveloped him – but it didn't matter; whatever was happening, real or unreal, it would have the same destination if the truck caught him: hell. And, real or unreal, the truck was there.

There were twin orbs of white staring at him, unblinking, every yard bringing the truck nearer and nearer until its lights would blind him and he would be devoured. Ronald looked frantically for a turning, but the road had suddenly become a single carriageway, hedges bounding both sides, the road ahead so straight and featureless that he could have been inside a video game.

On an impulse, Ronald took his hands off the wheel and felt no difference, the van continuing in a perfect line. He took his foot off the pedal. Again, no change. Without touching any controls, the VW was at maximum speed, following the only escape route – and losing the race. He turned back and looked through the rear window. An evil glinting mouth leered back, the monster truck lunging forward as it saw the terror in his face.

Ronald wrenched at the wheel but it was fixed, as unyielding as the onslaught from behind. He jabbed at the brakes. Pointless.

And still the truck came closer. He tried the door: the handle came off in his hand. He slammed at the window with his fist, screeching his terror, but the glass didn't crack, didn't craze. He pulled his foot up out of the footwell and kicked at the windscreen, but it also proved too resilient.

Then the truck sounded its horn, a deep bellow like some behemoth from the darkest watery depths breaking free into the world above and giving vent to its relief and long-denied needs. It was a terrifying cry of hunger, of anger, from a creature that Ronald knew would not stop until it had slaked its desires.

Ronald looked back again and found himself blinded. The truck was within inches of the van. It was over. Then there was a thump and the VW shook, tossing Ronald across the seats. Then another bellow of air horn, the angry growl of an engine and an odd noise; an out of place sound that seared into his mind like an icicle into flesh: a whistle, high-pitched and shrill, a sound from another age, another world.

There was another impact and Ronald fell into the footwell and banged his head. Pain joined his sensory overload and Ronald's scream became higher and higher pitched until it didn't even sound human, didn't even sound as if it belonged to him. Then there was light and shouting and he whirled up and screamed as he saw Cally standing over him, holding a knife.

'Will you shut up!' she hissed.

He stared up at her, expecting the knife to lance into his chest. Why had he trusted this mad girl and her stories? Hadn't he horrors enough of his own?

'Ron! Did you hear it?'

'What?'

'The train whistle.'

'What? What train whistle?'

Seeing he was able to give a coherent answer, Cally sat back on her haunches and put the knife down.

'Sorry,' she said. 'I had to stop you screaming. You were waking up the neighbourhood. What were you dreaming?'

'A nightmare . . .' He realized he was wringing with sweat but he didn't care. He sat up and saw the girl was shaking. 'Again. I keep having it . . . Come to think of it, there *was* a sound. It could have been a whistle.'

'It was. I fell asleep,' said Cally. 'Only for a minute or two but it was enough. I dreamt the train in the distance, coming here. When it blew its whistle I woke up but it blew a couple more times while I was awake.'

'I might have heard it. And I was shouting?'

'A lot. It was scary, Ron. I wouldn't want to dream what you were dreaming – and I've dreamt some shit . . .'

Ronald wondered how many times over the past few weeks he had shouted in his sleep, and how many people had heard him as they passed his van. Then he noticed the room was light.

'What time is it?'

'About eight.'

Cally stood up and went into the kitchen. There she filled a pan with water and set it on the stove, almost spilling it as her hand shook.

She had watched Ronald fall asleep at about midnight and had kept herself awake trying to work out all their options. She wasn't sure yet if she could trust Ronald; his story had been pretty weird. She didn't doubt what he had done; the van and his physical condition were evidence enough of that, but as for whether his truck was real . . .

In Handland she had met people who talked to flies, who believed their father was a wardrobe, thought they themselves were Mother Theresa . . . Their sincerity and passion didn't make their delusions any more real. So what if there wasn't a white truck? What was she to make of the shit in his van, all those polaroids and the map and stuff? And then to let herself fall asleep in the same room as him . . . Never mind her problems with the train; what if he had woken up with some weird ideas?

Ronald came into the kitchen behind her and splashed cold water onto his face. 'You know,' he said. 'I do think I heard a whistle, just before I woke up, but I was dreaming.'

'Yeah,' she said. 'Dreaming.'

'Where's Mark?'

'He got up to go to the toilet while you were asleep and he found his pad and pen in the bedroom and started drawing the garden.'

'In the dark?'

'No. It was light. He's an early riser. It was after I'd gone to sort him out I came back here and fell asleep.'

'So he's up there now?'

'Yes, the poor sod. I'd better get him some breakfast, been three hours now.'

Cally popped six eggs into the pan of water, soft-boiled them and made three cups of tea with the water. She then handed Ronald two eggs while she mashed up the remaining four, splitting the mush into two.

'Could you take this up to him?' she asked. 'Make sure he eats it. Once he starts drawing he doesn't notice a thing.'

'Okay,' said Ronald, adding a couple of slices of bread to the plate.

He walked up the stairs and found Mark in the back bedroom studying the view intently and muttering 'fug' softly.

'Hi, Mark, how's it going today?'

The first surprise was that Mark said 'fug' unprompted. The next was that he wasn't actually drawing, although three sketches lay on the bedspread. Even though he had only known the man the best part of a day, Ronald had never seen him *not* drawing and, by Cally's account, that was all he ever did do.

'What's up?' he asked.

'Fug,' said Mark again without looking at him, instead continuing to stare out into the field beyond the house. Ronald studied the view with him.

The wide expanse of the rape seed field, like a hallucinogenic Van Gogh painting, spread out before the two of them to a line of trees in the distance, as featureless as any desert. Glancing at the pictures scattered on the bed, Ronald noticed that all Mark had drawn, predictably, were the field, the trees and the windowsill.

Cally came into the room.

'Could you look after Mark?' Ronald said to her. 'Something's bothering him. Maybe he's ill.'

'You feeling off?' asked Cally, peering into Mark's face.

'Fug,' Mark said, staring past her into the field.

'Is he often like this?' asked Ronald.

'Never. You haven't—'

'I found him like this! Maybe he needs some fresh air. He's probably not been out of the house for days.'

'Could be. Okay, come on, Mark.'

The man acquiesced but Ronald couldn't help noticing that his gaze stayed fixed on the scene outside the window. It was rather unnerving, like a dog staring at a door as if it's privy to something its owner isn't.

After Mark and Cally had clattered down the stairs, Ronald sat at the window with Mark's sketches and surveyed the scene. The man had drawn the same picture three times, with hardly any difference between them. He was a true draughtsman. One picture did contain less detail than the others but Ronald presumed it had been drawn in the early light when fewer features could be made out. Maybe he had seen someone coming but, looking into the field, it would still be easy to spot anyone against that potent yellow. Besides, why should Mark react to people? He was in a world of his own – even if not of his own making, thought Ronald, remembering the scars on Mark's head. He lined the three A3 sketches up on the windowsill and flicked his eyes in turn from each to the scene in front of him.

It was a full two minutes before he saw the difference. It was small, but, knowing Mark's meticulous eye for detail, it had to be true. He remembered his dream and how it had ended and Cally . . .

He ran downstairs, through the back door and across the garden to the rickety fence that bordered the bottom of the garden, then over into the field. Rather than cut a swathe through the yellow sea, Ronald followed its perimeter to the right, then along a hedgerow up the slight rise to the line of trees at the top, two hundred yards away. All the time he kept his eyes on the tallest tree that had sat dead centre of Mark's drawings. The anomaly he had spotted had been to its left, and that was where he was heading. The day was already warm and soon he was sweating, but whether it was from exertion or apprehension, he didn't know; he just prayed that Mark had twitched and his pen had slipped.

Five minutes later and out of breath, Ronald found himself on the top side of the field, perhaps thirty yards from his goal, a swathe of bright yellow between him and the cottage. He stopped and held the stitch in his side. What the hell was he doing? Reducing the odds, that's what. He didn't expect to find anything but he was still there, his heart thumping, his body running with perspiration.

Ronald walked towards the tall trees then stopped, judging the distance from his memory of the sketch. Then, taking a deep breath, he turned and looked along a line directly back to the view from the cottage window. Oh Christ . . .

There in front of him the rape had been squashed flat in a long rectangular shape, the stalks charred and broken as if by some giant iron. Except this iron was a horse; an iron horse as American Indians called them in bad Westerns. A pattern of thin, deep parallel furrows advanced the length of the shape on either side: the kind of marks that heavy metal wheels would make on soft earth.

Ronald stepped slowly back, then turned and ran the way he had come, his mind full of terrifying possibilities every bit as vivid as those involving his white truck. The second of Mark's sketches had shown a thin wisp of smoke at the top end of the field, yet there was no house with a chimney to cause it. What had created it was now frighteningly clear and what he had heard as he woke up had been no imaginary train whistle.

Cally's story was true.

Ronald stumbled over the fence, tearing his trousers but ignoring the pain in his chest and ribs. He ran through the house and out through the front door shouting Cally's name.

He came to halt on the unkempt gravel path that ran along the front of the cottage and looked around frantically. In front of him were bushes behind which lay an untidy tangle of garden, beyond which were yet more bushes then the road. To the right were trees that effectively hid the rape field that ran along two sides of the cottage, and to the left was the driveway, again screened from view by a riot of bushes and trees. It served to hide the place from passers-by but it was also concealing Cally and Mark.

'Cally! Cally! Where are you?' he shouted, panic making his voice rise. Where was the damned girl?

Ronald ran to the driveway. The Ford Cortina was parked out of sight at the side of the cottage, his van invisible in the ditch behind shrubs. And still no Cally.

'Cally! Where are you?'

Suddenly a hand clamped him on the shoulder. He spun round. It was Cally.

'What's all the fucking noise, Ron? It's early!'

'Your train! It's real!'

''Course it is. But how . . .?'

'Mark's drawings. He saw it. Drew it. This morning.'

Cally's face drained of colour. 'Let's go inside.'

'Where is he?'

'He's sat drawing a tree.'

Once inside, Cally made them coffee and he told her what he had discovered.

'This is bad,' she said.

'You're telling me? I wanted to believe you, but it was so bizarre . . . but now I know.'

'It's the pills,' she said, pulling out a Tesco bag from under a broken floorboard and spilling the contents on the table, plastic rattling hollowly. 'I've been on so much shit over the last few weeks to keep me awake they don't work any more. And the stuff to knock me out's the same. What I take could kill you, but it doesn't affect me any more. This morning I fell asleep, not thinking about anything special, not hating anyone, and the train comes. Gantry's pushed me too far, I've lost control of it.'

'Couldn't you get stronger stuff?'

'I suppose so, but how? Gantry's the only one who would know what to do and I'd rather cut my throat than go back to him.'

'And it's not as if you can buy the stuff over the counter in a chemist. You'd need a prescription – and that needs a doctor. What about that doctor who put you in Handland in the first place?'

'Rogers? Why should he help? He couldn't wait to get shot of me.'

'But he tried to help at first, didn't he? Maybe he feels guilty.'

'That's why he visited me so many times to find out how I was doing?'

'I know, I know . . . maybe we could threaten him.'

'Into writing a prescription?' she said.

'Hmm, maybe not. But we've got to do—'

'He has his own drugs! He works from a clinic that looks like a house. He might even live there. He's got nurses, consulting rooms and a pharmacy all his own.'

'Where is it?'

'Falston, just outside town on the main road.'

'That's a fair way away.'

'Getting a car's simple enough.'

'Yes,' said Ronald shaking his head.

'So what do we do?'

'Need to get him on his own, so he can't get help, then persuade him to give you the right stuff.'

'What if he still refuses?'

'You take a nap in his surgery!'

There was a pause, then they both smiled.

'So, what next?' said Cally.

'We get Mark, pack up and you, er, find a car.'

Whatever Ronald's fears about his truck, the girl's problems with her train were far more pressing. If she closed her eyes too long anything could happen.

For her part, Cally felt a certain relief that Ronald now believed her, even though the means of his conversion scared her. Ronald had every excuse now to leave her to her fate but instead his first reaction had been to try and help her find an answer. Just like a teacher. Or a father, she thought, looking at him over her coffee cup. For all his paranoia about his truck, her future was his main concern now. She thought she liked this Ron.

They collected together what few belongings they had and, pooling their cash, found they had two hundred and eight pounds. It was decided that Cally, armed with a coathanger from one of the bedrooms, would 'find' a car and bring it back to the farm. Then the three of them would head for Dr Rogers's clinic in Falston.

'We'd best let Mark use the toilet before we go,' said Ronald as they walked out into the front garden. 'Then I'll take him up to the top of the drive and you can pick us up there. Just show me where you left him.'

They walked through the bushes into the jungle that had been a lawn to a broken bench that sat facing the cottage.

'I left him here,' said Cally. 'Never known him to wander before.'

'You go down towards the front, I'll try back near the car. He might have gone round the back.'

They split up but after five minutes of searching they couldn't find him. Ronald even ran through the place checking each room in case they had missed him, but the cottage was empty. The back garden also showed no sign of Mark or his drawing gear. Running round the side of the house, he found Cally checking the Cortina.

'Already done that! What about my van?'

'I shut it up.'

'So where the hell is he? You say he doesn't—'

'All Mark does is sleep, eat and draw. He doesn't do anything else unless you tell him. He should be on that bench drawing.'

'Well, he isn't.'

'Don't get ratty with me, Ron. It's not my—'

'Fault? Yes, it is! You brought him with you, he's your responsibility!'

'I got him out of Gantry's hands. He'd—'

'Doesn't matter, Cally. He's your responsibility now. Now let's just find him.'

'You bastard!' She was upset. 'It's not my fault.'

But Ronald was already off, trotting up the driveway to the road. Cally debated whether to follow or let the interfering sod sort it out, but her instinctive resentment quickly gave way to common sense; it was Mark was that mattered, not her wounded pride.

They reached the road together, Cally's youth more than a match for Ronald's flab. Looking up and down the road they were amazed and relieved to see Mark fifty yards away standing on the road, drawing a telegraph pole.

Just as Cally was about to shout, a car came into sight. A police car. She froze, but Ronald grabbed her hand and pulled her back behind a tree.

The police car passed Mark, slowed, then reversed back. It stopped and one of the two policemen in it got out and crossed the road to Mark and talked to him. Getting no response the cop walked back to the car and had words with his colleague. Soon they were both trying to talk to Mark but with an obvious lack of success. Cally wanted to run out and explain but Ronald held her back.

'What odds Gantry's reported you and Mark to the police?' he said.

'Not likely,' she hissed. 'If I told them about him . . .'

One of the policemen took Mark's pad, walked him to their Rover and put him in the back seat, as compliant as ever. Ronald and Cally ducked down as the car drove off.

'Can you believe our fucking luck?' said Cally. 'Of all the bloody cars that could—'

'Too late now. At least they'll look after him. We'd better get that car. You sure the Cortina—'

'Back wheel wobbles. Best thing is—'

'Oh, shit!' exclaimed Ronald. 'They're coming back!'

True enough, Cally saw the same Rover traffic car driving towards them. Ronald hustled Cally into the bushes on the right of the drive and they huddled down as the car turned down the track. Cally's bright blue floral dress and white socks and pumps – chosen to combat the attention her tomboy appearance tended to attract when she went 'shopping' in the local village – now served as an advert for her presence. Ronald shielded her, his green shirt blending successfully with the undergrowth. They could both see Mark in the back of the car – drawing, naturally – and knew it would be their last sight of him.

After the police car had turned into the driveway, Ronald and Cally cut across the field to the side of the cottage, keeping to the hedgerow that bounded the road in order not to be seen. Ronald then waited by the road, hidden behind bushes, while Cally hared off across the remainder of the field in search of a getaway vehicle.

Thirty minutes later – during which Ronald was alarmed to see another police car arrive rather than the car containing Mark leave – Cally pulled up in front of him in a red C-registered Renault 5. She had found the car in a lay-by used by anglers at a nearby lake; chances were the Renault wouldn't be missed for hours. Ronald climbed in and they drove off.

'What does it mean?' asked Cally when she heard about the increased police interest. 'For us?'

'Well, look at it from their point of view,' said Ronald, impressed by Cally's driving, especially considering she was a year away from the minimum legal age for taking her driving test.

'They've got an autistic man found wandering near a deserted country cottage that has obviously been lived in, so he wasn't alone. Is there any way they can identify Mark? Did he have a wallet?'

'No,' said Cally. 'But his clothes, they'll have labels, for the laundry. They should tell he's from Handland.'

'Pity. Once they contact the hospital, Gantry will have to say you took him, otherwise he's letting patients wander the country-side willy-nilly. So, they'll then know about you. Next they find my VW. Ha! They'll trace it back to me, and after they've had a good look inside . . . Gantry will try to cover his tracks; he'll say you're a misguided girl with delusions: why else would you skip with an autistic adult? But you're missing and who else was in the vicinity? Just a loony, who collects pictures of bodies and crashes. And he's disappeared as well . . . Now what do *you* think they'll think?'

'But you're not dangerous. Just a bit, well, warped.'

Ronald held his nose and imitated a man talking into a microphone: ' "All Units be on the lookout for deluded young girl and warped ghoulish adult." Sound hopeful?'

Cally giggled. 'Putting it like that . . .'

They fell quiet, the humour soon evaporating.

'Look, *you* haven't done anything Ron. At least I don't think you have. Why don't we just find a police station and give up?'

'They'll send you back to Gantry. And if you start telling them why you don't want to go back to Gantry, they'll send you back even quicker. Besides, there's still your train. You need the right drugs but you don't need Gantry giving them to you. Dr Rogers is our best bet.'

Cally had taken the remaining drugs from the farmhouse but all she had was Methylphenidate in solution, a couple of needles, and a handful of Dexamphetamine pills. By her reckoning perhaps two days' worth of peace of mind, and then . . . There was also a bottle of Nitrazepam, but what use were knockout drops?

'But what if they don't work,' she said. 'Or we can't even get the drugs, or—'

'Or nothing. It's you that counts, Cally, and until we can't do anything, we do what we can. Okay?'

With that they drove on in silence, Ronald surprised at what he had said. For the last few months he had thought of only one thing: the truck. But now he was worried for someone else. He didn't know how that made him feel – but it wasn't a bad feeling.

TWENTY

Children's laughter. Summer sun. Birds chittering, bees buzzing. Ronald could almost believe he was human again.

The old Falston Station goods yard had been changed into a playground. A wide, flat basin, it contained traditional swings and roundabouts, a slide, see-saws and a spotless paddling pool shaped like a cat's head. It was obviously a popular venue, teeming with rowdy children and relaxed parents. Good weather, safe playthings, no cars and nowhere nearby for perverts to lurk and leer.

Ronald parked the Renault 5 between two Fiestas, both boasting they had a 'Baby on Board', although plainly the children had managed to escape to the playground. Grabbing the Ordnance Survey map he had bought in town, Ronald and Cally followed their example.

Halfway across they both paused and drank in the scene. Right then everything seemed good and right. *Proper*. There was a point to existence; children were the be-all of life; innocence had a place in the world. Then, remembering where they were going, and why, the afternoon sun dimmed and the laughter became too raucous. They hurried on.

The old railway footpath was surprisingly overgrown, as if the jolly colours of the swings and roundabouts had stopped people venturing any further. Ronald checked the map just to be sure; there was no sign on the ground, just a wooden stile. The map showed a pathway running along the smooth curves and level contours of an old railway line, but it didn't shout about it. They clambered over and set off.

The path was made up of black cinders and short grass and was barely a couple of yards wide in places. The undergrowth had been left untamed and gave the journey a hint of the unknown. It was almost natural, only the flatness of the path and, here and there, the deep embankments cut into the hillside betraying its origins.

They passed one cheery middle-aged couple after half a mile, and a group of sniggering teenagers on mountain bikes a little after that, but for the rest of the journey they were on their own. It was to be a two-mile walk and, under other circumstances, would have been very enjoyable. A father and his daughter out for a pleasant afternoon stroll, talking about this and that, enjoying each other's company. But while Ronald was – had been – a father and Cally a daughter, there was no familial intimacy between them, no conversation.

After half an hour Ronald reckoned they were nearly there, despite the last mile having been free of any view. On one side, young trees effectively screened them from the hillside above while to their right the cutting rose some twenty feet high. Perhaps this was the reason for the path's seeming unpopularity: they might as well have been in a tunnel.

They had paused for a rest, Ronald in particular feeling the late afternoon heat. He took off his jacket and wiped his forehead on his sleeve.

'What was your daughter like?' asked Cally suddenly.

'Julie? She . . . why?'

'I don't know. No, I do. I like this. The country. Walking with someone I . . . trust. Someone I'm safe with.'

'How do you mean?'

'You're not after me for anything. We're just friends.'

'True. Well, Julie was bright, attractive, friendly—'

'Perfect, right?'

'No. She—'

'She was your daughter.'

'Yes,' he smiled. 'Exactly.'

They walked on.

A minute later the path opened out and, on their right, the steep slope changed quickly to a gentle rise, still high enough to obscure the countryside below but far less claustrophobic. The sun was low behind them so it would light up the view below when they finally got to see it. Ronald was just about to break away from the path and mount the rise when he caught sight of something hidden further along the track. He put his finger to his mouth and hushed Cally, his heart already thumping. He could see a wheel.

Slowing, he edged his way along the path until he had a clear view. It was a car. A Land Rover Discovery. 'M' reg. Purple. Empty.

Ronald looked around. The occupants were nowhere to be seen. He looked back, up and down the track. No tyre marks. He walked to the back of the car. It was facing onto the track and apparently had been driven up a very vague path from the field below. He stepped up the embankment to the side of the vehicle and came abruptly to a stop. He could see the clinic, just as Cally had described it; a modest Victorian pile with a walled kitchen garden and large lawn backing onto a wide grassy field that rose gently towards the railway cutting, sheep dotting the landscape like cotton wool balls on a deep green blanket. It was about half a mile down in the valley, directly down from the track three hundred yards further along from where they stood by the Discovery. Ronald's eyes followed the path that led from the rear of the car downhill until it reached the road a hundred yards to the right of Rogers's clinic.

He edged back to Cally, his look telling the full story. 'Looks like Dr Rogers's place,' he said.

'Any sign of police?'

'No.' He forced his mind away from the clinic. He tapped the rear of the Discovery. 'I wonder where the driver of this is. And why's it parked here?'

'Gone rambling? Off having a shag?' she said. Then she frowned. 'You know, I think I've seen this before.'

He peered inside the Land Rover. Neat, spartan. He walked round to the bonnet and felt the metal hood. Warm. But was it the sun or the engine?

Cally peered into the back. 'Ron, look at this.'

Ronald walked round until he could see what she was looking at. It was a briefcase, large and expensive.

'Bit of a risk, that,' she said professionally.

'Out here?' wondered Ronald.

'Thieves don't go for walks? Opportunity's what counts, Ron: we could take that now, the owner'd never know.'

'But we're not going to, are we?'

'We need cash. There might be—'

'No. We're here for a reason. Let's not get side-tracked.'

'Quite right,' said a man's voice behind them.

They both whirled round in shock.

Dr Gantry was emerging from a clump of bushes, his suit and bow-tie familiar to Cally. But now he also carried a revolver.

'Once you set your mind to something, Cally . . .' Gantry said as he eased himself onto the track and leaned against the bonnet of the Discovery. 'You stick to it, don't you? A veritable terrier. Or, given the carnage that seems to follow you around, perhaps that should be a pit bull.

'And you, I presume, are Mr Blakestone. The police are very interested in you; think you may be trying to harm our young Miss Summerskill here.'

'And you're Gantry,' said Ronald.

'Dr Gantry, if you don't mind. I presume Cally has been filling your head with nonsense.'

'Forget it, Gantry. I've seen Cally's train. She's no reason to lie about anything you've done, you bastard.'

Gantry was plainly surprised about Ronald's knowledge of the train. He turned his gaze on Cally.

'So. We've been dreaming again, have we?'

Cally didn't answer, instead asking: 'How's Mark?'

'Oh, he's fine. One of my people is collecting him this evening. Soon have him back, safe and sound . . . as long as his little friend comes back and is co-operative.'

'Fuck off,' said Cally.

'The scars on his head,' said Ronald. 'What are they?'

'We *have* been having a nosy, haven't we, Ronald? You don't mind if I call you Ronald, do you?'

'It's Ron.'

'Well, Ronald, Mark is quite a talented chap, as you no doubt have seen. Quite an artist. We've had him for years – his mother pays the extortionate bills so he stays.'

Ronald stepped towards the doctor but he levelled the gun at Ronald's head.

'As I was saying . . . As an experiment I once took him to a house owned by another inmate who'd had a breakdown,

claiming his home was haunted. I left Mark in the room where
the spectre was supposed to appear for a couple of hours, then
looked at his drawings. A superb depiction of the room, down
to the individual Jacobean panels and the paintings on the wall
and, there in the corner, a man in Puritan dress sat staring
directly at Mark, a look of utter hatred on his face. Exactly the
face described by my other patient. Mark sees what the rest of
mankind misses. The night your train wrecked my sleep
laboratory, Cally, I had Mark sitting in the corner, a reminder
to you to co-operate. But also, to keep him busy, he had a pad.
He turned out eight drawings of the lab inside two hours. The
last three detailed the train, even better than I remembered it.'

'All very interesting,' said Ronald. 'But—'

'About a year ago I decided to take a look inside his head. See
if there were any physical signs of his strange ability. Didn't find
anything. I was a bit clumsy, I'll admit it now, and, well, it
affected his speech. Used to talk quite well on the few occasions
he wanted to; not now. And he seems a bit slower. Still, he
wasn't that much of a conversationalist before so it's no great
loss.'

All Cally's claims about Gantry had now been proven; the man
was a monster. 'But why?' asked Ronald, still unable to believe
what he was hearing. 'You're a doctor. Your job is to care and
cure, not—'

'Not what? Surely Cally has told you of my interests? Her
gift is remarkable. Unique. It is my *duty* to understand it. The
power of the mind is the only direction science can go. Outer
space is too cold and expensive; underwater the same. The
Earth's resources are finite; the ecosystem unlikely to be saved
in time. All that is left is the inner being and the potential of
the mind to alter what supposedly cannot be altered. Movement beyond the laws of physics; vision in other spectra; life
after death; psychic insight.'

'So what are you going to do now?' said Cally, not listening,
concentrating instead on edging imperceptibly towards the rear of
the Land Rover.

'Stop right there, young lady,' said Gantry, pointing the gun at
her stomach. 'What am I going to do? Well, I have two choices.
Either you come back with me, co-operate fully with all my

wishes while I attempt to understand what you have to offer – and Ronald "disappears". Or . . .'

'Or you kill us both,' said Ronald.

Cally let out a gasp of shock.

'Indeed, Ronald, indeed. It's good to see you have a grasp of your predicament. And don't be so shocked, Cally. After all, what alternative have you left me? You, Ronald, from the cursory discussion I have had with the police about you on the phone, are more than likely a paranoid schizophrenic, obsessed with the death of your daughter. Easy enough to paint a more, how shall I say, dangerous personality. The police are always keen to have an explanation for unusual behaviour; something for their reports, you see. To be able to class you as a lunatic who had kidnapped Cally for purposes only those of a salacious disposition could contemplate would be very simple. And that you would then murder your young captive would not really surprise anyone, least of all myself, a psychiatrist. They would find Cally's body in a shallow grave, yours with a bullet in the head somewhere nearby. It would be one of those cases where the police state cryptically that "they are not actively looking for other suspects". Sexual interference would probably add weight to their understanding of the situation; *post mortem* sexual interference even better.'

Ronald gasped.

'What does he mean?' said Cally.

'He means that *after* he had killed us both he would . . . have sex with you to make it look like I did it,' Ronald said.

Cally cowered back, visibly shaken by Ronald's statement.

Gantry laughed. 'Crudely put but succinct, although I would have to be careful; forensic evidence, you know.'

'You'd kill a sixteen-year-old girl?' said Ronald, still unable to come to terms fully with the man's evil.

'As surely as I have this gun in my hand.'

Ronald almost threw up. He knew that Gantry was ruthless, but a killer? Then he remembered Cally's story about Nurse Bigg: a sacrifice on the altar of Gantry's ambition. Even so, Ronald was still desperate to reason with the psychiatrist.

'But you're a doctor. You took an oath.'

'Come on, Ronald. Words. They mean nothing against the

power of knowledge.' Gantry swapped the gun to his other hand and wiped a bead of sweat from his forehead, his eyes flicking from Cally to Ronald and back again, watching for the first movement. He continued his lecture:

'A surgeon is licensed to commit grievous bodily harm, a psychiatrist to brainwash his patients with and without the aid of drugs. We hold your very existence in our hands, even your soul. You're *meat*. And we are just butchers with suits and certificates. How many patients do you think die in this country because of incompetent care from so-called trained professionals? I have encouraged patients to *kill* themselves just to prove I can do it. Hanging, overdoses, open windows . . . One I even persuaded to drink himself to death. With water. Hydromania. I wrote a paper on it! No, Ronald, Cally means nothing to me other than an opportunity, and should that opportunity be taken away by your obstinacy then I *swear* I shall obliterate the evidence and carry on with someone else. How's that for an oath, Ronald?' Gantry sneered.

Cally fell to her knees and started to cry. Ronald stepped towards her but Gantry jerked the gun back to point it directly at him.

'You forget, Ronald, I have had care of Cally for four months. She's an accomplished actress. Girl, stop it!'

She did. Instead she spat at Gantry but missed. 'You won't kill me, though, will you?' said Cally. 'I'm too valuable. You know what I can do.'

'On the contrary, girl. You're no longer in control of your train. It took me a full eight minutes to rouse you the last time. The next time may well prove fatal for all concerned. I'd probably be doing myself a favour getting rid of you.'

'No!' shouted Ronald. 'Let her live. I'd rather you—'

'Kill you? No problem.' Gantry cocked the hammer of the gun.

'No!' screamed Cally. 'If you kill Ron I'll never work for you. Let him go and . . . and I'll do anything you say. Anything.'

'A tempting offer, dear, but, on reflection, a tad late. Whatever happens, Mr Blakestone has to die. Simple logic. I'm sure, as a teacher, Ronald can see my predicament.'

'I taught geography, not maths.'

'Well, in that case, you should be interested in a little feature

just down the slope a way. A little dell, hidden from everywhere else. Lots of soft earth and bracken. Perfect for a grave.
Move!'

Ronald started to pee himself, the warmth running down his
leg as surely as the blood would flow soon unless he did
something. But what? What could he do? He could jump the
man, but if he failed to disarm him, they would be doomed all the
same. He could only play for time and pray an opportunity
presented itself. He started down the path, Cally immediately
behind him, Gantry bringing up the rear.

It was an old cart track, with two deep ruts. An ordinary car
would have scraped bottom once too often but the Discovery
would have had no problem. Ronald desperately tried to think of
some course of action but short of simply running, there was
nothing. Gantry would have no hesitation in shooting them. Once
it suited him, Gantry would switch the two of them off like two
bunsen burners in a laboratory.

'How did you know we'd come here?' asked Ronald.

'Tally the quantity of drugs stolen by the days absent times the
available sources. Cally's bright but also desperate. She knew
Rogers would have the drugs she needed; only a matter of time
before she came here. I came as soon as I found out about Mark.
All my conversations with the police have been on a mobile
phone. I have a private detective sitting out front. Dr Rogers
doesn't even know I'm here and, when we've done, he never
will.'

'You're one sick bastard,' said Ronald.

'From you, a compliment.' He laughed but, just as Cally had
described it, it wasn't convincing.

They had been walking for a couple of minutes when Cally
suddenly stopped, causing Gantry to bump into her.

'Don't shoot!' she shrieked as he stumbled back out of her
reach.

He made to hit her over the head with the revolver but thought
better of it. 'One more trick like that and—'

'It wasn't a trick. I need a pee.'

'So?' was Gantry's curt response.

'I've got to go now.'

'No.'

She turned to face him. She needed to convince him. 'I need to go *now*.' A thin trickle of pee ran down her right leg to stain her white sock.

'All right, but be quick,' said Gantry with a look of exaggerated disgust completely at odds with the reality of the situation.

Gratefully Cally jumped behind a bush and crouched down. Now she could try and save them.

'And no tricks,' said Gantry. 'I've got the gun aimed at Ronald's head.'

'If you think you can make it, Cally, run!' shouted Ronald, staring Gantry in the eye. Ronald had never felt such hatred for a human being in his life. And he had never felt more protective towards another: whatever else happened, Cally had to survive.

'Bad idea, Ronald,' said Gantry.

Cally shouted: 'I'm not going anywhere, Dr Gantry. Just let me finish.' What she was doing was a long shot but it looked to be their only chance.

'Five seconds,' warned Gantry.

'All right, I'm nearly done.' She winced with the pain.

'Four, three, two—'

'Okay,' she said, stumbling from behind the bush and pulling her dress down.

'Right. Shall we continue?' said Gantry.

Cally slowly passed Gantry and walked up to Ronald, bumping into him.

'Careful,' said Ronald.

'Get on with it,' said Gantry.

Cally nodded but tripped again.

'Sssorry,' she slurred.

'What's up with you, girl?' said Gantry. 'And why's your sleeve rolled – blood! What have you – you little bitch!'

He grabbed her by the hair and spun her round. Already her eyes had ceased to focus and as her knees buckled she fell to the floor, leaving Gantry's hand grasping at air.

To Cally all was now a slow-motion dream: her troubles had suddenly evaporated, her mind trying instead to concentrate on a point of darkest emotion and channel it at one specific single target – Gantry.

'Drugs!' Gantry shrieked. 'Where did—?'

'They're in the car!' said Ronald, as perturbed as Gantry. 'I made her put them in—'

'In glove b-box,' said Cally vaguely. 'Took out bottle before Ron saw . . . needle . . . knickers,' said Cally, her neck muscles giving way, her head flopping onto her chest.

Gantry pushed them both onto the ground, then burst through the bush to where Cally had taken her pee. He returned almost immediately with an empty medicine bottle.

'You little bitch! You know what you've done, *you know what you've done*!' he wailed.

Ronald, now cradling Cally's head in his arms, was stunned at the sacrifice Cally had made, but as aware as Gantry of the consequences – and that Gantry had only one solution to the horror about to descend upon the three of them. But even as Ronald tried to think of some way of getting hold of the revolver, Gantry was shrieking his terror and outrage at the girl and levelling the barrel at her lolling head. Another second and a bullet would scatter her brains all over Ronald's shirt.

'No!' yelled Ronald as he hurled Cally to his left. Luckily Gantry let the revolver follow her collapsing form, giving Ronald a vital moment in which to launch himself at the doctor. But the shot rang out before Ronald made contact and he was horrified to see Gantry squeezing the trigger a second time as he threw himself headfirst against the shrink's chest.

There was a loud gasp followed by a second loud report and the two of them were on the floor, Gantry thrashing like an upturned beetle, desperate to get out from under Ronald's superior weight. He kneed Ronald in the groin and Ronald had to roll sideways, but he managed to snag the arm holding the gun. As the gun hit the ground and fired a *third* time Ronald balled up his right fist and slammed it into the side of Gantry's face.

Ronald caught a glimpse of the man's hand spasming open and the gun hanging loose. It would be his last chance. He dived onto Gantry's outstretched hand and buried his teeth into the doctor's wrist, biting deep and hard. Gantry squealed, his feet kicking underneath Ronald but having little effect. Ronald quickly tasted blood which only served to increase his efforts. He felt Gantry pulling at his hair but he ignored the pain. The cunt under him had shot at Cally; he was not going to get the chance to do it again.

Ronald reached up blindly with his hand and wrapped his fingers around the barrel of the gun and tried to wrench it free. It fired again, the barrel hot, the flash singeing the back of his hand. He stopped biting and, with a roar, sat upright. Then he brought both fists down together on Gantry's face – once, twice. The third time Gantry raised both his hands to protect himself and the gun fell to the grass.

Ronald immediately rolled off him, accidentally kicking the gun into a nearby bush. Putting himself between Gantry and the bush, he rolled over twice more until he came to rest next to Cally. For his part Gantry was lost, still batting away at some phantom figure above him. Then he stilled, realizing Ronald had won.

Gantry looked over at Ronald, blood smearing his face from his pulped nose. He tried wiping his face with his bloodied wrist but succeeded only in giving himself a clown smile in scarlet.

Ronald grabbed at Cally and shook her. He glanced quickly down at her.

Blood.

He began shouting incoherently. Gantry let out a yell of terror, then started to crab away from the scene. Ronald ignored him as soon as he knew Gantry wasn't going for the revolver. Instead he turned Cally over and examined her. She was unconscious and, to his horror, her face was covered in blood and her front carried a bib of deepest red. Frantically he felt over her dress but couldn't find a hole hidden amidst the seeming torrent of blood. Then he saw she had been shot in the left side of the head, blood pouring from the long wound. A warm pulsing on his hand told him the bottom of her right ear had also been shot off.

Ronald went blind with panic. The girl could be dying or dead. No, not dead. When you die, the blood stops flowing. No heartbeat: no pump. So she still lived, but the drugs? How much had she taken? How far down would she go? Far enough to keep the train at bay? No, that wasn't the point. She *wanted* it to come. To come for Gantry.

Ronald sat up and cradled Cally, tears blurring his vision, horror misting his thoughts. He saw Gantry on his hands and knees crawling back up the path towards the Land Rover, one hand clutching at his sides. A rib? It was a start.

The Land Rover! It could get them back into town, get Cally to hospital.

Gently he laid Cally down, feeling for a pulse, but in his panic not finding one, though the seeping from the side of her head indicated she was still alive. Ronald set off along the path in pursuit of Gantry who, hearing his approach, managed to stand up and stagger onwards.

It was an agonizingly slow journey for both of them but, as a winded Ronald finally reached the other man and slammed him against the Discovery's rear door, they heard the whistle.

'Oh, God,' they both chorused.

The whistle sounded again. Far off and to their right, but not far enough.

'Where's it coming from?' babbled Gantry.

'Don't know,' shouted Ronald. 'But I know where it's going!'

Before Gantry could react, Ronald punched him under the jaw and the man flumped onto the bumper of the Land Rover, cross-eyed. Ronald then hooked his arm under Gantry's armpit, hauled him to his feet, dragged him along the side of the Land Rover and pushed him out onto the old railway track. Gantry tried to get his footing on the shallow embankment but tripped and landed face first on the cinders.

The whistle sounded again. Nearer this time. How far? Ronald couldn't tell. Never mind the train. He had to get away and save Cally.

He staggered back to the girl and, checking that she was still bleeding, he hauled her over his shoulders and carried her to the Land Rover. He found the passenger door locked, so he carried her round to the driver's door. It wasn't locked, but there were no keys inside.

Ronald unloaded Cally onto the driver's seat, then hefted her over the gear lever into the passenger seat.

As he jumped down the embankment to the still prostrate form of Gantry, he heard the train again, terrifyingly near. He rolled Gantry over and felt in his pockets for his keys. The man's face was bloody and covered in cinders, his lips bleeding, his teeth coated in black grime. Ronald found the keys, dropped Gantry and ran back to the Discovery.

Firing the vehicle up he selected reverse but nothing happened. He stepped on the accelerator but still the vehicle wouldn't budge. He jumped out and immediately saw the problem. The Discovery had driven over a small tree which had snapped back up once the rear wheels were over it and tangled itself in the bumper. Without cutting the tree loose the vehicle wouldn't go backwards.

Getting back in, Ronald heard another whistle and now the hefty chugging of a train getting up steam.

He slammed the car into first and drove straight down the embankment. Gantry was standing in the middle of the path, staring up the track towards the sound of the train. Ronald tried to avoid him as he turned left but too late: he hit the man and sent Gantry cartwheeling five yards down the track to land on his back, his right arm pinned underneath him, clearly broken.

Ronald straightened the Land Rover out and accelerated away, his eyes fixed on the view in his rear mirror. The sound of the train was deafening, even over the sound of the Discovery's protesting engine – Ronald had missed a gear – but it wasn't visible. He saw Gantry struggling to sit upright, his arm failing him. Both arms broken?

Suddenly the windscreen shattered as a low tree branch banged into the cabin and then was gone. Ronald swerved too late, over-compensated and slammed into a tree on the opposite side of the track.

He reversed immediately, glad that this time he could make progress, then wheeled the Land Rover back onto the track and accelerated away. Now the bellowing of the engine and the deathly shriek of its whistle were joined by a vision from hell. Above and to both sides of the track behind them the sky turned black, the trees silver, the track itself became a matte mirror of the sky and there, between, came the train, its lone red light like a torch beam guiding the damned down into the Pit. He saw Gantry's small figure jump erect, silhouetted black against black, his arms windmilling like a spastic marionette, trying to fend off the monster but too late. The train was on him and in an instant Gantry had disappeared as the billowing smoke blasted its way through the undergrowth, levelling a path fully twice as wide again as the train itself. But still the whistle screamed, the engine boomed, the steam writhed and consumed all in its path. Still it came. Gantry wasn't enough.

Ronald stepped on the pedal and screamed at the car to move. In the mirror all he could see was steam and blackness and that one red light, the red of blood.

To the side of the Land Rover, night came rushing by to envelop them like a shroud tossed on a corpse. Only ahead lay hope: like hope at the end of a tunnel of despair, a small half-circle of sunlight and green, ever diminishing, hovered above the track. Ronald pushed the pedal to the floor and yelled with relief when he saw the semicircle remain constant in size. At least the train wasn't gaining on him.

He looked in the mirror. All he saw was red, a harsh probing glow that stabbed at his eyes like a blowtorch. He hunkered down over the wheel as if the nightmarish pursuer was about to pass overhead, but instead he felt hot breath on his back and inhaled the smell of death and the taste of thick tarry soot. The inside of the Land Rover became smoky, the bitter sting slicing at his eyes, making them water and his concentration waver.

On and on he drove, aware of trees and bushes slashing at the side of the car, the gritty slur of gravel and ashes spraying up and under the car, and the hell's breath of the train huffing and puffing at his tailgate.

And then, suddenly, just as it looked as if the pinprick of light ahead might be snuffed out forever, the Land Rover exited the darkness and hurtled full pelt into the light, crashing through the stile at the end of the path and on through the crowded children's playground, demolishing a swing and sideswiping a roundabout, children and parents screaming in terror and scattering any way they could.

Ronald slung the car to the left and, just missing four children playing on a see-saw, felt the car become briefly airborne as it hit the side of a paddling pool before landing with a crashing splash that washed all the darkness out of the car.

As the car slewed to a halt, Ronald looked back through the newly-clean rear window. The track lay some hundred yards the other side of a screaming shambles of children and adults. There was no darkness, no smoke, no piercing whistles, just bright daylight and terrified children. Ronald looked down at Cally, his breath laboured, his hands shaking uncontrollably. The blood was wet and plentiful but it wasn't moving.

No!!!

The car had stopped but not stalled and even as brave souls stalked towards him, intent on retribution for his insane driving, Ronald drove the car through the rest of the paddling pool, careful to avoid what children remained in it staring dumbly up at him. Then he bumped over the side and on through the park to the exit, a horde of gesticulating fathers now cantering after him, some waving improvised weapons, others just their fists. From what he could see he hadn't actually hit any children, but how could he know? Right now his priority was Cally, but he didn't know where the local hospital was – and she needed a doctor now.

A doctor! He might not know where the hospital was, but he sure as hell knew where Dr Rogers lived.

TWENTY-ONE

Ronald braked too late and the Discovery clipped a large green Rover 800 parked beside Dr Rogers's clinic, but he didn't care. He jumped out, dragged Cally out of the car, then carried her in his arms over the gravel drive round to the front of the house where he heaved open the front door and staggered into a large hallway. A middle-aged nurse in a white uniform came out of a side room.

'Get Rogers!' shouted Ronald.

The nurse was about to protest.

'Get bloody Rogers out here now!'

A man came out of an office at the rear of the house.

'Are you Rogers?'

'Yes,' said the small man warily.

'This is Cally Summerskill. Remember? Gantry's shot her and you're going to fix her.'

Dr Rogers nodded at the nurse. 'Call the police, Agatha.'

'And Gantry's dead. Cally's *train* got him. So forget the bloody police and help her.'

It took a moment for Ronald's words to sink in, then the man sprang into life. 'Agatha, show Mr Levine out. I'll look at this girl in Consulting One. When you're finished, I'll need your help. This way, the room on the left.'

Ronald stumbled after the doctor into a small surgery, his legs about to give out, and laid the unconscious girl on an examining couch.

'What injuries has she got?' said Dr Rogers checking her head, blood already staining his jacket sleeves.

'Shot in the head, don't know how bad, lot of blood lost. Drug overdose. Nitra-something.'

'Why didn't you take her to hospital?'

'*You* explain Gantry and her train.'

'See your point. Look, first priority is to save her. Go and get Agatha, I need her here now.'

Ronald found the nurse at the front door ushering an old man out. He managed to indicate that Dr Rogers needed her before he collapsed in the hall.

Ronald came to sitting in a chair next to Cally. Dr Rogers stood leaning against the door. The girl's head was bandaged and she was asleep under a thin blanket.

'You're okay,' said Dr Rogers. 'I checked you over. Just shock. As for Cally, she's lost a part of her right ear and I've sewn it up. She also has a bullet graze on the opposite side of her head; luckily it was only a scratch. Head wounds always produce a lot of blood but it isn't as much as you'd think. I've used various measures to counteract her drug overdose – good thing you knew what it was – and she's stabilized. The drugs slowed her metabolism which may actually have saved her life. Now, if you don't want me to call the police – and I'd advise you that Agatha is itching to dial – you'd better tell me the whole story.'

'No problem. And thanks. Could I have a drink?'

'Scotch, brandy?'

'Tea.'

Dr Rogers smiled. 'Very wise. I think I'll join you. It's a while since anything quite so exciting has happened.'

'I bet that was Cally's doing, too.'

Dr Rogers's smile vanished. 'It was, as a matter of fact . . . Your clothes?'

Ronald noticed his clothes for the first time. His shirt was covered in blood. 'I didn't bring a change.'

'I have some sweatshirts we printed up for charity upstairs. Have a wash and I'll fetch one.'

Five minutes later they were ensconced in Rogers's plush, panelled office – Ronald wearing a black Healthy Minds Start With Healthy Bodies shirt and very impressed by the large – presumably new – aquarium of coloured fish behind the doctor's desk: it was just as Cally had described. Sufficiently refreshed by their cups of tea, Ronald told Dr Rogers everything Cally had told him about her time at Handland under the tutelage of the late Dr Gantry, and their subsequent meeting with him on the abandoned railway barely half a mile away.

Dr Rogers was attentive and didn't interrupt, even when his eyes betrayed his incredulity. He was a small man, slim and compact, with a thick mane of yellowy hair. He was immaculately dressed in a dark three-piece suit and spoke English obviously designed to disguise a regional accent.

'Gantry told me he didn't give a damn about the Hippocratic oath, didn't give a shit about his patients, thought you were a weak-kneed amateur who ran at the first sign of trouble . . .'

'Mr Blakestone, I'm sorry for what I did to Cally. Truly. It was just that I had never . . . I've had patients commit suicide, threaten me, stab me . . .'

'Frankly, my dear, I don't give a damn. Just tell me Cally's train is gone for good.'

'Yes. I would think so.'

Ronald sat back, pleased with Dr Rogers's conclusions. Whatever black hole his life had fallen into after Julie's death, at least there was now light: he had helped Cally with her problems, a young girl who, now she had survived a murder attempt and her tormentor had met his deserved fate, had the whole of her life to look forward to. She might be able to make something of that precious gift that so many had tried to squander in her short existence. Whatever happened to Ronald now was unimportant when measured against what he wanted for the girl.

'And what of you, Ronald? What's your story?' said Dr Rogers, replenishing their tea cups.

'I wish I knew.'

'Why not try telling me?'

Ronald sat back and stared out of the window at the darkness. He had been unconscious for some hours and yet Dr Rogers hadn't called the police, so perhaps he could trust him. After all, whatever his failings as a man, he was a doctor. Whether Ronald's story revealed him as deluded or stark raving mad, Rogers would be qualified to deal with it.

'Where should I begin?' asked Ronald finally.

'The beginning's usually best.'

'Well, it was about a week after my daughter's funeral.'

'Ah.'

Ronald's newfound faith in Dr Rogers's abilities sank to fresh depths.

'Punishment?' said Ronald.

'Yes, punishment,' said Dr Rogers. He had dismissed his nurse an hour before, instructing her not to tell anyone about what had happened, and since then he had listened intently to Ronald's story.

'You say yourself that, apart from the death of this Annie Wilks, your truck never actually did anything material. It could have been a phantom. Your daughter's death made you realize how empty your life had become. Now, the obvious answer would be that you wanted to avenge your daughter, to find whoever you believed ran her off the road, hence your chasing up and down the motorway. But I believe you were also into self-flagellation: you wanted to punish yourself for having no goals in your life. Without your family, you see your life as a waste, with no achievements, no monuments, nothing of lasting value, and so your mind set itself a task that simultaneously gave you a goal you never had *and* punished you in your pursuit of it. Just look at your obvious suffering over the last few months: your lost job, spending all your savings, living rough, poor personal hygiene, weight loss, being shunned by society, your loss of sanity . . . it all adds up to punishment. The human mind is capable of almost anything, given the right circumstances. Just look at Cally . . .'

'Punishment?' Ronald repeated, mulling the thought over. He actually liked the idea. It had a twisted sense, a logical illogicality. It also had the added benefit of laying the truck to rest. It was over.

'It couldn't be as solid or real as Cally's train?'

'If it was, surely it would have done more? The very fact that it seemed to taunt you as you searched for it suggests that it was just a figment of your imagination.'

'But the photographs?'

'Precisely, Ronald! No one but you can see a white truck in the photographs.'

'What about Annie Wilks? She saw it. Named it.'

'You *thought* she saw it and named it.'

'But that's ridiculous. I found her, talked to her—'

'And she's dead.'

'Meaning either my truck is as real as Cally's train or . . . or I'm a what? Murderer?'

'Did Annie exist?'

Ronald stood up, his mind blazing with anger. 'Oh, I'm not having this. I could live with being screwed up over everything, but that I could kill someone . . .'

'You let Gantry die.'

'That was different. And you know it was different!'

'Sorry. It's just . . .'

Ronald stood up and went to the window, looking out into the garden. Dr Rogers's office was on the west side of the house and faced a patio and the drive that ringed the house. He rested his forehead on the cold glass and blinked away tears of frustration and rage. God, what was he going to do? Just then the front doorbell rang.

'Now who on earth could that be?' asked Dr Rogers, checking his watch.

He crossed to his door and opened it. Blue lights flashed across the landing ceiling.

'Oh, Agatha . . . It's the police, Ronald.'

Ronald heard the word but something caught his eye outside in the garden. He opened his eyes wide and stared down in disbelief. *Jesus*! He stepped back, his whole body jolted as if an electric shock.

'Not real?' he said. '*Not bloody real*?'

Ronald charged past the startled doctor and ran down the stairs into the long entrance hall. Ignoring the hammering on the front door, he ran to the back of the house.

Dr Rogers dashed over to the window to see what Ronald had reacted to so strongly.

It was a giant truck, blinding white under the glare of the security lights, its ugly cab pointing at the house, the huge white trailer covering the length of the lawn. Dr Rogers stared numbly at the intruder for several seconds before the insistent pounding from the front door nudged him back to the present. He cantered downstairs, walked to the front door and pulled it open to find two men in suits and three uniformed police officers.

'Dr Rogers? We have reason to believe you have a Mr Ronald

Blakestone and a Miss Cally Summerskill on the premises.'

Suddenly there was a shout of '*Out the back!*' from the kitchen. The policemen pushed past Dr Rogers and ran down the hall. Dr Rogers followed them.

Once in the garden everyone stopped. They heard a scream from somewhere in the house, but there was nothing to see – no truck, no Ronald and the immaculate lawn bore no evidence that a forty-ton truck had been parked on it barely a minute ago.

The senior detective sent two men into the house to investigate the scream. But Dr Rogers knew it had been Cally and that she, too, had seen Ronald's truck. Given that it couldn't have driven around the house, she had probably seen it disappear before her eyes – and Ronald along with it.

TWENTY-TWO

Cally's first sight on waking was of a poster of the Algarve but, confused as she was, she knew she wasn't there. She tried to sit up but her head throbbed furiously and she had to lower herself back down. She felt her head. There was a large pad on her right ear the size of a paperback book, which hurt like crazy, and a smaller pad on the opposite side held on by a bandage wrapped round her head. What the hell . . .?

Shot! That bastard Gantry had shot her after she took the . . . *The train*. It had come. She remembered. It had come for Gantry – and taken him. Good. Served the bastard right. So where was she? She looked around.

A doctor's surgery: desk, chair, filing cabinets and the examining table she was lying on, covered by a blanket. She was in her underwear, her face and top smelling of antiseptic soap. And her throat was raw; she might have been sick.

Cally rolled over and looked towards the window. All she could see was darkness and trees caught in the light from the building, wherever it was. Not a hospital, though, was it? This wasn't a room off a ward; this was a doctor's office. Rogers? Was she in Dr Rogers's house? It would make sense. So where was he, and where was Ronald, that brave idiot who had fought off Gantry? She owed him her life.

She edged her feet out from under the blanket and righted herself, her head aching. She had been shot. With a gun; bullets had whizzed past her head. Another inch and she could have been dead. Fucking hell . . . But, as they say, a miss is as good as a mile, and the number of deaths she had witnessed had dulled the emotional impact somewhat. But still . . . she felt the dressing. Wonder what it looked like. Wonder what *I* look like, she thought.

She took a wobbly step in search of a mirror. There wasn't one but the window would do for the moment. But, as she stared at her reflection in the glass, a movement caught her eye and she saw Ronald run past. She reached to tap at the glass, but then saw what he was running towards. A big white truck. Oh, fuck . . .

She saw Ronald run up to it and pause before the passenger door opened and he slowly climbed in. Then, as the door shut, the truck, instead of driving off, simply vanished into thin air. One second it was there, the next, nothing. Gone.

Cally screamed, ignoring the pain it caused in her head. Ronald's truck was real. But her screaming was cut short by several policemen bursting into the room, demanding to know what was wrong. She saw no reason not to tell them, not least when she saw that some of them were armed with revolvers.

'Ronald's truck. It just disappeared. He was in it!'

Dr Rogers came in then, picked the blanket off the couch and wrapped the semi-naked girl in it.

'Gentlemen, I think a little privacy would be in order?'

Mumbled apologies and shuffling accompanied the policemen as all but one left the room. The one who remained wore a grey suit and a friendly expression. He was probably fifty, his handsome face etched with worry lines.

'Hallo, you're Cally Summerskill, aren't you?' he said, his accent pure Liverpudlian.

'Yes,' she said, not sure who to trust.

'I'm Detective Chief Inspector William Palmer, but you can call me Bill.'

'The old Bill?' she said.

'Good one. Not heard that one before.'

'Not today no. Don't patronize me.'

'Sorry. Look, I need to talk to you. Are you up to it?'

Dr Rogers protested. 'As you can see, she's recently—'

'Let the girl answer for herself, doctor.'

'What about?' said Cally.

'Lots of things. Not least the whereabouts of Mr Blakestone.'

'In the truck,' Cally and Dr Rogers said together.

'And which truck is that?' said Palmer, walking to the window.

'The one that was out there,' said Dr Rogers, already seeing trouble.

'It disappeared just before you came in,' said Cally.

'Disappeared, eh? As in Paul Daniels's disappeared? Or as in land speed record acceleration disappeared?'

Neither answered.

'There was no truck out there for Mr Blakestone to disappear in. He's out there somewhere, probably running around the countryside. We'll find him soon enough, but until we do, I'd like to hear what you have to say.'

'I should remind you, Chief Inspector, that Miss Summerskill is my patient and—'

'I thought she was Dr Gantry's patient?' said Palmer, settling himself in the chair and gesturing for the other two to sit.

Cally settled herself in the chair opposite the chief inspector, Rogers choosing to remain standing by the couch, his discomfort plain to see. He hadn't changed. Cally only hoped he wouldn't bottle out again.

'Well?' said Palmer.

'I should also remind you that, as a juvenile, Miss—'

'She's an orphan, and Dr Gantry is unavailable. Besides, this isn't a formal interview; not yet, anyway.' The veiled threat was obvious to both of them, but it was difficult to tell who took it worst.

'Before we make it all official, I'd like to lay my cards on the table. My job is to solve crime; I don't judge the people I nick, I just find out who did it and bang them up. I have here a mess of a case and you are in the thick of it and I want some answers; a little light at the end of a very murky tunnel. It's in both your interests to cooperate because this is a murder inquiry and to me that's a pretty serious offence.'

'Murder?' said Dr Rogers, his mind racing.

'Who?' said Cally, certain that the policeman couldn't begin to grasp how Gantry had died.

'A woman called Annie Wilks.'

'Let me give you the facts,' Palmer went on after pausing deliberately. 'A Mark Cockett was found wandering outside Carnbury this morning. Subsequent enquiries revealed him to be a patient at Handland Hospital who had been abducted by a Cally Summerskill several days previously in a stolen car. Searching a nearby cottage revealed signs of habitation by this Mark, a girl and another male. A wrecked van in the grounds of the cottage was traced to a Mr Ronald Blakestone of Wilmslow, missing for several weeks from his home. The licence number of his van has been reported by various police forces up and down the country as being near the scenes of motorway crashes. Inside the van we found photographs of a dozen crashes as well as newspaper clippings and a map detailing more than thirty accidents on the M6 in the last couple of months.

'There were also reports logged of this Blakestone character pestering customers at service areas. He apparently had been looking for a woman, a Miss Annie Wilks. A photograph of the woman was found in the van. Miss Wilks's body was found four days ago in the Samson Retail Park, also near Carnbury. She had died violently. Tracing her movements we have information that leads us to believe that this Blakestone was stalking Miss Wilks for some time. It would appear that he found her. Debris found near her body appears to come from a Volkswagen van similar to his own.

'So far, so circumstantial. However, this afternoon Dr Gantry, the man in charge at Handland Hospital, went missing. Subsequently his Land Rover Discovery was reported careering around a children's playground a mile from here. Descriptions of the driver do not match those of Dr Gantry, but they do match those of Mr Blakestone, leading us to believe the car had been stolen. Routine enquiries concerning you, Miss Summerskill, led one of my officers to Dr Rogers's house here earlier this afternoon where he observed Dr Gantry's Land Rover, and the blood in it. I presume it was your blood but until forensics have reported . . . Additionally, there were reports this afternoon of gunshots on an abandoned railway just north of here. A vigilant motorcycle patrolman investigated and found a spot where a car had sped off in a hurry. Further investigation revealed bloodstains, a discarded container of drugs and syringes and a revolver, four shots fired – all within sight of this house.'

'All very interesting, Chief Insp—'

'How did Miss Summerskill receive her injuries?'

'As my patient—'

'I have a police surgeon coming.'

'Bullet wounds,' said Cally.

'Did Mr Blakestone shoot you?'

'No! Gantry did.'

'And where is he now?'

Dr Rogers and Cally exchanged glances which, unfortunately, Palmer saw.

'I don't know,' said Cally.

'Did Mr Blakestone kill him?'

'No!'

'So where is he, then?'

There was a long pause.

'Will Blakestone be coming back?' asked Palmer.

'Er, yes,' said Dr Rogers, anxious that they should remain in the house, not only so that he was there to advise Ronald but also because he had no desire to spend the night in the police station.

Again the Chief Inspector caught the look between the two but let it pass. 'Very well, we'll wait a while. Would either of you like a cup of tea?'

'Yes,' they both said, keen to delay proceedings.

'Good,' said Palmer. 'Go and make them, doctor. It's your house.'

As a reluctant Dr Rogers left the room, Cally sat back. Her head was hurting. She had been interviewed enough times by suspicious care staff and police to know that Palmer had told them what he knew so they would realize how seriously he was taking the investigation. Even if Ronald came back things looked bleak. And with there being no way of explaining Gantry's death, he might be better off where he was.

No! she told herself, angry at her defeatism. The man had helped her, she was going to help him. And she was not going to get him into more trouble by saying the wrong thing.

'Chief Inspector,' she said. 'Do you know *why* he was looking for Annie Wilks?'

'Not really.'

'Not really? What does that mean?'

'Well, the place she lived had one story, the service area staff say something else.'

'What?'

'I don't really see—'

'You want our help, tell me.'

'I'm not used to being blackmailed. He had a photograph, asked people if they could see a truck in it. No one could.'

'A truck no one could see? Like the one he left on?'

'Clever, but there was no truck.'

Just then a policeman came in and handed him a couple of sheets of paper. As the constable left, Dr Rogers came in with three cups of tea.

The inspector read the pages and pulled a face.

'News on Ronald?' asked Cally.

'No. It's about Annie Wilks, actually. Her record.'

'Ronald said she was a prozzie and took drugs.'

'That's here.'

'And?' said Dr Rogers. 'There's an "and" in there.'

Palmer let out a sigh. 'Annie Wilks's husband and daughter were killed four years ago by a truck. She named the driver but nothing was proven. When the case was dropped she started smashing up the owner's property and she was put on probation. She left the area and moved to Manchester.'

'Does it say who she accused?' asked Dr Rogers.

'Simmons,' said Cally before she could stop herself.

'Well, well, well,' said Palmer. 'It seems we do have something to talk about after all.'

'I'm saying nothing,' she said. 'Not until Ronald's back.'

Dr Rogers shook his head, a gesture which, unfortunately, Palmer took as a conspiratorial rather than condemnatory.

'I'm going to check on how things are going. I want you to stay in here. I'll leave a man on the door.'

'Aren't you worried, leaving us together?' said Cally.

'You should be more worried about being charged with conspiracy to pervert the course of justice; obstructing the police; aiding and abetting a known criminal; kidnapping; car theft; breaking and entering; accessory to aggravated car theft; perhaps accessory to murder; then there's illegal use of drugs . . .' Palmer continued the list as he walked out of the room and shut the door behind him.

'How are we going to sort this out?' said Cally.

'Telling the truth might help,' said Dr Rogers.

'Oh, I don't think it will, do you?'

Dr Rogers's grin looked as sickly as Cally felt.

TWENTY-THREE

When Ronald saw the truck through the window he decided there was only one course of action: confrontation. Insane or haunted, he was going to meet his nemesis face to face. He ran out of the room, barely registering the presence of the police, then dashed through a kitchen and out into the floodlit back garden – and he found the truck in all its ugliness.

Despite its sleek lines and brilliant white finish, there was something irrevocably dark and out of kilter about it. Like a samurai sword that, its metal folded a million times by a priest-blacksmith and engraved with the finest detail, remained a weapon designed to sever limbs at a stroke, for all its majesty. Ronald ran to within ten yards of the truck, then shuddered to a stop, his heart racing.

The nearside door opened and light spilled out making a square at his feet like a welcome mat. He could still run away, find somewhere to hide and tremble and pray. But Ronald had spent so long hunting this, this *thing*, that now he was within striking distance of an answer he remained unsure. Cowardice or commonsense, it didn't matter: he knew that if he stepped up into the cab he was doomed. But, fight the urge as he might, there was no stopping his foot rising to the step, no halting his legs propelling him into the cab.

It was only as he sat down and the door slammed that the light dimmed to a manageable level and he saw the driver. Ronald's shriek of horror was accompanied by a loosening of his bladder as he felt the truck move off, his heart beating a tattoo of terror. He tore his eyes away from the sight in the cab but he couldn't escape the smell of death and decay.

'Don't think of leaving,' said a rasping voice. 'Got to finish what you start. Like a good wank.'

Ronald turned to look at the driver, but when he saw the bony stumps of its fingers clawed around the wheel and the peeled skin hanging in tatters from its hands, and smelled the putrescence from the running sores that covered its naked arms, his voice was lost in a wave of nausea. His evident distress provoked cracked laughter that caught in the driver's throat like the gurgling of a patient after a laryngectomy. Ronald stopped retching and forced himself to look at the man's face, or what was left of it.

Badly burned and unhealed, it glistened black and green in the dull light of the cab, the nose eaten away, the lips pared back to reveal broken, blackened teeth and a tongue purpled and bulbous. The hair was sparse and yellow, both ears shrivelled like fried onions. But it was the eyes that stilled Ronald's heart. They were absolutely normal, clear and blue, almost beautiful but as out of place in the obscenity that was the man's face as diamonds set in a human turd.

Ronald finally found his voice, high and cracked though it was. 'Who . . . *what* are you?'

'Your Holy fucking Grail, Ronnie.'

The man prised a bony hand from the steering wheel and patted Ronald on the knee. As pus oozed from the naked nailbed of the driver's index finger and stained his trousers, Ronald scrabbled at the door, but there was no handle, no escape.

'Wh-what do you want?' he managed, pushing himself as far away from the thing as he could.

'Just sit still and fucking listen!' It spat dark green phlegm onto the windscreen as it shouted at Ronald. Then it stared at him, its eyes bright and baleful.

Ronald nodded. The eyes in the darkened wreck of a face continued to bore into him like torchbeams at twilight. It smiled – or at least its face cracked and teeth pegs glinted.

'I've been in this truck for months, though time don't mean much here. Dad and me had a deal going but we fucked it up. We was promised power like you wouldn't believe and all it was going to take was the blood of some kids. Four times a year for three years, then one extra. Thirteen brats and it would all be ours. And it was fun! Shit, you have no idea the good time we had. We'd take the kids back to the barn when we needed them and have us some fun. Fuck, did we have some good times using those little bastards . . .' His hands slapped the wheel and he giggled, just like an excited child.

'You're Simmons!' Ronald realized. 'From the garage.'

'Bright for a teacher, ain't you?'

'But what had the children—'

'—got to do with it? Fun! What we didn't do to those little runts! They'd scream and cry and beg for their fucking mummy-wummies. Wish their mummies could have seen some of the stuff we did. Christ, would there have been some screaming then! Good times. We could do what we liked, me and Dad, and it was all adding up to the big prize.'

Ronald's stomach heaved, his mind screamed denial. He wanted to block out the images that assailed him as the thing next to him revelled in its memories. He was sitting with evil, impure and simple. He'd met the parents of abused children in his time, one even went to jail, and he'd heard the evidence, but they had always appeared contrite, almost victims themselves – of their own abused upbringings or a pathetic inability to control their baser impulses – but this . . . *thing*. It *relished* misery, it *savoured* the horror.

'Thirteen little bastards we were to off. Then he'd reward us,' it said.

'He?'

'You know. Him. Satan. The big fucking cheese.'

Ronald gasped. Now this thing was trying to *justify* its sick perversions; to give reason beyond its own evil lusts.

'You thought . . .' he said. 'If you murdered—'

'*Thought*?' The finger stabbed at Ronald's face, the thick spittle flew. 'Thoughts fuck up your mind. Don't think, *do*. Want it, take it. Like it, get some more! No, he told me.'

'You met . . .?'

'No, not met.' It seemed disappointed. 'But he spoke to me. I heard him, understand? He fucking spoke to me. In the barn, late at night. On special nights. When me and Dad were together, messing, before we got the kids. He told us he appreciated all the wrong things Dad and me did to each other. He wanted to reward us, but it'd cost thirteen kids. We did twelve. All set to do number thirteen but just as we snatched the little cunt he fell in the river and we lost him. People started snooping and we had to run for it. We only had that night to do it. Nine o'clock and no kid. Dad went spare, sent me to town to pick up a kid, *any* kid. On the way I crashed. The old fuck had fixed me brakes! Went off the road, car caught fire, I caught fire . . .' It paused, as if reliving something unpleasant. Ronald was pleased it had suffered.

'Watching your hands on fire, trying to slap them out but you set fire to your trousers, then see the flames work into your crotch . . . smell your hair being frizzed off, hear the steam from your own skin . . . the pain, the fucking pain . . .'

There was a long silence, during which all Ronald could hear was the beating of his own heart. It was too fast. Ronald, however, realized that if he didn't keep talking to the Simmons thing, his mind would collapse in on itself, overcome by horrors; like a man hanging on to a rope held by his worst enemy, he needed to keep a grip for as long as possible, despite the seeming inevitability of the outcome.

'Why did he fix your car?' asked Ronald.

'Number thirteen! Dad was so fucking desperate he thought he'd get away with me being *his* kid. Didn't work. Not for him, anyway. Me, I got this. I remember heat and pain and the smell of burnt meat. Next thing I was sat in this truck, Dad sat beside me, pissed. He took one look at me and shit his pants. God, what a laugh. Teach the old fuck. I tried talking to him, he was me dad. But he wouldn't have it – that it was me, I mean. Any time I tried to talk to the old tosser – in the bedroom, the barn, on the road – he just freaked. Soon he was always pissed, eight in the morning job. So pissed he didn't care. Then he started talking and that's when I found out he'd fixed the brakes on my car. So I started fucking with his mind, suggesting he pay for what he'd done to me. He finally got the message. Topped himself in this very cab. Torched the barn, then came and sat where you are, poured petrol all over himself, then lit his lighter. I can remember him sat there soaked in the shit, blubbing his eyes out, looking at that little yellow flame, not sure whether to do it or not, then he drops the lighter and it's bye-bye dad. Crisped up nice he did, the old fart.' There was almost a note of affection in his voice. 'Screamed like a girl though. That's when I got the truck.'

'You drive this? You caused all those—'

'No, it drives me. I just get a front row seat. It looks after itself, does this truck.' He sounded disappointed.

Ronald wanted to kick out at the thing next to him, to argue, plead, beg, anything, everything. Instead he wept.

It sniggered as it watched the road unfurl in front of them. And, after his tears had dried up, Ronald did the same, his eyes fixed ahead, his mind blank, his emotions in neutral: a terminal case of white line fever. He lost all track of time.

The world outside the cab windows was red, the road stretching out ahead like a thin, endless graveyard, its occupants prey to be ground under the wheels of the truck. Night or day, he couldn't tell. It was like looking at infra-red film, everything stained the colour of blood. As for sounds, there were none; only a quiet like the stilled breath of a corpse. And the smell: blood, vomit, urine, shit, sour milk, stale semen, rotten meat, decay, degeneration . . . an indescribable melding of all the bad odours that could assail mortal man combined into a heady reek that clawed its way into his lungs and settled like thick dust, contaminating oxygen and saliva alike so that every swallow and breath became an assault on the senses. Ronald could see no escape from this new world he was drowning in.

It was difficult to judge speed or distance. Cars, buses, trucks, all came into view and disappeared like mystery objects bobbing in and out of sight in a horizon-wide bucket of blood. It took a while but he came to realize that what he saw outside wasn't any particular road but all roads; a montage of present and past – maybe even future – of minutes and days and flashes and moments, all mixed up, played and replayed, so that it all became a oneness. Time didn't mean anything. Outside could be any moment in the truck's life. A chill hand clutched his heart as he realized that he might see his own daughter's death. Or even himself looking in . . .

Ronald could see the truck was closing on a small car but couldn't tear his eyes away as it was rear-ended and shunted to the left and out of sight. Yet there was no sound, no vibration. It would be explained away as a blow out, a patch of oil, another sleeper at the wheel . . .

Escape, he needed to escape. He stared at his door. White metal, smooth, without indentation or extrusion – and no handles. He looked over his shoulder. A solid white wall stretched the width and height of the cab. He then forced himself to look over at the giggling monstrosity. It caught his gaze and he stared into its eyes and he remembered where he had seen them before. In his nightmares, where Julie had borne the same almost unnaturally bright blue eyes. It had been watching him through those eyes even when he was asleep. Suddenly it sniggered, the eyes flashed.

'Yeah, that's right, Ronnie. I was in *there*,' it said, pointing at his head. 'Rooting around, digging about. Found your precious fucking daughter. The fog? The crashes? Me. Got you so shit-scared you didn't know night from day. Got that Wilks bitch, too. Taught her a lesson, eh, teacher?'

Ronald didn't dare speak; like a child awaiting punishment, he hoped the promise of retribution might be forgotten if he kept quiet. Instead, he ran the last few months through his head. The sightings, the chases, the baiting, the deaths, even the nightmares, trying to find some weakness to give him an edge, but he couldn't think of any. And if there truly was none, then he was doomed.

'Why?' he blurted out, finally unable to contain himself.

'What?' it said.

'Why are you doing this? It's not *right*.'

'What the fuck's "right" when it's at home?' it shrieked. '*Right is what you want*. He told me that. If you want it, take it. You and your fucking right . . . you don't know what right is; all you do is say "no" to what you really want.

'Did you ever see your daughter naked? Ever see *her* face when you fucked your wife? Wondered about that pubic hair on the toilet seat? Did it come from her snatch, or maybe from a boyfriend while she was humping on his big cock?'

'*Shut up! Shut up! Shut up!*' Ronald covered his ears with his hands but wouldn't blot out the vile tirade.

It laughed insanely at his helplessness, obviously pleased to have an audience. 'Imagine it, Ronnie, coming home to find your precious little daughter on her knees sucking on your best friend's cock while some bastard reams out her—'

The shrieks from Ronald finally drowned out the thing's words but not the images that slashed into Ronald's thoughts like razors on a baby's face, destroying the beauty and the innocence of his daughter's precious memory. He screamed and yelled till his voice was hoarse and his eyes ached to loose tears that would no longer come. The mind that swamped his own was more depraved than any he could imagine. He'd do anything to get away from its rantings, anything to still the vomitous perversions that spilled from its broken mouth.

'Don't worry,' said a voice.

Ronald heard it, even though his ears still rang from his shouting.

'It will soon be over,' said the calm voice.

Ronald opened his eyes and looked at the Simmons thing. No change, still rotten, still stinking, but the eyes had calmed, the malevolence had receded, almost as if someone else was at home.

Again it spoke, its ragged edge softer, more controlled. 'Not long now.'

Ronald guessed the thing had a visitor.

'What do you mean?' asked Ronald, his voice almost as cracked as the burnt skin of the thing that kept him company.

'At two minutes past midnight tonight you will die and all your worries will be over.'

Ronald didn't need to voice his incredulity.

The lulling voice continued. 'You don't understand, do you? At 12:02 this truck will run over you and you'll die. A sad but sorry fact.'

Ronald couldn't speak.

'A place called Marlsden. You will see this truck coming and you will try and run but it will kill you. You see, Ronald, some people are unlucky enough to foresee their own deaths. Unfortunately, you have been one of them. All the time you have been hunting this truck you have been chasing the spectre of your own death. Ironic, for one who so much wished to die and now wants so much to live.'

Ronald tried praying but words wouldn't form – only images of the violent and lewd obscenities that the Simmons creature had sown in his mind. And all through his rage and anguish those calm blue eyes surveyed him, unimpressed and uncommunicative, a passive observer of his torment. What could help him, how could he get God on his side? He needed a holy eraser, something to rub out the darkness enveloping him.

'You need faith to beat death,' it said. 'But you don't *believe*. You have no faith.'

It was true. He had never been a churchgoer like Ruth, but had always held on to the agnostic's trump card that if a good and just God did exist He wouldn't condemn someone just for being unsure. However, when Ruth became ill, God became the doctor of all doctors but, as His medicine failed and Ruth slowly dwindled away, Ronald lost all hope of there being a benevolence at work in the universe. If God could let Ronald's decent Christian wife die so agonizingly, He had little for which Ronald could thank Him. And when Julie died, that was the final straw. At her funeral all he saw was a deluded man in a skirt spouting mumbo-jumbo to succour fools too stupid to see things as they really were. You're born, you die and somewhere in between you try and smile. Ronald had buried what little faith he might have had with his child; nothing would change that, even an encounter with evil. *Especially* evil; after all, what God would allow such a thing to exist?

Ronald looked into the visitor's eyes, but their blankness was even more chilling than the thing's insane stare.

'Not evil, Ronald. Just death,' it said, its expression unchanged. 'Just death. Now, get out.'

'W-what?'

'Get out,' it repeated, looking forwards. 'I release you. You'll die soon enough. For now, leave.'

Ronald looked through the windscreen. The truck had stopped. Then his door opened.

'Get out!' it squawked. 'Get out, you fucker!' Evidently the visitor had left and Simmons was back, angered by the turn of events.

Ronald edged himself towards the blackness outside the door. The thing that had been Simmons was hysterical.

'Get out, you bastard! I'm going to enjoy smashing your fucking head to pulp! Watching your brains squirt out—'

Ronald jumped.

TWENTY-FOUR

It was shouting from outside that attracted Cally's attention.
Looking through the surgery window she could see several police
officers running across the floodlit lawn towards a body. She
knew instinctively it was Ronald.

She shouted at Dr Rogers that Ronald was back and then she
ran into the entrance hall, only to be grabbed by a police sergeant
who ignored her pleas and herded them both back into the
room.

'Look, man, he may be hurt,' urged Dr Rogers as the policeman tried to shut the door. 'Where's Chief Inspector Palmer?'

'Trying to organize a helicopter. I'll tell him—'

'I'm a doctor, you fool. If he needs help . . .'

The sergeant considered this, then nodded. 'We'll bring him in
here.'

'Good, I'll get my gear.'

Two minutes later two policemen carried a dishevelled and
bloodied Ronald into the surgery. Several policemen crowded
around the door but Dr Rogers demanded they leave.

'Whatever he's done, he needs first aid.'

Once the room had been cleared of everyone but himself,
Cally, Ronald, the sergeant and a constable, Rogers set about
checking Ronald's condition.

The man was in shock, almost delirious, and his hands, knees
and face were grazed and bleeding. Rogers washed the cuts,
dabbed them with antiseptic then dressed them. They were
nothing to worry about. However, Ronald's mental state gave
cause for concern. And it was as Dr Rogers was checking his
pulse that Ronald suddenly found a voice to match his wild,
darting eyes, and startled everyone present in the process.

'Going to die,' he shouted. 'Tonight. I'm going to die!'

Cally tried to reassure him. 'No, you're not, Ron. You're here with us, you're safe.'

'Doesn't matter,' he said, his eyes darting every which way. 'The truck *is* death, don't you see? It's death.'

The two policemen tried to grab him but Dr Rogers waved them back. 'Don't you mean "deadly"?' he said, unsure whether he should be pursuing the matter so soon after an obvious trauma.

'No! I mean Death. That truck *is* Death. And it's going to kill me. Tonight. Just like it's killed others.' He was shaking with fear, sweat running down his cheek.

'What truck?' said the sergeant.

Dr Rogers waved him silent. 'How do you know?'

'The driver told me. He – it said I'm going to be killed by that truck tonight just after midnight.'

At this, the constable sniggered but Dr Rogers leaned over and whispered. 'Whatever this man says is no laughing matter. You can see he's distressed, he needs help.'

Suitably admonished, the policeman fell silent.

Dr Rogers returned his attention to Ronald, who didn't appear to have noticed anything, too tightly wound up in his own problem to care about the rest of the world.

'You mean that truck's going to come into this room at midnight and kill you?' he said, trying to sound reasonable.

'No. Near Marlsden.'

'Marlsden? Where's that?' said Cally.

'About twenty miles away,' offered one of the policemen.

'Twenty miles?' said Dr Rogers. 'But it's after eleven already. As long as you sit tight it can't get you, Ronald, isn't that obvious?'

'Eleven o'clock?'

'11:08, to be precise.'

'An hour. 12:02, he said.'

'That's it, then,' said Cally. 'Another half-hour and you couldn't get there anyway. You're safe, Ron. You're not going to die.'

For the first time Ronald showed something other than stark terror as Cally's calculation sank in. 'Really? Twenty miles?'

'Yes,' said the other policeman, pleased to see the man calming down. 'Up the A6, then over to the A65.'

'Maybe he was lying,' said Dr Rogers. 'Whatever he is or that truck is, there's no way he can kill you when and where he said if you stay here.'

Ronald sat up and started weeping, relief crashing through him like a flash flood. Cally put her arm over his shoulder and felt ripples of terror running through him.

'Oh God, I'm sorry,' he said over and over.

'S'alright, Ron,' said Cally gently. 'It's over.'

Suddenly Ronald stopped and looked into Cally's concerned face. 'What if it's like your train?'

'How?'

'Your train ran through his office, didn't it? Fitted through the damn door. What if the truck can—'

The two policemen looked at each other, their disdain all too obvious.

'Even if it could, Ronald, my office is on the ground floor. We'll take you upstairs. You'll be safe there.'

Even so, Dr Rogers stepped away from the dark square of the window, hoping Ronald wouldn't notice his cowardice.

Ronald leaned back and wiped his face with his forearm and apologized again as he squeezed Cally's hand. 'I'm sorry but that's what he told me . . .'

'Who?' asked the sergeant.

'The driver.'

'He threatened to kill you? That's a serious offence. Did you get the number of the truck. Did you know the man?'

'Man? I suppose he was . . .' Ronald was finding it difficult to concentrate, as if he was in a dream struggling to wake up. 'Simmons. His name was Simmons.'

'First name?' said the policeman.

Dr Rogers placed his hand over the PC's notebook. 'No need for notes. Chief Inspector Palmer will deal with this. He knows the full story.'

But he won't believe it, thought Cally, gripping Ronald's hand. He felt cold. What had Ron seen? Simmons was the owner of the garage Ron visited – and the man Annie Wilks accused of killing her family.

'But isn't Simmons dead?' said Cally.

'Yes,' said Ronald.

The policeman who had laughed now shook his head in disgust. He clearly felt he was guarding someone deranged.

Ronald ignored him; ignored everyone, in fact, his mind reliving his encounter, trying to put some semblance of reason to the dark void that had engulfed his mind and heart in that cab, with that creature.

Ronald continued: 'He told me he killed a lot of kids.' He shivered at the memory of the man's descriptions. 'Then he . . . it . . . said he knew when and where I would die.'

'Couldn't you have dreamed him?' asked Dr Rogers.

'You saw the truck,' said Cally. 'Why should he dream anything?' She turned to Ronald. 'Does he drive the truck?'

'No. He just sits and watches. He'd made a pact with . . . he didn't finish his side of the bargain. Whether it's a reward or a punishment . . .' He dissolved into tears again.

Dr Rogers gently eased Cally away from him.

The cynical constable uttered his disgust, stood up and went out of the room. The sergeant stayed where he was by the window, his face professionally blank.

'Well,' said Cally. 'What do we do?'

'What do you mean?' said Dr Rogers. 'He's in police custody, he's not going anywhere, he's safe.'

'But you do believe him?'

'I don't know,' said Dr Rogers, casting a wary eye at the policeman. It was neither the time nor the place to get into this; Cally's points of reference when it came to the supernatural were not conventional.

'But you saw the truck – it *must* be true!'

Dr Rogers was taken aback by the girl's resolution. 'All right, all right. Even so, he needs medical attention. And rest.'

Just then, Chief Inspector Palmer hurried in, accompanied by three other men, all in suits.

'So, we're back, are we?' he said to Ronald.

Ronald looked up at them but didn't seem interested.

'And where have you been, Mr Blakestone?'

Dr Rogers intervened. 'I've told you where he's been. The man needs—'

'The man needs locking up. And don't come it with that truck bullshit again or you'll find yourself in deeper trouble than you already are. There's one woman dead and Dr Gantry's missing. Forensics have confirmed the blood found on the embankment, the track *and* on the Discovery matches Gantry's. Despite proclaiming his innocence, first chance Blakestone gets he does a runner. Well, no more. I'm taking him into custody.'

'But he's ill. He's only just—'

'I have the police surgeon,' he said, indicating the man at his right shoulder. 'I also have a warrant for his arrest and the necessary documents to have him admitted to a prison hospital for observation and security.'

'Prison hospital!' said Dr Rogers with a sneer. 'You may as well throw him in a cell for all the—'

The inspector was angry. 'Dr Rogers, this is not a debate! The doctor is going to make sure Blakestone is fit for transfer and then he will be moved. Your presence – and that of the girl – is not required. I ask you to co-operate or he may not be the only one taken into custody. Now, do I make myself clear?'

Dr Rogers was about to protest but Cally shook her head. She looked at the watch on the inspector's outstretched hand. 11:14. There was no arguing with the man and pretty soon Ronald would be safe from his appointment with the truck.

'He needs treatment, you said it yourself. Doesn't matter where he is, does it?' she said.

Dr Rogers shrugged his shoulders and looked at Palmer. 'The wisdom of youth.'

He allowed himself and Cally to be escorted from the room and back into his own office. The same two policemen were stationed outside and he and Cally were left alone. As he sat down he felt his strength ebb away like a deflating balloon. It had been a long, tiring day.

Cally lay on the couch on her side, her energies as yet undepleted. 'So, what now?'

Dr Rogers was too tired to try falsehoods. 'They will examine him, declare him fit enough to travel sedated, take him to prison, lock him in the hospital wing and he will then be questioned. He will not change his story, so they will bring in psychiatrists to examine him and then . . .'

'Yes?'

'Chief Inspector Palmer wants blood; he believes he has two murders, he needs a murderer. He will charge Ronald with the murder of Annie Wilks. Ronald will be remanded in custody, leaving the inspector free to question him whenever he likes concerning Dr Gantry.'

'And?'

'And . . . and, to be blunt, he will be convicted of Annie's murder but probably allowed the defence of insanity and will be sent to a psychiatric hospital.'

Cally lay back and let out a long sigh. That was it, really, she thought. There wasn't anything else they could do. Next time she would see Ronald would be on visiting day, assuming she kept her own freedom. For once, she didn't care. She was used to being used, let them use her some more. At least her train had gone. What was it Gantry had said once? The wheels of reason run on very narrow tracks. Hmm, true enough. And, it seemed, the wheels of justice followed the same route. She tried to cry for Ronald but it wouldn't come. Instead she closed her eyes and thought of ways they could help him, but there were none.

Ten minutes later DCI Palmer came into the room. 'Mr Blakestone is fit to travel. We will be taking him to Greybank Prison.'

'And us?'

'I'll have you escorted back to the police station for statements.'

'When will you be taking Mr Blakestone?' said Dr Rogers.

'An hour.'

'Can we see him?' asked Cally.

Palmer opened the door. 'What do you think?' he said and left the room.

Dr Rogers looked at his watch. 11:23. An hour would take it well past midnight and the threat would be over, if threat there was. In the cold light of tomorrow, sitting in a grey police station interview room with a twin-tape deck running and a solicitor present, things might seem a whole lot different. As indeed they might to Ronald when he woke up and found himself strapped to a prison bed, his date with death long passed.

Five minutes ticked by to the sound of a grandfather clock and the static babble from various police radios, both inside and outside the house. Cally found she needed to visit the toilet. She opened the door to explain and one of the policeman outside led her to a bathroom off the hall entrance and waited outside.

It was as she left the toilet that she came face to face with Chief Inspector Palmer, two other uniformed policemen, the police surgeon and a tired and drawn Ronald in a straitjacket, all making their way to the front door.

Outraged, she flew at Palmer but was soon bundled back to her room, the detective hurling angry insults at her.

Inside, she grabbed Dr Rogers's wrist and checked his watch. 11:31. Dr Rogers tried to calm her.

'Cally, Cally, so they're taking him away, but Greybank Prison is nowhere near Marlsden. I've visited it several times. He'll be all right!'

Cally tried to calm down but she couldn't. The adrenalin was pumping and her mind wouldn't settle; it flicked through the possibilities as if they were CDs in a rack: heart attack; car crash; diversion; breakdown; the truck driver lied; Palmer lied; or everybody lied, including Dr Rogers. She turned to look at him.

Could he be in on this? The way he'd dumped her the first time and yet fell for Ronald's story right from the start. Okay, so the truck had appeared, but . . . *stop it, stop it, you're getting paranoid, girl*! She walked to the door and knocked on it. One of the policeman standing outside answered:

'Yes?'

'Sorry to bother you. Could you tell me when Chief Inspector Palmer will get to Greybank Prison? I'd like to know if Ron . . . Mr Blakestone arrived okay.'

'There's been an accident on the A6; it's closed off, so they're taking an alternate route, but they should get there in about forty-five minutes.'

'Another route? Which way?'

'The M6.'

The name of the motorway hit Cally with the impact of an obscenity shouted in a silent cathedral. She dashed back to the startled Dr Rogers.

'Where is Marlsden? Where is it exactly?' she demanded.

'Twenty miles away, like the policeman told you.'

'Is it on the M6?'

'No. It's off it, though. You have to take Junction . . . Junction 34, I think. Then it's a couple of miles east.'

'What junction would you use to get to Greybank Prison?'

'Junction 34.'

'And do you have to go through Marlsden to—'

'—get to Greybank? Yes . . .'

They both looked at his watch. 11:35. How far could a police car get on an empty motorway in twenty-seven minutes? Far enough.

TWENTY-FIVE

Ronald was driving slowly along a motorway. Very slowly, almost as if he was in a film that was winding down. Smoke drifted across the road ahead, occasionally thinning to reveal the carcasses of wrecked cars, their remains the deepest burnt black and the shiniest chrome. Cars, vans and trucks, all were smashed open and ruptured like corpses at a post mortem, littering all three carriageways as far as he could see, with just enough space between them for his van to weave a careful path over shattered glass that reflected the rainbow colours of spilled fuel. His mirrors showed the same scene to his rear. All was quiet, like the aftermath of a battle, as if Nature itself couldn't comprehend the destruction wrought in its presence. As Ronald continued to drive, his mind raced over the possible events that could have caused much mayhem, but his hazy thought processes were distracted by a figure up ahead. As the distance between them closed, he saw it was a girl.

Slight and scruffy, she was carrying what looked like a toy train under one arm, her other raised above her head waving him on. He slowed until they were both moving at her halting pace, the only sound now the gentle vibrato from the van's engine and the crisp grinding of glass under his wheels. Then there was another sound, distant, threatening, and then he saw it in his door mirror: his white truck was powering towards him along the carriageway, its bulk batting the wrecks out of the way as easily as if they were made of cardboard. Its engine roared, its smokestack billowed and it charged towards him, nothing resisting its speeding onslaught.

Ronald instinctively stepped on the accelerator but raised his foot as he saw the van surge towards the girl still walking in front of him.

He searched desperately for a way past her but to no avail. He pushed at his horn but was rewarded with silence. He shouted but could offer no sound. He tried to wind down his window but there was no handle. Then he saw the truck was closer! He had no choice. It was him or the girl, he had to do it. He had to escape . . . but still his foot hovered above the pedal. How could he just run over the girl? What harm had she done? He looked in the mirror. The truck was almost on him, its ugly form blotting out both the carriageway below and the sky above. He looked back to the girl, but now a policeman was standing with her, both of them waving him on. What could he do? Suddenly he felt something on his knee and, looking down, saw a skeletal hand forcing his foot down onto the accelerator.

As it made contact with the rubber pad of the pedal he began to scream and as his foot was pushed lower his silent scream rose higher, and then he saw the road was littered with the bodies of dead children and his panic burst forth like a living thing, taking hold of his limbs, making him shudder and jerk, desperate to shake off the thing gripping his leg. *No no no no no no no . . .*

He felt a slap on his face, but it didn't mean anything; it was a sensation from another universe. But the pain persisted and he felt his face being slapped several more times until he heard himself screaming and, opening his eyes, found himself totally unable to move, an angry man staring into his face.

'Any more of that and I'll have to sedate you completely. Understand?'

Ronald nodded although he didn't understand. His mind was still trying to get its bearings; like a sheepdog rounding up its flock, his brain slowly brought together random images and memories. A truck, a girl, a policeman. A cackling corpse. Dead children. Blood. A promise. Calmness delivering a death sentence.

He looked beyond the man and saw the blue of a motorway exit sign, then the word 'Marlsden' arrowed ahead, and suddenly all became clear and he started shouting again, but there was pain in his strapped arm and although the urge to shout why they should turn back still hammered in his head with all the persistent fury of a pneumatic drill, his mouth and limbs stubbornly refused to co-operate, instead offering gibberish and jerks.

He caught sight of the clock on the dashboard between the police driver and another man. 11:38 it greened at him. Twenty-four minutes to live and here he was, unable to move, with eyes unable to avoid the countdown to doom.

11:39. Twenty-three minutes.

'We've got to do something,' hissed Cally, grabbing Dr Rogers by the lapels as he sat on the bed.

'But what? They're long gone. Besides, if—'

'Besides nothing, you arsehole. Ron knows when he's going to die and he knows where and he's on his way there right now! We've got to stop them. Now get to that door and get one of those cops in here.'

'Then what?'

'Let me worry about that. Now move it!'

Dr Rogers reluctantly walked over to the door and tapped on it lightly. Cally glared at him and he knocked harder.

'Yes?' said a voice.

'It's Dr Rogers. I . . . I need some pills. For me. From my bag. Heart condition. Have to take them each night.'

There was a pause.

'Where's the bag?'

'In my room.'

'I'll go get them.'

'No! No, I'd best get them. The case has a lock.'

'I'll bring the case, then.'

'Look, it's rather urgent. I don't feel too well.'

'What's it look like?'

'For God's sake, man, I'm not a prisoner! Let me get them!'

Again there was a pause, then the door opened and one of the policemen looked in.

He didn't have time to speak before a metal bedpan was smashed onto the back of his skull with a resounding clunk and he dropped like a stone at Cally's feet.

'Oldest trick in the book,' she said shaking her head at the pillows stuffed inside the bed covers.

The other cop had heard the commotion and came in the door just in time to receive the bed pan full in the face.

He fell to his knees clutching his bleeding nose, unconcerned about Cally's and Dr Rogers's exit from the room.

As they ran down the corridor, Cally asked for Dr Rogers's keys.

'What keys?'

'For your car. Trust me, I'm good.'

Ronald jerked awake. Damn, he couldn't concentrate. The figures on the clock kept trying to fly off, his eyes rolling as if they were at sea rather than in a car.

The men in the car were ignoring him now, confident that he was drugged enough not to bother them. He tried to pull his hands free but the straitjacket was too tight.

Straitjacket? He tried to struggle but nothing happened. Like corn popping in a microwave, all inside was energy but all outside was unaffected. He gave up and looked at the clock again.

11:52.

He might as well be on his way to a hanging, his companions a priest, guards and the prison warden.

On their way out to the car, Cally ran into Dr Rogers's surgery, grabbed a large plastic medical case and, ransacking his drugs cabinet, threw any pills, ampoules and syringes she could find into it. Then, snapping it shut, she thrust it at Dr Rogers and made him carry it out to his car.

After she had slotted the ignition key into the Rover 800 and rammed the seat forward so she could reach the pedals, she gunned the engine and set off, gravel flying. It was only as they skidded onto the main road that she bothered to check if Dr Rogers was still with her in the passenger seat. He was, but plainly wished he wasn't.

Thirty seconds later they passed the sign for the M6. She checked the dash clock. 11:52.

'Map! Find a map!' she yelled. 'Need to know how far!'

Dr Rogers panicked for a moment, then checked his glove compartment. It was awkward with the medical box on his lap, but he found a road map. Flicking on the internal light he found the relevant section.

'Let's see. Two miles to the M6 – nearly there – then it's ten, twelve miles on the motorway, then exit 36 and another three

miles. Fifteen miles.' The car slewed to the left and Dr Rogers
was slammed into the side door. G-forces kept him there until the
car snapped back to the straight and plummeted down a slip road.
They were on the M6.

'Thirteen miles,' he managed to say before he had to cough
down the bile. He tried to avoid looking through the windscreen –
he had always hated speed – but seeing the speedometer arc
through the 100 was no comfort.

Cally was calculating. If she was to reach Marlsden by 12:02
they had up to thirteen miles to cover in ten minutes. She floored
the accelerator, grateful that it was night and the motorway was
nearly empty.

11:53. If only they knew, if only they knew.

Ronald remembered the thing in the cab and its delight at the
pain and suffering it had caused. He remembered its promise
about his death.

11:54.

His fear was slowly being replaced with anger. Anger at the
stupidity of his captors; anger at himself for his persistence in
seeking a truth he didn't want to know; and anger at the thing
that was to have the satisfaction of killing him. Like the con-
demned man he had imagined himself to be, he would rather his
executioner was some anonymous civil servant than some pervert
who lived for the moment he could open the trapdoor and hear
the snap of the rope.

11:55.

Cally hunched over the wheel, her foot to the floor, praying that
any vehicle in her lane would move in time. She had no wish to
start weaving at this speed. Dr Rogers was also hunched over, his
head resting on the large medical box in his lap, his hands
trembling, his stomach quivering its distress.

11:56.

A distance sign came up. No mention of Marlsden. Damn. She
wondered how far ahead Ronald and his escort could be.
Assuming they would reach Marlsden at 12:02 – they had no
reason to have already got there and stopped – she still had a
chance to intercept them before they reached the town. But then

what? And how could she get them to listen? Maybe just delaying them for a couple of minutes would be enough. As long as Ron wasn't in Marlsden in – *shit* – five minutes.

Ronald could see Julie. She was sitting next to him, smiling, playing with a kitten. She was eleven. The kitten had been called Bodie after one of The Professionals. She was wearing her school uniform, her hair was long, the cat purring. He remembered how she used to rush home from school to feed Bodie. How she used to paint pictures of him and collect photographs of other ginger tabbies from magazines. She had pasted them all over his basket and would often lecture him on how he had to grow his stripes just right if he wanted to be in cat shows. Little girls and kittens: they were created to make a proud father's heart ache.

11:59 flashed.

Ronald then remembered what had happened to Bodie and as the memory of that bloody smudge on the road came back, the cat in Julie's arms turned inside out and she turned to look at him, tears coursing down her face. But they weren't salt water, they were acid and in seconds they had eaten through the flesh until her skull was revealed and her eyes widened and then he realised he was looking at Simmons.

'Ever heard a skull pop, Ronnie?' it giggled. 'From the inside?'

12:00. They were out of time and they hadn't even reached the damn exit. Cally started to keen. She could hear herself and wanted to stop but she couldn't. She was whining like a bloody baby. Why? Why?

There was a police car ahead in the middle lane, its light flashing. Cally was touching 120 m.p.h. as they passed it and she saw, inside the Vauxhall Senator, several men, including one in a white coat on the back seat.

As soon as the image had registered she slammed on the brakes and let the other car catch up with her. When it was within distance, she swung the Rover into the middle lane causing the other driver to serve towards the inside. To a chorus of shouts from a terrified Dr Rogers, Cally slammed on her brakes again to let the other car draw up alongside. Then she broadsided it. The initial impact bounced the Rover back across the carriageway but, using all her strength, she wrenched the wheel hard to the left and slammed into the Senator again, forcing it into a row of cones which flew into the night as if fired from cannons. Locked together, the two cars roared up a dusty sliproad through more cones and then up a steeper incline until they ran out of tarmac and bumped onto a wide open area of dirt, covered in ruts that rattled both cars, tossing their occupants about.

The cars broke apart and Cally swung the Rover in a wide curve until it had turned through three hundred and sixty degrees and come to a halt in a cloud of dust. The police car managed to stop in a straight line, its front tyres digging into loose earth.

'Have we stopped?' begged Dr Rogers, eyes as tightly closed as his fists.

'Yes,' said Cally, wrestling the medical kit from his constrictor-tight arms. She didn't want to do what she was going to do, but she only had seconds before they were swamped by angry cops.

She pushed open her door and threw the bag outside, rolled out after it and, fumbling the fasteners open, spilled its contents onto the ground. Finding what she needed, she ran round the back of the car and, aware that the other car's doors were opening, yanked open Dr Rogers' door and pulled the man out. He fell to his knees, whimpering.

'Get up, you sod, we've got two minutes,' yelled Cally. 'Do what I say or I might just do what I say.'

'What?' he asked, oblivious to his new location, his mind still stuck in a car being driven by a suicidal teenager at twice the legal speed limit.

The sound of shouting and swearing made him look up. Cally tugged at his armpit and he stood up on shaking legs. He belched and swallowed back vomit. What had he done to—

'Stop right there!' screamed Cally. 'Any closer and the doc gets it!'

The men didn't stop immediately but as they came closer they could see by the flashing blue light what she was threatening to do and they all stopped, Chief Inspector Palmer in the lead.

'Don't!' he shouted. 'Let him go, Cally. Everything will—'

'Everything won't! Not yet! Get Ron out of the car. I want to see him now!' Cally shouted, pushing as hard as she could at the doctor's neck without breaking the skin. She had seen it work in

Terminator 2 and she hoped it would work now. 'If I don't see
Ron inside five seconds, the doctor gets a vein full of air.'

Dr Rogers fell limp in her grasp and crashed to his knees, but
Cally went with him and, squatting beside him, pressed the
needle to his neck, her thumb poised on the plunger.

'Get fucking Ron out here NOW!' she screamed.

Ronald had to get away from it. He couldn't just sit and let
Simmons take him, he had to fight. But he couldn't. His legs were
numb, his arm unable to move. He closed his ears off to the
shrieking demon beside him and looked forward.

12:00.

Then he noticed the car had stopped, and that the men were
leaving. Leaving him to *it*.

He started to struggle, but whether he was actually moving or
just imagining he was kicking out with his legs he couldn't tell.
The adrenalin surged, his mind re-awoke, he became aware of
the here and now. Suddenly the thing was gone and he could hear
a girl shouting. He looked through the open door of the car and
saw a group of men standing still in front of a girl and a man on
his knees.

Ronald tried to move but he was stuck, like a drugged virgin on
a satanic altar, waiting for the blade to descend at the stroke of
midnight. Except, for Ronald, it would be two minutes past
midnight – but the outcome would be no less painful and no less
final.

Then he felt hands grabbing him and he was being dragged
out of the car, his feet scraping tarmac as he was taken towards
the girl, again like some sacrificial offering. He thought he
knew the girl and the man beside her but his mind was still
doped and there was pain to distract him. And then he was
dropped onto his knees and he and the other man knelt staring
at one another.

'What now?' said one of the men who hadn't dragged him.

'We wait,' said the girl.

'Wait?'

'Yeah. You deaf?'

'Wait for what? Not . . . not that nonsense about—'

'Yeah, that "nonsense",' said Cally, annoyed by Palmer's tone.

'Two minutes past twelve at Marlsden. When it's passed you can do what you—'

'We're five miles from Marlsden and it's . . .' He looked at his watch. 'One minute past twelve. Even your driving wouldn't get you there in time, so let's just stop it all right now before it gets really silly.'

'We wait.'

Ronald heard the man tell the time. One minute. *Oh God, help me, help me*! Then he remembered the visitor reminding him that he had no faith. Suddenly Ronald, even in the company of five men and a girl, found himself the loneliest man on the planet. He leaned back on his haunches, trying not to overbalance because his hands were still strapped behind him. He tried to shout but it was useless. Instead, he concentrated his efforts on getting his legs to work. Precious seconds ticked away as he urged himself to rise, to get his left leg out from under him.

'Help him up,' said Cally, seeing Ronald struggling in his straitjacket.

One of the men hauled Ronald up just as he had summoned the energy to do it himself. The result was that Ronald knocked over his helper. As the man staggered back, his arms wheeling, Ronald started to run. He tried to get to the girl, she seemed in charge, but his own balance was unreliable and he found himself running at a diagonal between the men and the girl until he bumped into the Rover's wing and fell over it, banging his face on its bonnet. He rolled himself over and blinked away the sweat in his eyes. His strapped arms meant he was again unable to lever himself up and he slumped back and found himself staring up at a large sign that had been erected by the side of the area the cars had stopped in.

'Twelve-oh-two, Miss Summerskill,' announced an angry Chief Inspector Palmer. 'Can we stop this bloody charade—'

He was cut short by a shout from Ronald, all the louder for having been denied the last few minutes.

'Oh no,' cried Ronald. '*Oh God, no!*'

His eyes had finally focused on the sign and his hopes that Palmer was right about their being five miles from Marlsden were instantly dashed. Even as he rolled off the bonnet and hit the ground and heard Palmer announce the time, he saw headlights in the distance and heard the throaty rumble of a large truck.

Cally turned to look at Ronald, then followed his gaze to the headlights, then looked back at Palmer. This time he too could see the monster. It was about a hundred yards away, only its lights clear. It was revving its engine.

Cally forced Dr Rogers to rise and walked him to the front of the car where she saw Ronald lying on the ground repeating the word 'no' over and over. She looked up at the sign that loomed behind the car. It was a site information board, telling people of the various contractors who were working on the new service area they were parked in.

THE MARLSDEN SERVICE AREA.

The truck roared, Ronald screamed, Cally dropped the syringe and dashed to Ronald. Palmer and another policeman ran at her, the other two rushing to protect Dr Rogers who had fallen back against the car. But just as Cally got to Ronald, the two policemen grabbed her and hauled her back, keeping her feet off the ground. She lashed out, trying to kick at them, but they wouldn't give her the room.

'Now, Miss Summerskill, I think we should have a talk,' said Palmer.

'Fine,' she said, eyeing the truck. 'Do you want to talk to him as well?'

The truck revved its engine again and smoke poured into the night, a luminous fog that shrouded it like a small cloudbank.

'Some driver taking a rest. He—'

It started towards them, the gears crunching, the ground vibrating as it rumbled across the empty car park towards them, the gap closing by the second.

The policemen distracted, Cally managed to bite Palmer on the nose and he let her go. She then kicked the other in the shin and as he too let go, she swooped on Ronald and forced him to stand.

The truck was almost on them, with no sign of slowing. As Cally hustled Ronald across the front of the Rover and under the sign, she yelled at the others to get Dr Rogers.

Then the truck hit the Rover head on. The noise was horrendous, a deep roar and a metallic smash followed by silence and then the sound of the Rover flipping end over end down the side of the truck's trailer, wheels and glass and twisted metal dancing

across the arena of the car park as dramatically as if the car had
been wired with explosives.

The truck rushed on, a fiery wind in its wake that scorched
their skin and made their eyes smart. A whirl of dust spat at their
faces and hands, as rough as sandpaper, and then the truck was
gone, its sound receding down the slip road, its rear lights twin
mocking red eyes of evil.

Cally rubbed frantically at her eyes until she could see, then
looked around for Ronald. He was lying on his back, blood
pouring from a cut over his right eye. He was conscious but
clearly dazed. She looked over at the four men and Dr Rogers.
Except there were only three men and the doctor. Palmer was
picking himself up.

'Where's Blane?' he shouted. The other policeman pointed
down the slip road.

'The truck. Hit him. He . . .'

Palmer looked over at Cally. 'What is this? An ambush?'

Dr Rogers, who was dusting himself down, suddenly stopped,
walked over to the inspector and slapped him across the face.
'You bloody moron. That's his truck. It's here to kill him.
Anyone who sees it dies. Understand? It's not going—'

As if on cue, they heard the roar of the truck and as one they
looked down the slip road. Several seconds passed as the sound of
the engine grew louder and more threatening and then, suddenly,
it was there, its headlights blazing, its radiator grinning, the black
hole of its windscreen patterned with the cruciform remains of
their dead companion.

'Jesus Christ,' said Palmer.

'He's about all we've got left,' said Dr Rogers.

'Don't bank on it,' managed Ronald.

Everyone ran. Cally and Ronald struggled away up the slope
behind the sign, Palmer and the others scattering in various
directions.

The truck was on them in moments, screaming across the dusty
field of the car park. It clipped the police car and sent it spinning
like a toy. The careering car caught the other policeman and
bowled him fully thirty feet into the night. The truck hurtled on,
colliding with the carcass of the Rover which exploded on impact,
flaming debris raining down over a wide area and starting a dozen

small fires, each of which lit the car park up like campfires on a battlefield. Then the truck slowed and began to wheel round.

Dr Rogers and Palmer stopped beside the second car, the police surgeon running away into the shrubbery at the side of the slip road. The fourth man lay on the ground where he had landed on his back and didn't move. Palmer was about to run out to help him but Dr Rogers grabbed his arm.

The truck set off again, aiming straight for the prone man. Just as it reached him he sat up but he didn't even have time to scream as the truck's front right wheel ran over him full length, squashing him flat, the tractor unit's twin rear wheels smearing him wafer-thin before the trailers' wheels ground him into the dirt. Then the truck swung to the right and ploughed into the trees and long grass beside the slip road, its engine roaring like a hungry dinosaur in search of prey. There was a barely audible scream and then it reappeared a couple of hundred yards further on slamming down a slight rise onto the dusty slip road and disappearing down onto the motorway.

Cally watched the truck drop out of sight down the slope. There were only four of them left now. They hadn't a chance. Where could they run? As far as she could see with the flickering light from the burning police car, the whole area was flat. No buildings had been constructed, just land levelled in preparation for a car park. In the distance there seemed to be a large canopy structure, probably the service station forecourt, but other than that there was nowhere that wasn't within the truck's reach. Even the surrounding land failed to offer any cover, just gentle slopes and inclines, some planted, some still scraped bare.

She turned Ronald round, undid the straps on his jacket and helped him drop it on the floor. Ronald hugged her, even though his arms stung with pins and needles.

'I'm sorry,' he said. 'Just let it take me and everyone else will be—'

The truck let out a taunting blast of its horn somewhere over the crest of the slip road.

'Forget it, Ron. We've all seen it. You said it's Death. That means we're dead too.'

'I'm sorry.' He couldn't think of anything else to say.

Chief Inspector Palmer and Dr Rogers came trotting over. The detective looked frightened. Cally refused to say 'I told you so.'

'What are we going to do?' asked Dr Rogers.

No one answered. Then the truck was coming again. Each looked frantically around for somewhere to run but there was nowhere. Then Cally spotted something and it gave her an idea. She sprinted back onto the car park.

'Cally!' screamed Ronald, stumbling after her, but the other two held him back. What was the stupid girl doing?

The truck coursed up the slip road, its dead roar making their very bones ache. They watched as Cally ran straight in front of it. As if it had caught sight of fresh meat, the tone of its engine rose and it speeded up. Then they had to watch in horror, each of them letting out an involuntary yell, as the truck reached the running form of the girl, catching her in its headlights like a blue moth.

Then she was gone and the truck sounded its horn in triumph. The dust in its wake rushed over them, forcing them to turn away and shield their eyes.

As they heard the truck slow, its air brakes hissing it to a halt, they looked back at Cally. Her slight figure was lying on the ground in a ball. As one they ran across to her, oblivious of the truck turning to face them once again.

It was when they were halfway to her that she leapt up and waved them back. She had something in her hand but rather than follow them she stayed where she was. The three men paused, midway between her rescue and their own safe haven on the incline, unsure what to do.

'Get back, get back!' she yelled. 'I've sussed it. We only have the time it's on the slip road. Got to get it down there again.'

'What are you talking about?' shouted Palmer.

'Cally, come on, there's still time. Run!' shouted Ronald but it was too late.

The monster belched exhaust fumes into the night, black on black, crunched its gear teeth as it let rip its horsepower and charged at them again.

The three men scrambled back up under the sign, but the truck ignored them and targeted Cally instead. Only this time the girl didn't run; she stood her ground, her face set hard against the relentless juggernaut speeding towards her, a lamb squaring up to an enraged bull.

'*Come and get me, you fucker! Come and get me!*'

The distance between them narrowed in an instant and then the truck was on her. Cally hoped her judgement was right. One time when she had been in care she had fallen in with a bunch of losers who liked to play chicken with trains. They would wait by the line, then, when it was too late for the driver to react, they would run onto the track and wait till the last second before jumping out of the way. Cally had proven herself to be adept at the stunt, even though she only did it to keep in with the morons who thought it cool. Predictably one of them eventually mistimed his run and lost a leg: end of game. But she thought the experience could help her this time.

As the truck thundered towards her, Cally waited until the last possible moment and then, on an impulse, instead of leaping to the side, she dived headlong towards it instead. As she hit the ground and the image of torn limbs splayed across the radiator's teeth like psychotic hood ornaments seared into her mind, she tasted dirt and felt the heat as it screamed over her, the riptide of its downdraught all but tearing the dress off her back, its wheels inches from her head, grit scorching her face with the force of a sandblaster. It took barely three seconds for the truck and its trailer to fly over her, but it seemed as long as any train they had challenged. And then it was gone.

Apart from the stench of rubber, oil and choking dust that clogged her lungs, Cally was unscathed. Without wasting another second, she ran over to the men, each of whom was aghast at her action. As she reached them she turned and saw the truck slowing as it plunged down the slip road. She grabbed Dr Rogers.

'I don't want any shit. When you said my train had gone, did you really mean it?'

'Your train?' said Dr Rogers.

'Your train?' said Palmer.

'Your train? *No!*' said Ronald.

'Shut up, Ronald. You've saved me twice already. Payback time. Well, has it really gone?'

'I honestly don't know.'

'I thought you were lying.' She held up a syringe and a handful of ampoules that she had taken from the abandoned medical case. 'Will any of these knock me out now?'

'I don't see—' started Palmer.

'I do,' said Ronald, and he couldn't let her do it. 'No! You know this might be the last time. Look what happened with Gantry.'

'Gantry? Train? What is going on?' said Palmer.

The truck sounded a warning blast on its klaxon. Plainly it enjoyed the chase.

'Cally, no!' pleaded Ronald. Better that he at fifty sacrifice himself than Cally who had her whole life ahead of her.

'Ron, I'm doing this! Five seconds, doc. Choose one that'll get me out and dreaming or I'll choose one myself.'

'I don't think—'

'No, you don't think, do you, doc? That thing out there isn't real, is it?'

'Looks pretty damn fucking real to me!' said Palmer to no one in particular.

'It's not really real, is it, Ron? Only you could see it,' said Cally.

'Yes.'

'And my train's not real, is it? Eh, doc?'

'Well, it does manifest—'

'*Cut the crap*! If that thing's not real there's fuck-all we can do about it, right? So why not use something else that's unreal to beat it?'

'Train? Unreal?' Palmer was lost.

The truck was charging up the hill again, its bellowing even more vehement than before.

'A phantom to kill a phantom?' said Dr Rogers.

'Yes, yes!' said Cally. 'Now choose the fucking stuff!'

'Cally, I—' but Ronald received a knee in the groin and had to bend double, pain creasing his abdomen.

'Sorry, Ron. *Choose!*'

Dr Rogers looked at the ampoules in the light from the fires and, to his horror, found each label easier to read than the last – because of the headlights from the fast approaching truck.

'This one should . . . are you—'

'*Run!*' shouted Palmer and they stumbled further up the incline, a good thirty feet now from the killing ground of the unfinished car park. It made little difference to the truck. It aimed straight for them, its lights blinding them, the roar from its engine sucking all sound out of the night.

Inches. It missed them by inches, its wheel carving a channel in the soft earth of the slope, its backwash strong enough to knock them all off their feet. Then it ploughed on through the incline and burst out into the car park, plants and clods of earth flying in its wake as it drove on until it could swing round to attack them again.

'Last chance. Next time . . .' said Palmer.

'*Do it!*' shouted Cally to Dr Rogers.

He took the needle, plunged it into the lid of the ampoule and started filling the syringe.

'Look, what's all this about a train? I don't . . .'

'Forget it, Palmer,' said Ronald. 'You didn't believe *this* bloody thing. No way will you cope with her train.' Ronald almost laughed. He could feel hysteria poking at him.

'I don't want, I can't . . .' Palmer was exasperated, unable to focus his thoughts. Three men dead, this unbelievable truck, the destruction, the drugs . . . 'Look, this truck was supposed to get you at 12:02. It didn't, so why—'

'Oh, shit,' said Ronald, staring at Dr Rogers's wrist as he squirted spare air from the syringe.

'What? What?' said Palmer.

'The time.'

They looked at Dr Rogers's watch. It said 12:02. Chief Inspector Palmer checked his own. It also read 12:02.

'But this has been going on for *minutes*. It . . .' Palmer gave up.

Cally grabbed Dr Rogers's arm. 'Forget that. Do me. The lot.' She could see the doctor begin shaking his head. 'Worry about that shit later. Just get me under. It's the only hope we have!'

Dr Rogers took her arm.

'Quicker in the neck,' she said, pulling down the collar of her dress.

'Oh, Jesus,' said Ronald.

'I think—' said Palmer.

'You don't think, that's the fucking problem,' said Cally. 'Now shoot it up!'

Dr Rogers teased her neck then, finding the vein, injected her. Even before he had emptied the syringe her legs had given way and her eyes were rolling.

'You've killed her!' screamed Ronald.

'Not yet I haven't,' said Dr Rogers. 'This stuff, she's maybe got ten minutes. I just hope it works.'

'I don't believe I just let you do that,' said Palmer.

'What are you going to do? Arrest me?' said Dr Rogers, tossing the syringe aside. He'd as good as murdered the girl, but the inability of the detective to understand their true predicament was annoying him.

'Why don't you try arresting the driver of that first?' he said, pointing at the truck as it revved, announcing its intention to launch another assault on them.

Ronald, meanwhile, trying to ignore the pain in his groin, had knelt down, cradling the girl's head in his lap and wiping the dirt from her face. The drugs had taken effect far quicker than the last time when they had been confronted by Gantry. Too fast, it seemed. She might as well have been punched unconscious. He shouted up at Dr Rogers.

'She's gone! She's not dreaming, you fool. She's gone!'

'If anyone can dream through that stuff, Cally can.'

Palmer interrupted, his voice betraying his panic. 'Look, I don't know what's going on here, but that bloody truck's not going to stop just because the girl's taking a nap. Now, let's pick her up and get out of here.'

Ronald gently lay the girl down then squared up to the inspector. 'It's your bloody fault we're here. If you'd just kept us at Rogers's place—'

'That truck's after *you*!' shouted the policeman, aware that at that moment he was accepting everything Blakestone had told him. The realization halted his tongue. He looked over at Dr Rogers for help, but he was feeling Cally's pulse and shaking his head, all the time staring over at the truck as it gunned its engine on the other side of the dusty field, its lights glowing and dimming as if they were the eyes of a predator focusing on fresh meat.

'I don't know,' Dr Rogers said. 'There's just a chance—'

The truck's horn blasted the night, baying like an enraged

beast; it was not to be denied its kill. Then there was another sound, almost lost on the wind.

A train whistle.

Chief Inspector Palmer didn't hear it, but Ronald and Dr Rogers caught it. Ronald immediately knelt down to Cally. Grabbing her hand, he rubbed it vigorously.

'Cally, you're doing it, you're doing it. Come on, girl, make it work!'

The truck's engine roared again and it set off.

'Oh, God,' said Palmer, looking round for somewhere to run. But, terrified as he was, he was still aware of his duty to protect his companions. It was all four of them or none.

The best option seemed to be to continue up the slope behind the sign, though he suspected the truck would plough through it this time as easily as if it was a bank of snow.

Palmer stooped and, with Ronald's help, dragged the limp girl up the slope. All the time the truck was thundering towards them. They were nearly at the top when it reached them.

It rammed into the slope and lunged up at them, the sign's wooden legs snapping with a loud crack, the board flipping back onto the cab roof. The truck's front wheels left the ground as the momentum of the trailer forced it onwards and it rose above them, its light beaming over their heads into the night. then it came crashing down, its bloodied radiator missing them by inches, its engine screaming in protest, wheels spinning in the dirt, frantic to make progress towards its chosen target. But it had lost its advantage. It stopped, chrome incisors bared at them, lights blinding, the impenetrable black of its windscreen like a doorway into space. The stink of its exhaust wafted over them, making them retch and their eyes water. Then its screaming engine died and stilled. Silence reigned.

The three men scrabbled backwards, dragging Cally with them, but their progress was minimal, the loose earth shifting them back as soon as they gained precious inches. Eventually they had to stop and watch, almost paralyzed with fear and exhaustion, to see what the truck would do next.

A full minute passed. None dared speak, though each was desperate to voice the hope that the truck had stopped for good. Dr Rogers glanced at his watch, 12:02, the second hand still pointing to five. Then they all heard the whistle. Much nearer now, its high shriek rending the night; like the truck's klaxon, it too was the sound of a beast in search of food.

'What the hell is that?' asked Chief Inspector Palmer.

'That is Cally,' said Dr Rogers, already looking round for a glimpse of the monster that had killed his fish as sure as it had destroyed his self-respect.

'Don't worry, Palmer,' said Ronald. 'Just hope you didn't upset Cally too much.'

Another whistle blast stopped the detective asking what Ronald meant. Suddenly the truck roared into life and, crunching its gears, slowly edged backwards. After ten feet it stopped, then slammed forward, devouring eighteen inches of the bank beneath them.

As one, the men turned and crawled on hands and knees up the remainder of the slope, each struggling to haul the rag doll that was Cally.

The truck reversed, its horn blasting their senses, engine screaming in frustration. Then it hurled itself at the bank again. Again it gained inches, the shockwave tumbling the men and their cargo back, but they continued. It was their only hope. Three feet they would crawl up, then the truck would hurl itself at them and the resulting jolt would send them slipping back two feet. Again and again they made progress, only to have the truck slowly suck them back.

But suddenly Dr Rogers made the rise and the truck's impact didn't dislodge his hold on a small tree growing on the ridge. The others saw his handhold in the blazing headlights and they too grabbed branches and together heaved Cally up between them. Had she been heavier, they might have failed, and had to watch her roll down into the jaws of the truck. But they managed to pull her up and shove her over the top of the slope, then haul themselves after her.

Turning, they saw the truck pull back, ready to mount another earth-shaking assault. Instead it stopped and waited. It was as they turned to see where they could next go that the train whistle blasted again, this time within feet of them. Each man fell screaming to the ground clapping his hands over his ears, desperate to blot out the terrible cacophony that bore into their minds.

Just as suddenly as it had started it stopped, though its echo continued to buzz in their minds, confusing their thoughts. Then they saw it, crouching behind them like an enormous Rottweiler waiting to pounce. The train.

Its whistle sounded again, the shattering shriek kicking at them anew. Ronald cupped his hands to his ears and howled in pain. Then, suddenly, the sound was gone again, and silence rushed back like crashing surf. Yet the train was still there, black and menacing, blotting out the night.

It seemed to be floating on a bed of steam which crawled and rolled its way along the ground, obscuring its wheels. Its ugly, oversize, rectangular buffers pointed at them from the large riveted plate at the engine's base like blunt accusing fingers. In between hung three giant rusted chain links, clunking ominously. Above sat the boiler, its locking handles set at five o'clock. The engine was an odd design, with a small central boiler cylinder surrounded by a semi-circular metal collar about two feet wide that ran around its top like a hideous page-boy haircut. On top of this was the stunted funnel, barely a foot high, its cloying black smoke ugly and venomous. A small, battered rail beneath led back to the cab, where twin windows sat, dark and sightless. The only colour on the engine's scabrous oil-stained carcass, other than black and rust, was from the single red lamp squatting in front of the funnel.

There the train sat, its insides turning over, hissing and gurgling like some incontinent giant's digestive system, its breath rasping in sharp snorting whooshes, as if preparing to charge. Each man knew instinctively that was exactly what it intended to do but the knowledge did nothing to move their feet, or avert their eyes, or start their hearts. They were mesmerized; death again held them in its sights.

Then the oversized links rattled loudly, steam billowed higher like a rising curtain, the single red Cyclopean eye of the lamp flared into life, and the engine let out a huge rush of steam and started moving forward.

Behind them the truck had started to back away and Ronald shouted to the others. Picking up Cally, they ran to their left as the train began slowly to lumber forward. Convinced it was going to come after them, they continued to run, not realizing until it

was too late that they were running down the side of the slope
back into the open area that was home to the truck.

It was Palmer who called a halt, his mind just this side of
reason. 'I can't . . . I . . . no . . . a train? Here? It's . . .'

'That train. It's Cally's,' said Ronald dropping to his knees and
gasping for breath. 'She's controlling it. We hope. It's a long
story . . .' He dissolved into a coughing fit. There was a pain in
his chest again, but he was already too scared to worry about
what it might mean.

Their only chance was the petrol forecourt they had seen in the
distance. They weren't even sure how big it was, the light was so
vague. Odds were it was only a canopy on columns, offering
about as much protection as a tent, but it was all they had.

The truck had continued to back across the arena as the train
slowly shooshed its way down the slope where, reaching level
ground, it paused.

Ronald looked at Cally in the dim light from the truck's
headlights. Unconscious, maybe dying, how could she be in
control of the train? And if she was, who was she going to use it
against? She had reason to hate everyone here – hate the whole
damn world for that matter – there was no guarantee she would
use it against his truck. Even worse, there was no guarantee it
would actually work . . .

The whistle shrieked again, drowning out the guffaws of the
train's boiler. Ronald could see that the cab was lit up red and
orange by the hellish blaze in its belly, but it was clear no one was
driving. It hissed and gurgled, the stink of oil and smoke now
swamping every sense. What would it do?

Ronald looked down at Cally again. What was it about her
face? *She was smiling*! She had said she felt she was going to join
the train. She must be on it now, savouring the moment. As if
reading his terrified thoughts, her face broke into a broad grin
and her body shook as if suppressing laughter. And the train
roared into life.

The injection had hurt, but Cally hadn't dared flinch. Then, even
before the needle was extracted, light exploded in her head and
she felt herself on a steep slope racing down into darkness,
cascades of blue and green and yellow flashing past faster and

faster until there was a final explosion of a billion red sparkles. Then she was floating in space, no up, no down, no way of telling direction at all; just her and infinite blackness and a safe, soft feeling as if she was floating in the biggest womb in existence, her every need catered for, all worries removed, just ultimate peace and comfort. How long she floated there, her body caressing nothingness, she couldn't tell and didn't care. She had forgotten why she was there. It was nice. Too nice to leave.

It was a memory – or was it the outside world? – that had stirred her. Fear suddenly swept across her like a tsunami, obliterating all warmth, overwhelming her with the coldness of terror. She heard voices, high-pitched with panic, pleading for her to help. Her? How?

She shivered. All the kindness had been washed away and she could feel an entity approaching, something wrong and unrepentant. So why was she here? What was she supposed to do? Then she felt it, and her heart raced and her mind begged it to stop but it would not be denied. She knew it was a part of her, that it had been wrenched from some dark corner of her soul, but she couldn't stop it now. It had been called; it would not be denied. She felt herself squirming even though she couldn't move; heard men's voices even though she was deaf. Then she saw it through blinded eyes: her train.

She was above it, looking down, like a child with a toy. It was confronting a knot of cowering people. She could see one of them was a girl – it was her! She could see herself. Across the open space behind the group sat another vehicle of evil, a truck, its whiteness a lie. Now she remembered, now she knew. She needed her train to save them all from the truck. She took control. She began to hate and she directed her hate at the truck. It had to be destroyed and only she had the power.

She blew the whistle, she raised the control lever, she felt the wheels turn, heard the engine rumble, smelled the oily steam, saw the fire in its belly, enjoyed the motion, anticipated the outcome, *wanted the kill*.

The men could only watch, breath held, as the train bellowed into motion, its wheels gouging deep furrows in the earth, fighting for a grip, steam blasting into the night, its boiler huffing deep breaths. The truck was in direct line with it and sat, its engine now drowned out by the train. Slowly but surely the train gained purchase and, as its awesome power was transferred to its heavy wheels, it began to move forward. Inches at first, then surer, with more confidence, its pistons travelled a full cycle, then a second, then a third. Soon it was lumbering across the open area, building momentum.

The truck waited, its lights brightening and dimming, seemingly undecided what to do about the train. And then its exhaust stack vibrated, it spat dark smoke into the night, the engine whined and it accelerated towards the train.

The distance between them shortened as they gained speed. They were going to hit head on, their speed not very high, but their size and weight destructive forces in themselves.

Closer and closer they came until just as they were about to collide, the truck swung left, as if it was playing a game of chicken, but it was too late.

The train ploughed into the rear of the tractor unit and on through the full length of the trailer, its thin sides unpeeling like a banana, flimsy metal sheeting scything into the air. The train devoured all it hit in an enormous burst of white light and a thundercrack that battered the men to their knees. The trailer's panels exploded into pieces, the chassis disassembled, its wheels and stanchions bounced about the arena as if they had been held together with glue. The cab, although it escaped a direct hit, lost its twin rear wheels and, rudderless, careered in a tight circle until gravity flipped it onto its side and it broke up, the radiator exploding outwards, razored metal shards shooting across the open ground like multiple arrows, spearing the ground feet from the terrified onlookers.

The train carried on along its unstoppable course, the red glow of its boiler the only clue to its whereabouts as it thundered on into the darkness, the remains of the truck still settling with metallic clumps and heavy thuds.

The three men were transfixed. The remains of the cab had come to rest thirty yards from them. It was on its side, the body ruptured and misshapen, but the windscreen unscathed. Only when the train had disappeared, and the debris from the truck had finally stopped moving and there was silence, did they react.

Chief Inspector Palmer sat down with a thump, unable to speak. Dr Rogers just stood and stared, his hands in tight fists, nails drawing blood from his palms.

Ronald slowly lowered himself onto one knee and looked at Cally. *Brave girl. Brave stupid girl.* She was still smiling and, placing a shaking hand on her chest, he found she was still breathing. Good, that was something. He tried to speak but his throat was dry.

He looked at the wrecked cab. The truck may as well have exploded, there was nothing left, whereas the train hadn't even slowed. But where had it gone and, God forbid, had it taken Cally with it?

Ronald was just about to hoist the girl up onto his lap when he saw the cab door on the top of the wrecked unit open and fall back with a crash. Then a bony white hand appeared, groping round the door frame. *Oh God, no . . .*

Cally guided the train to its target, her hatred for the truck and what it contained as solid as the vehicles themselves. The impact had been glorious, a gorgeous fulfilment of desire, more powerful than any orgasm. Her senses touched new heights and she remembered the other times the train had claimed victims – and she remembered how good that had felt. Maybe she had secretly wanted this all along, however much she might protest otherwise. Perhaps, deep down, she was every bit as much a murderer as her train. It was as she contemplated this that she began to lose control of it.

During the run up to the crash she had been overhead, a spectator, but now she found herself on the footplate of the train. She could feel its heat red on her face, hear its throaty power and smell the stink of its oil and coal. She tried to lift herself away but it was useless; her feet might as well have been riveted to the patterned metal platform beneath her. She looked ahead through the small window, but it was grimy and the night was dark. She looked to her left and saw shadows rushing by which could have been trees. Then she looked to her right.

Gantry stood smiling at her through blackened, broken teeth. 'Hallo, Cally,' he lisped. 'I think we need to talk.'

★ ★ ★

'Oh, God, no,' Ronald managed to voice.

Palmer ignored him, his mind still sifting for possible explanations, but Dr Rogers heard him and saw what he was pointing at.

'I presume that's Simmons.'

'Yes. And we've no way of stopping him this time.'

Ronald stared into Cally's face, then slapped her. 'Come on, Cally, come back. Bring your train back. Please, love.'

He looked up as Simmons hauled himself out of the cab and sat looking across at him, his piercing blue eyes visible even at this distance.

Dr Rogers nudged Palmer in the back. 'Time to leave, inspector.'

Palmer looked up at Simmons and their eyes met. The policeman couldn't comprehend what he saw, the skeletal figure in rags with rotted flesh and oddly attractive deep-set eyes. But Simmons understood.

'Oh, good,' it croaked. 'Ronnie's brought me a copper.'

He might as well have said food.

The train rumbled on in darkness, no lights, no sounds other than the hissing steam, not even the comforting clatter of rails; it was in a world of its own, with its own rules. Even so, Cally had tried to jump but found she couldn't move. Gantry laughed; it was still unconvincing, especially with half his face shredded and his top teeth missing.

He leaned back against the side of the cab, his clothes intact but stained with blood, his shattered arm limp by his side, the hand twisted the wrong way. One of his feet was missing and he was resting on a bloody stump where his ankle should have been; he had the slumped posture of a drunk propping up a bar.

'No jumping, Cally. This is *your* train, remember. You can't leave it.'

'So why are you here? You're dead. It killed you,' she said, surprised at how calmly she was reacting. Maybe she was just too tired to care any more.

'Perceptive. Yes, it killed me, but as long as it lives in your mind I get to travel. Speaking as a professional, it's extremely fascinating. After a lifetime studying the insane mind, I'm actually resident in one, travelling the highways and byways; keyhole surgery taken to the infinite degree. I've poked my way round many a retarded brain, including that moron Mark's, but this is, as they say, "something else". By the way, you are one mixed-up girl, but we've plenty of time to put that to rights. Plenty of time.'

Mention of Mark managed to hurt Cally more, but she still didn't know what to do.

'Don't worry. It took me some time to get used to this but I've accepted it.' He leaned forward and caressed her face with his hand.

Cally tried to pull back but couldn't move.

Gantry laughed again and shook his head. 'Oh Cally, Cally, Cally. We're going to have such an *interesting* time together. And I promise not to forget how I got here . . .'

She tried to leave, to cast herself adrift from the train, but she couldn't. The train might as well have been a mobile prison and she chained to its tender.

Cally felt herself weaken suddenly. Her knees buckled and she fell to the floor, her head narrowly missing one of the levers that adorned the front wall of the cab. She rolled onto her back and looked up at Gantry.

'You can't fight it, Cally. Your train will disappear into the labyrinths of your mind, taking me with it until the next time you fall asleep and feel hatred and then we'll ride it together. And no one will believe you when you protest. No one. In fact, they'll probably lock you up for good, and then we can really get to work.' He looked out of the side of the cab along the length of the train, the wind whipping his thin hair. He laughed again. 'It really is jolly exhilarating, you know, going in for the kill.'

Cally ignored him. She could still hear other voices. It was Ron, pleading. Then Gantry heard them, too.

'That's the bastard who killed me, isn't it? Got problems, has he?'

'That truck. I didn't kill it.'

The word 'kill' brought a light into Gantry's eyes. His mouth widened and he licked his lips. 'And you want to go back and save him? And that fool Rogers?'

Cally managed a nod, but her muscles felt like lead. She couldn't even flex her fingers now. She felt as if each limb was strapped to the floor of the cab.

'Why not?' said Gantry looking ahead again. 'They say travel broadens the mind.'

The Simmons thing leaned forward, his eyes wide even within their dark sockets, and spat phlegm as he jabbed his finger at each frightened man in turn and catalogued the atrocities he would soon inflict on them.

'You, Ronnie, I'm going to cut your ears off so you can hear better when I slice the old fart's dick off and shove it up the cop's arse. Then *I'm* going to listen to the noise you make when I pop out your eyes and make you swallow them. Oh, shit, that's a good one. Then maybe I'll hack off the cop's tongue and stick that up your arse, Ronnie, so's he can give you a real rimming!'

The taunting continued, each man unable to move, but more than able to comprehend the agonizing tortures they were being promised.

Cally stopped fighting her muscles and concentrated instead on focusing her mind. She listened to the voices. Heard Ronald. Saw what he was seeing, the Simmons thing squatting like a starved toad on the remains of the truck's cab, taunting the men with what he was going to do to them.

She fixed her mind on the train, imagining rails leading it straight to the truck; long, silver rails like lasers leading from underneath the train across the darkened night straight to the crashed truck. White lines, white lines, wheels locked onto them, unstoppable, unswervable . . . She heard Gantry whoop as he saw that they were indeed heading for the wreckage at high speed.

Cally tried to look at him but even that small movement was now denied to her. *Concentrate, girl, concentrate.* All that was left was her mind and it was fast absorbing everything she had to offer. She knew what it meant and it didn't worry her. As long as the train lived in her mind, Gantry said he would get to travel, but without a mind, the train couldn't live and Gantry would cease to be a passenger. *The truck, that thing, get it, kill it, smash it*!

'That's it, girl. When we've dealt with that thing, we'll get the others and then . . . then we've got us a railway!'

'I don't think so,' she whispered as she envisioned the crippled truck ahead of them.

'And why not?'

She managed a smile in her mind. 'What use is a railway without a train?'

She couldn't speak any more. Existence for her now was a pinhole through which she could only see the fast-approaching truck and, ahead of it, three men, too exhausted to run, standing over a girl's body.

The distance closed and, as the train let out a last triumphant scream of its whistle, Gantry joined in, shrieking his denial of Cally's words.

They hit the truck, the Simmons thing instantly obliterated and, happy that she had finally saved Ronald, she let go. The train continued to hurtle on towards the men who, seeing its approach, threw themselves to the ground. But before it reached them it ceased to be. Its whistle became Gantry's scream and then an indefinable sound that drifted away on the night breeze.

The three men felt a hot rush of air over their heads, followed by an intense blast of cold. And then all was still. Braving a glance up, Ronald saw the last vestiges of the truck hit the ground, no piece bigger than an inch across, with no evidence at all of Simmons. Yet the train hadn't hit them; its headlong rush towards them had been as unstoppable as that of a real train and yet . . . and then he realized.

Cally's train had died. Because Cally had died.

TWENTY-SIX

Dead silence surrounded the men. There were no night sounds, no motorway hum, just a total absence of noise, as if the train had carried away their hearing.

'Rogers!' shouted Ronald. 'She's dead! What do we do?'

Dr Rogers knelt down by Cally. He checked for a pulse in her neck and her wrist, and listened to her heart.

'Not a lot I can do,' he said, thumping her chest. Then, tilting her head back, he covered her mouth with his own and forced air into her lungs. 'If it's the drugs, they're still working, fighting anything we do. If it's her heart, there may be a chance. Either way she won't make it out of here.'

'We need an ambulance,' said Palmer, holding his head, trying to clear the fuzziness clouding his thinking. 'What about the stuff you gave her? Is there an antidote?'

'If you find the medical case there might be stimulants.'

They all looked across the darkened field. Some chance. Ronald set off down the slope towards the wrecked Vauxhall Senator. The Rover had been obliterated but there was still a hope the remaining car might have a radio.

'Palmer, did your car have a radio?'

'What?' said the inspector. He had found the medical case but it had been run over. 'Yes. Yes, it did.'

'Well, see if it works,' said Ronald, realizing he wouldn't know how to use it.

'Oh . . . okay,' said Palmer. Shock was fast approaching.

A minute later, Palmer shouted that the radio seemed to work but he couldn't get a reply; he just hoped his transmissions were being monitored. All they could do was wait.

Meanwhile, Dr Rogers had found a pulse. It was fitful but at least it was back; all he needed now was for Cally to breathe. He continued his mouth-to-mouth resuscitation while Ronald looked on, helpless and guilt-ridden.

'My fault,' he said. 'All my fault.'

Dr Rogers shook his head. 'No one's fault, man, these things happen. Look, I'm getting tired. Can you take—'

Ronald took over immediately, following his instructions, all the time quietly urging Cally to come back to him.

And that was how they continued, Palmer repeating his demand for urgent assistance, and Dr Rogers and Ronald taking it in turns to apply artificial respiration to Cally. How long they fought to save her they didn't know, but all of a sudden police cars, ambulances and bright lights were everywhere, as if they had been hiding round the corner all the time waiting to make a dramatic entrance.

As soon as the paramedics reached Cally, Ronald collapsed, a last wish fading on his lips:

'Cally, don't go . . .'

It was as they were in the ambulance, two paramedics continuing their desperate efforts to save Cally, that the thing that had invaded Simmons in the truck again spoke to Ronald.

As they massaged the fragile girl's naked chest and hooked her up to an intravenous drip, the eyes in her lolling head opened and stared, soft and blue, at Ronald as he sat huddled in a blanket on the other side of the gangway.

'Ronald, you have been very lucky,' it said, although Cally's mouth didn't move. 'Few foresee their deaths. Everyone must die, the cause sometimes unpleasant, the timing inopportune, but it happens to all. You could have died tonight, but this girl saved you. The truck would not have stopped but Simmons interfered with its efficacy.

'The punishment for his abhorrent activities was to be in the truck and witness but never participate in its grim task. Imagine a glutton forever able to look at food but never to eat. Or a bigot never able to express his hatred. So it is with Simmons and his kind, but his presence in the truck allowed things to change, and this girl's own instrument of death was able to destroy a destroyer.'

'But what will happen to me? When will—'

'—you die? You have seen that once, you will not see it again, rest assured. Nor will you remember. Death is not vindictive, it just *is*. It is as natural as birth, as life itself. All that happens has an ending. A curtain is drawn over every existence; it is just that you saw the hand pulling it sooner than most. Do not worry. You are a good man, despite your fears to the contrary; it will make no difference to when you die but it will help afterwards.'

'Afterwards?'

Even as the visitor left and Cally's eyes closed, Ronald thought of Ruth and Julie and immediately his heart soared. *Good enjoys an afterwards. Ruth and Julie might have—*

Just then Cally coughed. It was weak, but it was life.

'Got respiration!' shouted a paramedic. 'I think your daughter's going to make it, mate.'

'She's not my . . .' *Shut up, Ronald*, he thought. *Or should that be Ron?*

DESTINATIONS

As Simmons's visitor had promised, Ronald's memory of the truck faded, though not before he had been able to give Chief Inspector Palmer a detailed account of what Simmons had told him about the murdered children.

Subsequent excavations at the garage at Lane End – based upon 'information received' – uncovered the remains of six children, two girls and four boys, aged between six and thirteen. The Simmonses, father and son, were considered prime suspects but there was no way to prove it. However, police now consider the cases of the six murders to be closed. Eleven other disappearances have been linked to the pair.

None of the survivors of the attack by the truck could throw any light on its origins including, after a few days, Ronald; only that it had seemed intent on killing them all. No one mentioned the train, maintaining instead that the truck simply blew up. Forensic evidence was inconclusive, failing to establish the make of truck, the cause of its destruction or, indeed, the identity of the driver. The inquest on the two policemen and the police doctor returned verdicts of murder by person or persons unknown.

No charges were brought against Ronald concerning the death of Annie Wilks as the evidence was purely circumstantial. Nor were any charges brought concerning the disappearance of Dr Taylor Gantry, who is still listed as missing and wanted in connection with the attempted murder of Cally Summerskill and assaults on various patients in his care at Handland Hospital.

However, Cally was charged with assault on the two police officers she attacked at Dr Rogers's house and was put on probation for two years, Chief Inspector Palmer acting as a character witness in court. She was also returned to Handland where, a month later, Dr Rogers was appointed Chief Medical officer. (The vast array of dirty linen that would have been washed in public had he not been given the post was a major factor in his appointment by the hospital's board of governors).

Tests conducted by Dr Rogers confirmed that Cally's train had died when she had, and hadn't returned when she was revived. Consequently, she was released. Over the next five months, Dr Rogers reviewed the cases of every single patient in his care and released or transferred no fewer than twenty-seven, including Mark Cockett, who now lives in a home for autistic adults near Southport – and is visited regularly by Ronald Blakestone and his adopted daughter.

Two years on, Cally Blakestone is in college studying catering and Ronald works as a teacher at a nearby crammer college, helping Geography GCSE failures to pass their re-sits. He's proud of the work he does, but even prouder of his new daughter. He even approves of her girlfriend.

THE END